THE MOURNING NECKLACE

Also by Kate Foster

The Maiden
The King's Witches

Kate Foster

THE MOURNING NECKLACE

MANTLE

First published 2025 by Mantle
an imprint of Pan Macmillan
The Smithson, 6 Briset Street, London EC1M 5NR
EU representative: Macmillan Publishers Ireland Ltd, 1st Floor,
The Liffey Trust Centre, 117–126 Sheriff Street Upper,
Dublin 1, D01 YC43
Associated companies throughout the world
www.panmacmillan.com

ISBN 978-1-0350-5205-9

1 3 5 7 9 8 6 4 2

A CIP catalogue record for this book is available from the British Library.

Typeset by Palimpsest Book Production Ltd, Falkirk, Stirlingshire
Printed and bound by CPI Group (UK) Ltd, Croydon, CR0 4YY

Visit www.panmacmillan.com to read more about all our books
and to buy them. You will also find features, author interviews and
news of any author events, and you can sign up for e-newsletters
so that you're always first to hear about our new releases.

For Ruby

Public Notice

Notice is hereby given that, on 2nd September 1724, at the Grassmarket Gallows, Edinburgh, at eleven o'clock in the morning, there will be an Execution by Hanging of sundry criminals, for miscellaneous offences, including Murder, Coining, Robbery and Concealment of a Pregnancy.

Public Order will be kept, and rioters arrested.

Any of the Hanged criminals whose bodies are unclaimed by next of kin will be taken by the Anatomists of Edinburgh for dissection at the Incorporation of Surgeons and Barbers.

PART ONE
HANGING DAY

Chapter One

The Sheep Heid Inn,
Duddingston, near Edinburgh
2nd September 1724

Oh, I am supposed to be dead!
My breath catches in my throat, the way it does when I'm jolted from a deep sleep. I try to cry out, but my mouth burns. My tongue is fat and dry. My hands are laid upon my chest as if in prayer. I unclasp them. Prayer was never that much of a comfort to me.

I've just had a dream so vivid I could have sworn it was real. I dreamed a snake had coiled itself tight around my neck and was squeezing the life out of me, pressing my veins and making my eyes bulge. A snake with a taut shiny skin, scales the colour of good hemp rope. It hissed my name. *You will die, Mistress Maggie Dickson.* It tried with all its might to strangle me. But at the last moment I grasped the creature and managed to drag it off me and toss it away.

I am supposed to be dead, so where am I? I am lying on my back, and everything is dark. Is this heaven? Hell? Purgatory? Will they come at me with flights of angels or with fire and brimstone?

My chest rises and falls. I am breathing. I lay my hand on my heart to feel the pulse of me. It gallops under my fingers faster and harder than it has ever done. *I am alive*, it says, *I am alive*. There are no angels or demons or serpents or snakes. Just one living, breathing woman.

My hands are stiff with pins and needles and my gown feels wrong: too loose and too thin and stiffly ruffled at the neck, like a child's dress. I squeeze and unsqueeze my fingers, searching for the familiar ridge of the glass ring Spencer gave me. The ring isn't on my finger, but of course I knew it wouldn't be. For did I not hand that ring over to Joan yesterday? As she bawled and howled, but took it anyway and pushed it onto her pinkie, blinking away her tears and pretending not to admire how the glass beads twinkled. She had always had her eye on that ring.

There is something else I must do now. Put my hand to my throat and touch the place where it throbs. The fabric of my collar is gauzy. This is definitely not mine, not the good dress I was wearing earlier, but – *oh, above the ruffles is the raw welt of my skin!* A swollen wound. A bruise that curves from ear to ear. Slashed with rope-burn. The mark of a thick hemp noose. It must look awful. If Joan could see it, she would shriek and shriek.

The hanging hasn't worked. But dear God, I am marked for life.

And according to the *Courant*, I should be meeting His Judgement right now, followed by an eternity down below with the Devil himself. But this is not heaven, nor hell, for – *hear that?* – the muffled snorts of horses chewing hay, and I could swear it was the chime of a kirk bell that roused me and sent the dream-snake slithering away. *I've survived!* I am supposed to be at my rest, but I have never been more awake.

They said I would swing for the crime, and I did. I stood on the gallows convulsing with fear, and the floor gave way and I dropped, and I tried to scream, but the scream caught in my chest as my neck tightened and everything went black.

The scream bursts out of me now. I gasp like a fish on a riverbank – like a baby on a riverbank, but I'm trying to forget what that looks like. I would scream again, but my throat has seized up.

Still your heart. Think. The sun creeps through the cracks in the wooden planks that cover me. *I am in a coffin!* The parish coffin of St Michael's. They had argued whether it was even proper to cart me home in the common coffin, but in the end decided it was cheaper, and less of a fuss than buying one. But sunlight through gaps means they haven't buried me yet. I was due to go back to Musselburgh and be buried beside all the other dead Dicksons, all the fishermen and fishwives who went before me, to save me being laid to rest with the Edinburgh criminals, for who could ever rest in peace in an Edinburgh graveyard? But we are not in Musselburgh. Not yet. I can't hear the gulls.

My fingers press against the coffin lid and nothing moves; at first I think it might have been nailed down for safety, for I know there were apprentice surgeons in Edinburgh who'd wanted my corpse for dissection and there was a worry they might steal me and take me from Ma and Da altogether. My heart pounds even harder, but no, the lid heaves up and over on its hinge, the sunlight blinding me now. I sit up, which is not as easy as it ought to be. My legs ache at the hips and knees, which must have been the jerking at the noose. *Look how she dances! Hang, bitch, hang!*

No one shouts or panics, so no one has seen me. I am thankful for that. I don't know what I am doing yet and I need a moment to suck in fresh air and think. My eyes come to, and I know where I am straight away. I am under the shadow of Arthur's Seat, in the yard outside an inn. The whiff of boiled mutton hangs like a fug. The horses are nose-deep in their troughs. Ahead of me is a kirk, where the clock has just chimed one. I was hanged at nine. I have been dead four hours.

I have been dead long enough.

I clamber out of the coffin and ease myself slowly off the cart. Looking down at myself, I see that I am in a burial shroud. I am barefoot too, for I had said Joan could have the lot – my gown and boots – but I do regret that now, for a breeze lifts my hem and it billows up. Everything feels different. My legs creak and tremble as though I have aged four decades in these last four hours. Perhaps I have. No one is about, only a crow that eyes me from the roof of the inn with something more than curiosity. Crows know things, don't they? He has a knowing look about him, this beady fellow, and he has not flinched to see a corpse spring to life, not so much as twitched an oily wing, as if he was waiting for it to happen all along.

It strikes me now, in this moment between the coffin and what I do next, that I have a choice. *There's always a choice to be made*, as Spencer would say. Even when you think you're all out of options, there is always something. That's Patrick Spencer for you. A schemer to the last. But haven't I learned the hard way that my judgement is not always the best?

Arguably, as Spencer might say, chewing on his pipe, I have already paid the price for the crime, and God has decided to give me a second chance. I could put back that coffin lid and make a run for it. To Leith Port and get on the next ship out. Find a smuggler and go wherever he is going. Wouldn't be the first time I've made a run for it. But here I am, stood in horse-shit in nothing more than a thin smock, with not a penny to my name, and I can't risk being caught like this. Imagine what would happen to me if a band of rogues came along. Worse if they realized, from my rope-mark, where I had come from. And there are plenty of rogues on the roads into Edinburgh. So I walk, my neck throbbing, with stones piercing the soles of my feet, into the inn.

Later, in the weeks that follow, they will talk of this day same as they talk of ghosts and highwaymen and grave-robbers and murderers. They will say how I leapt from my coffin and appeared at my own wake, and how everyone nearly died of fright themselves. Ma sobbed and took me into her arms, and Da choked on his mouthful of ale, and Joan shrieked and shrieked and dropped her bowl of sheep's-head soup on her lap and ruined her brand-new mourning-dress, and some men took me straight back to Edinburgh to be hanged again. They will say that, at first, my family took me for my own ghost until Joan said, 'We can all see your privies through that smock, Maggie. Will someone cover her up?'

But that is all to come. For now, on Hanging Day, in the courtyard of the Sheep Heid, there is only this: my name is Margaret Dickson, though everyone calls me Maggie. I am two-and-twenty years of age, a fishergirl who never became the fishwife I was supposed to. I did not want that harsh sort of a life. I wanted better. I was supposed to be executed, but I am still alive.

I was hanged for the death of my baby.

Chapter Two

I open the door slowly and stand at the entrance, wondering how long it will take for someone to notice me. My legs tremble. A ram's skull is mounted onto a plaque next to my head and I wonder, briefly, what the anatomists might have done with my skull if they'd had the chance. Ma is the first to see me. She screams, a piercing scream that could shatter glass, and clutches her chest. Da sees me next and his mouth falls open and he shakes his head over and over again. Some men I don't know, who are sitting in a corner at the back of the inn, slowly put down their ales.

'God save us all, she has risen,' cries Da.

'It cannot be true,' says Ma.

'Is it you, Maggie? Is it really you?' Da asks. The men stand up and walk towards me, moving carefully and, when they get to me, take me by the arms.

'Living and breathing,' one of them says. 'Living and breathing,' he repeats, louder, to all in the room, laughing like a lunatic. He smells of ale and onions.

'Careful,' shouts Ma, 'that's my daughter you are touching.'

'You said she was hanged,' cries the innkeeper. 'Well, she has defied the Grim Reaper today.'

'It was a botch job,' declares another of the men. 'They must have cut her down too quick.'

I try to pull away from him, but he grabs me even more tightly.

'Hey,' shouts Ma. 'She has had an ungodly ordeal and needs a sit-down and a tonic, not more rough handling.'

'She needs sent back to Edinburgh,' says the innkeeper, whose name I learn later is Mr Prat, which suits him to a tee. He has blanched deathly pale and has spilled the drink he's holding. 'They say the hangman at the Grassmarket has become a drunkard not fit for the job, and she is living proof, God save us all.'

'There'll be a reward for taking her back,' puffs the man gripping my arm too tightly. 'Good coin in this catch. See the bruising. A beauty. A shocker.'

They pause to admire my neck, which I cannot see, nor wish to. I want to speak, but my tongue is swollen big as an ox's on a butcher's stall.

'Do you remember it?' Joan has risen from her chair too, an explosion of soup across her lap, but for once she cares not for her appearance. 'The hanging, Maggie. Do you remember being hanged? And being dead? What was it like? Did you see God Almighty himself? Or did you reach the Pearly Gates and get turned away? Did you see Granny Dickson? Or any of the dead Dicksons?' The kerfuffle stops, as they all wonder the same thing.

Truth is, I saw no dead people. I was only looking for one – my poor babe – searching for her with a rising panic that I would never find her, and the most awful guilt about what I'd done. But I did not see her at all. I must have seemed dead, good and proper, or they would never have released my body to my family. And come to think of it, I do feel there's something different about me now, although I can't quite place it. Not just the throb at my neck. It's not a physical change. I feel that something of the essence of me is different. As though my soul has left and come back wiser.

'We'd best get their cart ready,' says another of the men. 'Back up to the courthouse.'

'Wait,' says Ma. 'She needs a physician first. Look at the terrible state of her. She is dazed and confused. Sit down on that stool, Maggie, before you faint. Is there a physician in Duddingston? Or mibbie we should take her to a medical man in Edinburgh. Get her examined there.'

I sit, feeling suddenly in desperate need of a chair, as though my legs can no longer carry me. As though I have been walking for miles and could not take another step. Someone puts a shawl over my knees and another shawl over my shoulders, yet still I shiver.

'An Edinburgh physician, are you mad?' cries Da. 'We don't have that kind of money.'

'Well then,' says Ma, 'she should come back to Musselburgh to get seen there. The constables can come and find her, if they want to arrest her.'

Joan speaks again. In truth, our eyes have hardly left each other all the while. She avoids lowering her gaze to my neck. 'What do you think we should do, Maggie?' It is the first time my sister has ever asked my thoughts on anything. She has never sought my counsel, only told me what to do or bickered and fussed all the way through our years together.

The thought of going back to jail terrifies me. Days I sat in that shithole, waiting to be hanged with all the other criminals. I try to say something, but the words are stuck in my throat. I grip the shawl to my breast. The snake flashes before my eyes again and I shake it away.

'Say something, Maggie,' says Ma. 'Let us know you are all right.'

But I cannot. I shake my head.

'She is struck dumb,' says Da. 'And disobedient too. She was never like this before.'

'Perhaps being struck dumb is her punishment,' innkeeper

Prat replies. 'And branded too – look at the gash on her throat. That will leave a scar.'

'It will,' says Joan. 'It looks rotten, Maggie. You'll have to wear a kerchief over that for the rest of your days.'

'It should fade in time,' murmurs Ma. 'Bruises do, even the worst ones. Now will someone pour the poor soul a drink: a whisky or a rum, if you have it. That might help her to talk.'

The innkeeper does as he is told.

'She will be hanged again,' says one of the men. I can't tell how many there are, nor who is who, for they buzz like blue-bottles around me. He says it slow. I think I hear a bit of pleasure in his voice too.

'We can't take her back to Musselburgh,' says Da. 'It will cause a riot. The house will be mobbed. We'd better go back into town.'

Da looks at Ma, and Ma nods. She always does what he says. She's had too many slaps from him. Too many of her own bruises.

'Perhaps for the best, Maggie,' she says.

I see it now in both my parents. Joan too. The same look on their faces they've all had since the first day they came to visit me in jail. The lowered eyes and the bowed heads. The shame of it. When I walked into the inn and stood there, unnoticed at the door for a moment or two, their faces had been different. Lighter. Ma had been supping her soup heartily and Da had been sitting pondering his ale solemnly, but with no great look of sorrow. They looked relieved it was over. They looked relieved I was gone.

I can hardly blame them, either.

I am handed a nip of rum. It slides like liquid fire down my throat. I hold out my cup for another drink, but the innkeeper shakes his head nervously. He wants me gone before I attract a crowd.

The men hoist me up and start to walk me out. Da fumbles in his pocket to pay for the unfinished meal and I wonder whether he will resent spending the money.

Finally my words come, thick and bruised-sounding.

'I will go,' I say. 'You've no need to drag me. But I want a physician. The best they can find. When we get to Edinburgh I want to go straight to the courthouse and I want to speak to the sheriffs directly. We must make good time, before it shuts for the day. I don't want to be accused of avoiding the law. And I want my gown and boots back. Joan, where are they?'

My family looks at me with renewed surprise. They have never seen me make such demands before. I always did what they wanted, until I met Spencer.

'Your gown and boots were stolen clean away, Maggie,' Joan says. 'As we were tending you under the scaffold – taken away from under our noses.'

'My Sunday gown, the one I was married in? Surely you could not be so careless?' Suddenly I start to cry at this, of all things. The tears prickle at my eyes and I think, *Do not lose your grip now, Maggie.* 'My Sunday gown gone, and me left in this ghoulish shroud?'

'Ah, but there's money in rag and leather, and even more money in anything taken from the gallows,' Mr Prat comments, with the air of an expert. 'Your good clothes will be fetching top bids, as we speak. Some folk collect things like that. Gentlemen of a certain persuasion. Particularly a hanged lady's dress.'

We all shudder, and Joan looks fit to vomit. 'This has been a truly dreadful day,' she whimpers.

Ma puts an arm about her shoulders and whispers, 'There, there, hen.'

No one puts their arm about me.

After an age of organizing the horses and untying the coffin from the cart, and a fraught argument about what to do with it for the time being, and finding me a pair of borrowed shoes and a gown, cloak and bonnet from Mistress Prat, which are too big, we all get onto the cart. Our sorry party consists of the men, who are both called Mr McIvor on account of being brothers, on my side of the cart and my family on the other. *I should have taken the road out to the port instead. I should have fled when I had the chance.*

Mr Prat takes the reins. My da had apparently driven the cart out of Edinburgh. 'But I am in no fit state to drive a cart now,' he complains, downing the last of his ale. 'No fit state to do anything.'

'It will be all right,' says Joan, patting my knee and reading my thoughts. 'They hanged a man at the Grassmarket for murder last year and he survived his hanging too, and he lives in Newhaven now.'

'How would you know something like that?' I retort.

The cart begins its journey: past my coffin, which lies open like a gaping mouth, and past the crow that has not moved from his spot, and past the kirk, then onto Royal Park where dozens of sheep graze, ready to be slaughtered for the tables of the Edinburgh gentry, their offal and heads sold cheap to the poor. It is an hour or so back under a blazing September sky, and Edinburgh looms larger and more horrible with every squeak of the cart's wheels. Joan, who has recovered her dignity, fusses at her stained skirts, and by and by Ma leans in to help her with a kerchief wetted with spit, and Da sighs and helps too, until my parents are so busy with Joan's damned skirts that they utterly forget all about me heading back to my doom.

Or mibbie they just don't know what to say to their daughter.

'Did you want rid of the baby, Maggie? Why did you not come and ask us for help?'

My stomach grumbles and heaves at the same time. Hunger and fear. They might take me straight back to the gallows. The scaffold is likely still up.

'Are they always like that?' mutters the McIvor on my right, nodding at my oblivious kin.

'Aye, sir,' I tell him.

'It's no wonder you turned out the way you did, hen.'

I decide to save my raw throat for my pleas to the sheriff rather than talk to anyone on this godforsaken journey. 'Tis true, though, what Joan said. True as anything, for I knew that story of the half-hanged man and had remembered it as soon as they sentenced me. The story of it came from the Newhaven fishwives some time back and spread to us in Musselburgh. Fishwives gossip. We are famed for it.

Legally dead, that man was, when they cut him down from the gallows, with no signs of life. No breath nor heartbeat. Sentence had been passed. They said the hangman took a bribe from the man. Sometimes a hangie can be bribed to give you a way out. Cut you down quick when you're still faintly alive and then you can come to some time later. Things like that.

Finally we reach the ominous city walls and pass through the towering gate of Netherbow Port into the heart of Edinburgh. The gentle royal pastures and the dazzle of the afternoon sunshine give way to the shadows of the tene-ment-lined street that snakes up the hill, and my heart darkens too. The cart slows, for there are a dozen or more carts around us now, piled with logs and bales and poultry cages. Men shout and swear at each other for taking too long or blocking the way. Water-caddies hunch under barrels strapped to their backs, which look even heavier than fishing creels.

We all stare now: me and Ma, and Da and Joan, and the McIvors. We cannot help it. There are market stalls set with weighing scales, and shops with signs and flags and patrolling high constables – they make me flinch: all of these sights pass us as we ease up to the Tolbooth Jail. I have only ever been on this street as a prisoner, but there are sights you cannot help but be astonished at. Buildings ten storeys tall. Wynds and closes crammed with inns and taverns and roaring drunks. Boys and girls collecting the gardeyloo waste thrown from the tenements, bundling it onto carts for compost. It is not a place for the faint-hearted.

We come to the forecourt of Parliament House. It is a commanding square, where men in sleek black hats mill around, carrying polished silver-handled walking canes that match the silver buttons of their coats. We are the only folk here on a rickety cart. Me, Ma and Joan are the only women. I have come to know the world of men in power these past weeks. It is a world of confidence, even amongst those who lack the good looks or wisdom or godliness to have earned it. It is not a world I am comfortable in, but I have had to find a way through. Theirs is a black-and-white world of certainties: of good and bad, and right and wrong. To them, I am wicked. So they strung me up in front of a baying crowd. But none of them had ever been in my shoes. If they had, I am not sure they would have reached such an easy judgement. For who can say what any of them would have done, if they had been me?

Before I get down from the cart, I turn to my family, who are putting kerchiefs to their noses against the stench of Edinburgh: the chimney smoke and gardeyloo and the rotten fallen fruit and veg. For a moment I think of uttering something profound to them, for again it might be our last conversation, but I don't. Instead I look at Ma.

'Have you my death-certificate,' I ask, 'for I might need it in there? The sheriffs like official documents.'

Again, they look surprised at me, for I was never one for knowing about certificates or documents or parchments because there is no call for that amongst fishwives.

Ma digs in her creel and brings out a scroll, wrapped in a black ribbon. She holds it aloft, between two fingers, as if it might bite.

I take it from her, my hand clasping the thick parchment and wondering at the absurdity of it all – that I should have the written proof of my own death in my hand whilst my pulse beats next to it. But I can do all my wondering later. Now I must think and be clever. I turn to Joan.

'I shall take my nice glass ring back now, if you please, my dear,' I say. 'It is mine, after all, and you have always been given plenty more nice things from Ma and Da than I ever was.' They all shift uncomfortably at that, for it's true, but not something we ever said out loud before.

Joan takes the ring off and hands it to me, inspecting her fingers. She opens her mouth and I think she is about to ask Ma if she might ever be allowed another ring to replace it, but when she looks up, she catches my eye and scrutinizes me up and down in my borrowed clothes, and my bruised neck, and thinks better of it.

But I am still furious with her about what happened in the court that day, and that ring is mine and I might need it. It is almost the only thing of mine that they did not lose under those damned gallows, so I consider it lucky. I have come to learn that everything is currency. A death-certificate. A glass ring. A smuggled package. A terrible secret.

Chapter Three

I walk into the courthouse, a McIvor on each side, but the brothers are not so sure of themselves now and no longer grip me, intimidated by the pomp. I do not turn back to catch a last glimpse of my family because I don't want them to see the terror in my eyes. That was a bold show I put on, out there – bolder than I feel.

A man in a black robe and cap with a florid nose bursting with whiskers sits at a desk, surrounded by larger-than-life oil paintings of men with swords and kilts and feathered hats. The window behind him is stained glass, and the high ceiling above our heads is held aloft by so many dark wooden beams it reminds me of an upturned fishing boat. The man glances up, and I can tell he is about to dismiss me when he sees my neck and his jaw drops.

'Sir, this is the condemned criminal Maggie Dickson,' announces the McIvor on my left. 'Hanged this morning, but returned to life at lunchtime. We witnessed her revival and brought her straight to you. One minute she was in her coffin, the next minute she was up and walking.'

'If this is a trick, I will have you all hanged,' says the court man, rising to his feet. But I can tell he knows it is not, for the welt on my throat throbs mercilessly and he can't take his eyes off it.

'No trick, no con, just God's will,' says the McIvor on my right.

'Was she revived by a physician? Or either of you?' asks the court man, narrowing his eyes with suspicion. 'For that would be a crime in itself.'

The men tremble and shake their heads vigorously. 'We are as shocked as you are now,' one says. 'She walked into the Sheep Heid Inn as though she had been woken from a slumber. I almost dropped dead myself with the shock of it.'

The other McIvor murmurs in agreement. 'Is there a reward,' he asks, 'for bringing her back?'

The court man is still gawping at my rope-burn. Eventually he speaks. 'The sheriffs are at their victuals in the White Hart Inn, where they have been since this morning, it being a Hanging Day,' he says. Then he clears his throat and gathers himself back to full gravity. 'When the sheriffs are at their victuals, particularly on a Hanging Day, they do not like to be disturbed. In fact it is their expressed desire to be left alone to ponder the weight of the law.'

The McIvors shuffle a bit and I think they are going to start begging for a reward, but never mind them. Now is my time to start being courageous and sharp. I put my hand to my throat and lower my eyes.

'Kind sir, if you will assist me, I should be most grateful,' I say, for I know how court men talk, and it is a steady game of good manners and pretended humbleness, but always with the courage of your convictions. 'I can tell that seeing me here, before your very eyes, is a shock to you. But trust me, sir, waking up in my own coffin came as an even bigger shock to me and I am forced to throw myself at your mercy. I was indeed hanged this morning, in accordance with the law, and I make no complaint about that. But as you can see, I remain alive and what happens next is a matter not for you or I, but for the sheriffs.'

He stares at me with no emotion, so I continue. 'I think it is imperative a physician is brought to check my health, for I have not eaten since my last meal yesterday, which I could barely manage, sir, but I make no complaint about that either, only to ask that the physician comes quite swiftly and perhaps I am offered a cup of clean water and mibbie a rum to revive me – whisky if you have no rum. Oh, and a bit of meat too. And to ask that the sheriffs are summoned from their victuals at the White Hart Inn, sooner rather than later, to make comment on this predicament I have been left in.'

The man is frowning now, but listening, quite intently. I take another deep breath and talk through the burning hoarseness in my throat. 'You see, aside from my own discomfort at not knowing what is what, my poor family outside do not know what to do with themselves: mourn or celebrate. And I am afeared that if they carry on standing out there, it is only a matter of time before they are noticed, and the balladeers and newspaper men get to hear about my revival and come rushing to this courthouse with their quills, asking my family all sorts of questions. And that would not reflect well on anyone.'

For a lass with a near-broken neck, it is quite the speech, but I want a swift decision from the sheriffs. And for good reason: they will have been eating their veal collops and mussels, and drinking their wine, since the hour before my drop, as they are renowned to do on a Hanging Day. The White Hart Inn is near the gallows and the first-floor private room affords a fine view, with no danger of mixing with the unwashed. And as it's now near three of the clock and the sheriffs opened their first bottle at eight, they will be drunk.

And that means I might just have the upper hand in arguing my case with them.

The court man looks horrified at the balladeers getting wind of it all and nods vigorously and stands up, then tells me to come with him. He walks me across the hall and puts me into a side-room and locks the door behind him. On the other side of the door I hear his footsteps click across the hall and then the murmurings of voices and the creaking of the great doors, and then nothing more than a long, still silence.

I am alone again, briefly. The side-room is a small cubby with a writing desk and a chair, which I sit down on. This might be one of the rooms the law men use. Mibbie they sit here and sign things like death-papers, and pay bills for hangmen and floggers and jailers. I know what lies beneath my feet too. Another set of rooms where the condemned live out their last days. They will be empty now, cleared out this morning, awaiting the next lot. I think of the woman who lay on the mat next to mine. I think the anatomists will have her now.

Time passes. I am brought a plate of cold but decent bacon and cabbage and a large cup of ale. By the time I have finished it, I do feel a lot better and, dare I say it, human again.

The window in the side-room is not stained glass, but is small and grimy with cobwebs and soot. It peers onto a narrow close that no one seems to frequent, so I have no idea of what is happening outside. They might take me back to the gallows again. And then what? The bacon and cabbage that seemed so welcome a few moments ago now churn in my belly and I have to breathe slowly to keep them there.

A sharp rap at the door tells me the sheriffs have been persuaded from their victuals. I am summoned to the court-room. It is the same man as before. This time he makes no comment, but leads the way. We turn through a series of corridors and, when we get to the courtroom, I realize it is the same courtroom too, the one they tried me in. Then it was crammed with all manner of folk come to see the spectacle. Now it is eerily quiet.

The sheriffs have pulled on their robes and wigs and stand unsteadily, three of them, behind their bench, with faces so dismayed I think it a shame the balladeers are not here to record the scene.

Eventually one of them speaks. The one who was my sheriff, a man called McAllister.

'She looks fairly unscathed, apart from that rope-mark. Her colour is good. I dare say she doesn't even need a physician,' he says.

His colleagues murmur and stare.

'Sirs,' I reply, 'I have come to you willingly and most humbly. I was revived naturally, or by some Act of God, in my coffin some hours ago, but I didn't abscond.'

Sheriff McAllister raises his eyebrows.

'I could have taken off and gone into hiding, but I did not. Instead I have come to you in honesty. For what kind of a life would that have been – to be forever hiding?'

'With that gash on your throat, you would not have been able to hide for long,' notes another of the sheriffs.

I press on. 'I have come to beg you to consider my case. To tell you that I have served my sentence, for I was hanged this very morning, as you will have watched. And I am here to beg you to judge that now I am free to go.'

Once I was terrified of men in robes and would quake at the sight. But that was before I saw with my own eyes that they are simply men who like to argue and debate and can be persuaded of the most unlikely things. They have a habit, see, of arguing with each other on every point. If one says *black*, another will say *white*; and if one says *wrong*, another will say *right*. It's a habit they learn at their law schools and it can be most irritating. But now I hope it will serve me well.

'You were sentenced to death,' says Sheriff McAllister. ''Twas me who made the pronouncement. And you stand before us alive and well. Too well.'

'I was sentenced to be hanged,' I reply. 'And hanged I was. Look, here is my very own death-certificate.'

I offer the scroll. They do not reach out for it. Instead another sheriff takes the bait.

'Hanged she was,' he says slowly.

'And yet she stands before me, begging for her life,' says Sheriff McAllister, 'telling me she could have run away instead, and expecting me to have mercy.'

'But her ramblings are irrelevant,' says his pal. 'What matters is that the sentence was carried out. We might have to retire to the library and see what the books say on this topic.'

Now the third sheriff chimes in. 'This kind of thing has happened before. The hangmen need to get their act together. This whole affair is an embarrassment.'

'Where is your legal representative?' asks Sheriff McAllister. 'The solicitor who spoke in your defence. You should not speak for yourself. You should have your man of the law speaking on your behalf on a matter as grave as this – the one who pleaded your case in court.'

On this point, they all nod and agree.

'We shall send for him if we need him,' I say. 'But I hope we do not, for I only ask you to consider that my sentence has been served. Did you not all sit in the White Hart Inn and watch me hang?'

'I think,' offers the third sheriff, 'that this is a matter for us to debate in private.'

This is as much as I could have hoped for. A reconsideration.

'And in the meantime, what will become of me?' I ask. 'Might I go back to my home in Fisherrow? I will be safe there and looked after too. My family is waiting outside on my news.'

'You will remain here in Edinburgh,' says Sheriff McAllister. 'For the likelihood is that you will be hanged again before the week is out.'

They all nod then and call for me to be taken from their courtroom, and I imagine they will head straight back to the White Hart Inn to debate the matter in earnest, supplemented with even more victuals to calm their agitated nerves.

I am led back to the Tolbooth Jail by two bullish constables, and I start to dread what awaits beyond the gates. The prison is only a short walk from the court, back across Parliament Square, but it is a walk from the civilized world to a dangerous one, for the Tolbooth has its own codes and rules. Ma, Da, Joan and the McIvors are standing by the cart and, when they see me come out, Ma, Da and Joan rush over.

'Wait,' says Ma, 'don't just hurl her back in there. What did they say, Maggie?'

The constables stop, but I know they won't give us long.

'They're still deciding what to do. I don't know how long that will take.'

Da shakes his head. 'I need to get back out on the boat,' he says. 'Or there'll be no fish for us to sell.'

Ma looks fit to collapse at it all and I feel a stab of guilt.

Joan looks away from me and fiddles with her bonnet ribbons. The constables start walking me towards the jail door.

'We'll try to visit,' offers Ma. But she says it weakly.

And that is how we say our goodbyes, with the same embarrassment and shame as we felt when we had our last visit before I was hanged.

If I have been a terrible disappointment to my family, they have been a disappointment to me. If I feel guilt at what I have put us all through, then surely they must feel guilt too?

But I can't think of that now. It is too much. I have to steel myself for prison life again.

The constables bundle me back inside and push me up narrow stairs and through low-ceilinged passageways, then finally they hand me over to the turnkey in charge of the women's cell.

'You will recognize this woman,' one of the constables says. 'Survived the hanging this morning. Keep a close eye on her.'

It is the turnkey that I don't like. The one who offers tipples of gin and smuggled pies in exchange for things I don't want to give. The passageway is dim, but there is no mistaking the shock on his face.

'This is the work of the Devil,' he says. 'To have escaped death. This woman must be a witch.'

The constable tuts. 'Then she is in good company in this cell,' he says. 'For it is full of wickedness and wantonness and she shall rot in here a while.'

'I shall want extra coin for guarding her,' the turnkey says. 'For who knows what pact she made with the Devil.'

'You can take that up with the sheriffs,' the constable says. 'For they are deciding what to about the debacle, but it is more likely trickery than witchery – you know that as well as I do.'

With some hesitation, as if I might bite, the turnkey puts his finger to my chin and tilts my head up. They all suck in their breath, gazing at my neck in the lamplight. I want to shake him off, grab his finger and stick it in his eye, but I daren't flinch. I am outnumbered.

'I shall keep an eye on her,' he says. 'But if there's any sign of devilment from her, I am out.'

That turnkey kept his eye on me before. Only days ago he watched me in this cell as a cat watches a mouse, and he has seen more of my body than any other man, except Spencer. He watched me lift my skirts to piss and thought lewd things.

But his gaze is different now. The lust has gone. I am macabre. A spectre come to life. Mibbie I consort with demons.

Oh, if only they knew the truth, and how wracked with guilt I am and that I pray desperately for my poor babe's soul.

He opens the gate to the women's cell. Faces stare from the gloom, five women and girls in various states of torn petticoat-flounce and filth. Most of them I recognize from before. The sleekit little pickpocket is still here, waiting for a public whipping. She scratches at her flea bites and looks terrified to say anything. The whoreish one – Molly, the turnkey's favourite – is here. She crosses herself and edges as far away from me as she can get.

They mutter amongst themselves and, at first, they avoid talking to me. I catch them trying to see my neck and glancing at my ill-fitting gown. They have all heard the conversation that just occurred: Maggie Dickson survived this morning's hanging. Words pass easily through cell gates; they slip between the bars. Words and whispers and bribes, and slices of pie and bottles of gin, and slender hands that can unbutton a turnkey's breeches and earn a favour quick as you like. Initially the women let me sit quiet and gather my thoughts. I know the questions will come, though. I am marked, now. I have been on the other side. Some of these women might be destined for their own hangings, once their cases are tried. They will want me to tell them how I survived – whether it was witchery or trickery. The others will be like Joan and will want me to tell them if I saw God, and who was waiting for me.

I don't know. I only know that I am changed inside and out.

I was someone else, once. A lover. A dreamer. But as the cell darkens into a night I thought I would never see, and the other women fold in on themselves, back to their own troubles, and eventually nod off and twitch and grunt and snore and weep in their dreams, I thank my lucky stars. For the shawl, the thin blanket, the gristle they toss me for supper, and even the rustle of rats. Every time I move my head, my neck hurts. I would have asked for a looking glass, to see the rope-burn. One of these women will have a pocket mirror stashed. Rouge too, and I have even smelled contraband scent in the Tolbooth. These are the novelties that help prisoners remember they are human, when they are treated as less. But asking for anything will draw attention and, besides, I don't want an audience when I do survey the damage to my flesh.

The glass ring twirls easy on my finger, that's how gaunt I am. Once I was a little sturdier. A sight dafter. A fishergirl who dreamed of running away from the sea.

When I sleep, finally, lightly and achingly on the prison mat, I dream of snakes again. Snakes and serpents and ropes.

When the serpent came to Eve, she gave in to temptation. 'Tis easy done.

In my dream, I find myself searching for my babe again and wake up with a start. Then it comes to me: I will never sleep soundly again and, worse, will never rest easy in my grave – unless I can be at peace with what happened.

And that means I must think back. Remember how it all started and where it all went wrong.

PART TWO
BEFORE THE HANG

Chapter Four

Fisherrow, Musselburgh
One year earlier: September 1723

Back then, I lived with Ma, Da and Joan in the tiny cottages at Fisherrow Harbour in Musselburgh, on the Firth of Forth. We lived in close quarters – too close. They call Musselburgh the *Honest Toun* on account of the nature of its folk, which is by and large true, for it is a town of fishwives and fishermen and mill workers. Industrious, from riverbank to beach. By day it hums with machinery that makes coarse, cheap cloth for servants' gowns. By night it thrums with the waves that bring the whitefish home from the shallow estuary waters to the wooden pier at the harbour.

An honest toun. But I don't think you could say honest types came in and out of our particular cottage. It was barely even a cottage, just one big room with a box-bed, like all the others on the row. Da was out on the water five days a week, dawn 'til dusk when the weather allowed it, and when he was not on the water he was at the Mussel Inn. He was part of a crew of men who worked one of the Fisherrow boats and we were all glad when he went and dreaded his return, for the certain thing you could say about Da – whether he was out on the estuary or whether he was on shore – was that he was an angry man. He carried resentment around with him like a companion. He was angry at his lowly status in life and had schemes afoot to try to get himself out of it, but they never came to anything much.

Me and Joan helped Ma clean the lines and fix the bait, then sell our share of the catch on a stall at the harbour, where fishmongers from all around would come each morning, so our hands were more often than not red-raw and tinged with whelk and mussel brine and cuts from the hooks.

Ma's hands were the most weather-beaten and work-beaten you have ever seen. She would hide them under soft suede gloves, which she bought from the haberdasher on Musselburgh High Street, when she went to kirk or whenever she ventured out of Fisherrow. None of the other fishwives bothered. Ma was different, like that.

One day she came home with a new pair that looked soft as a baby's skin. Palest pink, they were, and long too, so that they stretched halfway up her arms.

'Summer gloves,' she said, showing them off to me and Joan. 'The haberdasher says ladies wear them on day-trips.'

Joan and I cooed over them, although I could not think of anything worse than having to wear gloves on a hot day. When Da saw her put them on the next Sunday morning, just as we were about to leave for kirk, his face soured. He was already hungover and grey and was looking for a fight.

'Who do you think you are, buying fancies like these?' he scoffed.

'I can't take these old hands into the kirk,' said Ma. 'These mitts are light and airy.'

'You're ashamed of your work,' growled Da. 'Embarrassed of who you are.'

I pretended my boot laces needed tightening and cowered over my feet. I could hear Joan swallow nervously next to me.

'God knows I'm not ashamed of myself,' said Ma.

Da held out his hands for the gloves. Ma hesitated, for she knew that if Da took them, she might not get them back.

They stood there like that for a moment or two. We were all crowded near the front door, and I did not dare stand up or say anything.

'Please don't take the gloves. They were expensive,' said Ma.

'Keep them then,' he said. 'And use them to cover those ugly hands of yours.'

If it sounds unpleasant, it was – watching him leave the house in a bad mood and seeing Ma wipe tears from her eyes, staining her new pink gloves. But at least he had not hit her that morning, likely because he might have felt guilty about it, sitting in kirk.

But now you will be wondering how Ma could afford such nice gloves from the Musselburgh haberdasher. Well, the fishing life was only half our story. By night, visitors came to our cottage. Folks from near and far. Folks we knew, and others who were strangers who knew of us. For we were not just fisher folk. We were caught up in the world of tea-smuggling, which I suppose sounds very daring, but to me was simply ordinary life. The visitors would bring sacks of black tea from the Orient that had slipped their way to Scotland via Gothenburg, in the Swedish empire, and these folks always stayed for a cup to sample it. Da – or Ma, if he was out – would hold on to these sacks for a few days, hiding them in a cavity under the box-bed, which was in a cupboard off the kitchen side of the room, then pass these sacks on to other folks that came a-calling for them with codewords.

I say it was ordinary, but of course there came a time when I realized Ma and Da were part of a gang of criminals, of sorts, but we never seemed to make great monies from it, nor live in a merchant's house somewhere grand further away from the river;

and Ma's hands stayed red raw, although covered sometimes in a nice pair of gloves, and Da stayed discontent. So I suppose the part they played in the smuggling of tea from the Orient to Great Britain, by way of the Scottish shoreline, was trivial. There's no customs post at Fisherrow, for it is considered too small a port and the waters too shallow for decent foreign-ship trade. So smugglers can come and go as they please. Up and down the coast of Scotland and England fine and fancy goods are brought ashore on secluded beaches and at quiet ports. Coffee berries, aniseed, snuff; haberdasheries from India. They are hidden in casks and canisters and buried in caves or stored in trusted safe houses. For our part, it was tea, and it was stored under our box-bed for a time, then collected and, according to Ma, sold on the black market.

But whatever Ma and Da earned from their part in it all was pennies and just enough to keep the roof over our heads and put a joint of meat in the pot on occasions, which was a welcome change, and sometimes some nice whisky and fancy goods like kerchiefs and rugs and gloves.

Da also kept a pile of these pennies behind a brick in the wall, in case a press gang came calling and he could bribe them to ignore him. But the press gangs never came as far as our cottage; they merely roamed the alehouses. I often wished they would come for Da, for he was fearsome when he was in full temper, and he was in full temper quite a lot of the time. He was loud when he was being merry with the tea folk and loud when he was angry with us, and would switch between the two in a flash.

Joan is younger than me by two years and spoiled rotten. We all took an ague not long after she was born, and she almost died. Since then Ma has doted on her. I don't remember the sickness, but Ma tells the story. It was a fever that swept

Fisherrow, brought in on a boat full of smuggled tea. I shook
it off in a day or so and was taken in by a neighbour, as those
three tossed and turned in the bed. Da slept deep, but Ma
was fitful and thought Joan would not survive, so poorly she
was. She would not suckle and at first she mewled like a kitten,
then even the mewling stopped.

'But you did survive, precious hen,' Ma would say, stroking
Joan's cheeks, 'for God had already taken three of my bairns
born before the two of you, and He had taken enough. You
and I slept off that fever together, and after three days we
were both well enough to take milk and a bit of broth.'

And then Joan would likely say something like, 'Can I have
a bit of broth now, Ma, is there any in the pot?' and Ma would
reply, 'Aye, Maggie'll fetch it, won't you, Maggie?'

Joan would always eye me as she let Ma stroke her cheeks –
a look that said, *I'm the favourite*. I hated her for it, yet I
wanted into that embrace. I didn't want to fetch a cup of broth,
I wanted to dive right into the middle of them and feel them
stroke my cheeks. I never did, though, and stood awkwardly
watching them; and for that they thought me surly, until Ma
would say, 'Fetch the broth, hen, for the wee one, and put the
kettle on for all of us.'

So from birth Joan was doted on by Ma and even a bit
by Da, which meant that as a young bairn she became the
dreadfulest telltale, who would run to Ma with all manner
of trifles that I had done this or that, and we spent all our
days squabbling and our nights pinching each other; we must
have driven Ma and Da quite mad, for when the rows erupted,
they were nasty. Joan would shriek and I would shriek back,
and Da would always blame me, saying as I was older I
should know better, and he would smack me around the
head and threaten me with the workhouse at Eskmills, where

girls like me could lose a finger easy as anything in the big machinery.

It was a horrible life, really. But I dare say there were horrible lives being lived up and down the coast, between the vicious sea and the loom of poverty, if you did not work all the hours God sent. So we had things to keep us going. Da had his drink. Ma had her gloves. Joan sang in the fishwives' choir and tripped out to practice twice a week, with Ma polishing Joan's face clean with a cloth and making sure her little boots were shiny too. And I had my dreams, which back then were filled not with snakes, but with plans of how I might escape it all.

As I said, there had been five babes born, of whom me and Joan were the last two and the only ones who lived. There was another pregnancy, when I was around the age of six or seven, and that was how I learned how babies are made and that losing an unborn babe is a trauma of blood and grief. I didn't know Ma had been with child, for she hadn't said anything, but one morning there was blood in the bed and Ma was doubled over herself in agony, and Da went out and came back with some of the other fishwives, and they sat me by the hearth as they got Ma organized. Someone bundled the bed sheets away and brought fresh linens, and Da went out again and was gone for a long time. One of the women brought Joan and me some porridge, which we ate sitting on the Turkish carpet by the hearth, which we would never normally be allowed to do.

One of the women said, 'Now, girls, let your ma rest.'

And we did. For the blood had frightened us.

Later on Ma got up and started on the dinner. She sighed and sniffed as she chopped and boiled, and her face was grey and her hair a greasy mop. Joan went to her and Ma put her arms around her, and then her arms around me.

'You poor girls,' she said. 'You have all of this to come.'

After that, I don't think Ma was in the mood for any more baby-making. We all shared the box-bed, and Little Paws – our tabby mouser – too on cold nights, so it was likely she and Da rarely had the chance anyway. I think that suited Ma, for I only ever saw her clothed. Buttoned tight from her neck to her tiptoes. Grey nightie at bedtime, and striped skirt covered with a black apron by day. She was a woman who took a slap from her man and accepted it as well deserved, and we were girls who tried to avoid Da's temper at all costs. Joan avoided it better than I did.

And that was how it was until the day Patrick Spencer first came to our home. I was one-and-twenty years old, and it was as though someone had lit a candle in the darkness.

I remember the evening as clear as if it was yesterday. It happened under a blushing sunset that had that first crisp sniff of autumn about it, with the Forth shimmering pink under the sky. I had just been out the back after supper, bringing in firewood, and my hands and apron were grubby with wood-shavings. Little Paws was by the hearth, her favourite spot, sleeping on the small square of Turkish carpet that was one of the various imports we had come by. Joan was doing needlework, which mostly consisted of sewing variations of her own name onto fabric scraps in ever more elaborate designs – *Joan, Joanie, Jo*, and so on – and admiring seeing herself embroidered. Ma always let her fritter her evenings away whilst I was set to housework, even though Joan was nineteen by then. But when Patrick Spencer walked in our door, my sister put that girlish needlework away, lightning-quick. And, now I come to think of it, she never took it out again.

Spencer had a head of curly hair and a freckle-spattered face that made him look like he was up to mischief. He had a tendency to wink too – enough to make him cheeky, but not so much as to make him appear a sketchy sort, like some of the men that visited us. He was not tall of stature, nor needed to be. His merriness more than made up for it. That's what caught my attention. I felt almost as though he was inviting me in. With just one look.

'Well, this is a cosy scene,' he said as he stood at our door. 'Like something straight out of a painting. And that is a sight for sore eyes, for I've been travelling so long I'd quite forgotten the comfort of a good hearth and a welcoming family.'

'We do try to be welcoming,' said Da warily, eyeing the man's expensive greatcoat. 'But I am not sure how you come to have knocked upon the door of this house, out of all the houses in Musselburgh.'

That was Da trying to make sure Spencer had proper connec-tions and was not out to steal from us, or set a trap by which Da might have got into trouble. But Spencer introduced himself formally and said he had spoken to Mr Neptune at the Mussel Inn, which is a code they all used, on account of the Roman god of the sea, and Da relaxed after that and offered him a dram of whisky.

'I hear you can look after things,' Spencer said, after Ma had taken his greatcoat. Then he paused, assessing us.

Ma was nonchalant, brushing the dust off the collar of his coat. Da's brows were raised, waiting to hear what this man's business was about. I saw Spencer taking in the smallness of us all. The low-ceilinged kitchen, where the smell of smoking fat from the hearth and its blackened griddle always lingered. The curtain, an offcut of fabric from the mill, which barely covered the entrance to the box-bed or concealed the musty scent of its blankets. The piles of fishing line in a crate, which gave off the whiff of old bait. The gloom we lived in, with one tiny window and candles stuttering about the place. Yet look at those china plates, shining away on the tall dresser. Pockled from a trading ship, of course. Best-quality Scotch whisky too. And Joan and me, our hands rough and raw; our eyes alight with the thrill of a mysterious stranger in the house. Oh, Spencer took it all in, and I was not surprised that his eyes lingered longer on Joan than they did on me, for she's a bonny thing and she knows it.

'I can look after stuff, for a price,' said Da. 'But nothing stolen nor counterfeit.'

Spencer laughed as though Da had told a great joke, then once he had gained his composure again, he looked at us girls and winked.

'Well, if it's neither stolen nor counterfeit, what would anyone want it looked after for?' He spoke with a voice that had a burr, if that is the right word, of softness to it. He was not from around here. At a guess, I would have said he was from well over the English border. Gosh, didn't his eyes twinkle. And he was not afraid of Da, was he? Not intimidated at all. I admired that about him too.

Da took a dislike to him at that, for he did not pour another dram, as he usually would for visitors. Instead he let Spencer's cup run dry as he took the parcel and his payment and put it away in his hidey hole. The parcel was nothing to look at, merely a small box wrapped in brown paper and tied with string, although I couldn't help but guess what might be inside it.

'I'll be few weeks or so,' Spencer said, toying with his tobacco pipe. 'Got a bit of other business to attend to, then I'll be back for it. If anyone comes asking, you don't know anything about it and you've never met me, understand?'

He glanced then at me and Joan and the mischievous look was gone.

'The girls understand,' Da replied.

We nodded, for the moment seemed a deadly serious one and there was an undertone of Da's temper in his words. The fire crackled in the hearth and a sea-breeze got up, just enough to brush at the window. 'Tis a wicked blast that comes off the Forth sometimes and makes you think of the sea-creatures that roam there and beyond. Humpbacked whales and seals and dolphins and the like. Once a whale washed up on the beach and the stink of it was so high you could smell it all the way into town. We were told not to go near it, but Joan and me did, right up close. It was magnificent in its decay, but when Ma found out we had been down there, she said it was bad luck — bad as a curse. Da slapped us both.

'Are you off to sea?' Joan blurted, blushing pink as all eyes turned to her, for it was not like either of us girls to ask questions of the strangers who came a-calling.

'As it happens, I am not off to sea, no, young lady, but am journeying on land, as I have to see a man about a job,' Spencer answered.

Joan narrowed her eyes and pouted a bit, which I suspect was her attempt at being a flirt. 'That will be a long journey,' she said. 'For there aren't many jobs around here but fishing jobs. Are you headed north or south?'

'You are an inquisitive lass,' Spencer replied, sounding unimpressed. I liked him more and more now. He seemed to take no nonsense.

Joan shrugged, but this was the moment at which Spencer seemed to have made a decision, for despite his previous interested glances at Joan, he then turned his attention to me. 'But I shall look forward to seeing you all when I come back,' he said. And then he winked. Right at me.

Joan never forgave me for that, but she only had herself to

blame for speaking out of turn and making it look like she was the sort of girl who would ask too many questions. Men don't like girls like that.

The next few weeks dragged. I went about my chores and did half of Joan's as well. I let Joan tell me all the gossip from the fishwives' choir: the fallings-out and bickerings, and the rumours about which girl fancied which boy.

But, quietly, I made some changes. It was time I started looking after my appearance a bit. It was nice when a man winked at me, a good-looking man like Spencer, and I wanted more of it. I trimmed the split ends off my hair and made sure it was brushed morning and night. I bought a cheap scented hand-cream from the general store. I made sure my gowns were always laundered and free of snags and tears. Each morning, on waking, I could not help but wonder, *Will Patrick Spencer come back today?*

Chapter Five

There's another thing that I've not mentioned yet, on account of me being embarrassed about it, but I suppose now is as good a time as any. Joan and me were as bad as each other for it, but we both had our own little secrets, a bit like Da's stash. Joan's secret was a scrapbook, full of curiosities. A picture of the Palace of Versailles and a sample of smuggled white lace. Pressed flowers. Sea shells. Paper cuttings. Tucked into a pocket at the back of this scrapbook were sketches of men's breeches with bulging crotches. She must have sketched them herself, although I never asked, for then she would have known I'd gone peeking; and it was very bold of her to have sketched such vulgar things, considering what Da might have done, had he found it. But she must have been curious about men, mighty curious.

My stash was simpler and consisted of two things. One was a tin with coins in it – coins I had saved up over the years. Tips from the fishmongers for saving them the best of the catch, or coins I had been tossed by a tea man for luck. But it was not a huge savings pot, only a few pennies. The other item in my stash was a map of the British Isles, which I folded and unfolded time and again, so much that its creases were worn thin. I'd got the map from the general-goods store at the Mussel Inn. And on that map was one place that sung to me as a mermaid might sing to a sailor: London Town.

I could trace the route of the Great North Road to London

with my finger. Past York, Selby and Doncaster, then Grantham, Stamford and Stilton. Or another, longer route that meandered through the west of the country, through the towns of the Scottish Borders and Carlisle, Penrith, Leeds and Sheffield. And then I was there. For although I was a girl of creels and mussel beds, gulls and gannets and beached whales, I craved the metropolitan things I had heard about from the tea men. The Season. Musical theatres. Pleasure gardens. Events that needed admission tickets, plus a handsome chaperone and a dash of rouge.

My destiny was laid out before me, you see, like a fisherman's line. I was a fishergirl, becoming a fishwife like Ma, and soon a fisher lad would propose and I would be a proper wife to him. I would wear a striped skirt and apron every day except Sundays. I would toil when my husband was ashore, looking after him, and I would toil when he was on the Forth, repairing and baiting up his lines. I already knew how to gut and dress cod, halibut and flatfish, singing all the while as my fingers got redder and colder and sliced with cuts. Singing the same songs my grannies had sung, of good winds bringing the men home; although my voice might not be as high and sweet as Joan's, I still enjoyed those songs. If I had a babe, whether it lived or died, I would be back at the market within the week, calling 'Fresh fish' into the harbour wind. I would never leave tiny Fisherrow, and I would never go to London or see a play or walk in a garden of showy blooms, or let a gent kiss me hello in the foyer of a theatre. One day I would realize that I needed to hide my roughened hands with a pair of soft suede gloves, if I was ever to be seen in kirk.

Finally Spencer returned, a month or so later on a Sunday evening as it was darkening. He arrived much as he'd done the first time he came to our cottage, merry and cold, smelling of pipe tobacco and sharp peppermint and a spiced cologne. The nights had got shorter and our cottage had got even darker and gloomier, with a bigger pile of logs now hissing and crackling in the fire. But when I opened the door and saw him standing there, I shivered – not with cold, but with excitement. Here he was. Something different from my ordinary life. And even handsomer than I had remembered.

Ma had been at her darning, stockings in a creel at her feet, shooing Little Paws away from the wool, and Da was out for a Sunday pint, which he liked after his Sunday lunch.

'You've just missed Mr Dickson,' said Ma as I brought Spencer into the room. 'But you'll find him down at the Mussel Inn.'

'Ah, that is good luck, for the Mussel Inn is where I am staying,' Spencer replied, 'but never mind, I have only come for my parcel.' He gave a pause then and looked at us all expectantly, which obliged Ma to be hospitable by offering him a mug of tea. He nodded heartily and sat in Da's chair, looking comfy as you like. Joan had been set to washing the pots, but she cut that task short to pour Spencer's tea, so we all sat round the fire as he sipped. Joan played with her hair, which hung in two messy plaits, and I guessed she wished she'd had the time to brush it through. Mine gleamed. My hands were soft. My gown was pristine.

The pots will be half cleaned and I'll have to do them later, I thought. And after watching Joan preen for a bit, Spencer looked towards me.

'Are you girls not with husbands yet?' he asked. He asked it gently but it was as direct a question as we had ever been asked in our lives.

We both blushed bright pink. Ma stiffened.

'I still need my girls around the house for a bit, helping me

with the bait-collecting and the chores,' she said. In truth, she
only needed one of us – that is, me, as Joan was lazy and far
too mollycoddled. She sniffed and looked uncomfortable. But
Spencer was breezy.

'You should see what girls like you pair can earn in London,'
he went on. I was all ears now. 'Working in big shops and
selling buttons and hats and bodices to the ladies. Or making
tassels, or painting fans in the nice little workshops they have
set up there. Why, the earnings for girls like you are ten pounds
a year, so I'm told.' He sipped his tea. Politely, with not a hint
of a slurp or a sigh.

Ma stiffened again and reddened too, for I don't think we
had ever heard the word 'bodices' uttered by a man, and
certainly not by a stranger.

But I spoke up. I could not help myself. 'And how do they
get such jobs?'

'Apprenticeships,' Spencer replied confidently. 'Same as
fishing. Same as that mill up the road. Fishergirls like you
would get a job anywhere, with your handiwork skills. But
you've got to know the right people, of course.'

'I should never like to work as an apprentice,' said Joan. 'It
would be hard work from dawn 'til dusk.'

'You should never like to work as anything,' I retorted.

'But I would like to have a nice trunk of fans and buttons.
And bodices,' Joan added slyly, not meeting Ma's eye.

'That's enough talk of undergarments,' Ma said.

I could have died on the spot. But Spencer was a man who
had heard far dirtier talk than a girl yearning for a cotton
bodice, and thankfully the comment bounced off him.

'Is it true what they say about London?' I asked. 'That it
grows bigger and bigger by the day?'

He nodded, fiddling with his mug and crossing one leg over

the other, then settling into a story. 'Every time I go back there, something has changed,' he said. 'Something new has been built or opened. There are great brick town houses five storeys high. The Thames is crowded with ships' masts and sails and rowing boats. We are no longer England and Scotland, two separate nations, now. We are truly Great Britain, with London as our beating heart. There is a fortune to be made there, which is why I have returned for my package. I trust you have kept it safe.'

'We have, sir,' says Joan. 'Shall I fetch it?'

'There's a good girl, Joan,' commented Ma, for she was always praising Joan for trifles and never praised me for anything.

Joan bustled around fetching the package. Ma tidied away her darning. Spencer caught my eye and smiled. I could have died on the spot again. Joan gave the package to Spencer, who stood up and gave more money to Ma.

'I shall be off then,' he said, brushing his fingers through his unruly hair. 'But I shall be down the Mussel Inn for the next two days, having meetings with a couple of my acquaintances about a thing or two before I head back down south, should Mr Dickson fancy joining me for an ale.' He said this to Ma, but he glanced at me as he said it. He wanted me to know where he would be – I knew it. He was giving me his whereabouts on the off-chance I might want to skip out and meet him for an ale, or a walk or a talk. Mibbie find out more about the fortunes that can be made by girls in London Town. Or mibbie even get to know him better.

I skipped out first thing the next day, when Joan was still in bed and Da was off on the boat, so no chance of him going to meet Spencer – not that I thought he ever would, for Ma had said, 'He's a fast one' as soon as Spencer had left, and the door was locked behind him.

'What do you think was in that package?' I'd overheard Joan ask our ma that night.

'Well, I never speculate, Joan,' Ma had replied, a tone of pride in her voice, for Ma and Da's lack of curiosity about the things that came and went from our house was the entire reason they had such a trusted job in keeping things safe.

'The parcel had a peculiar scent to it,' said Joan, 'a scent I could not place. And it seemed overly small for the big, enormous fuss he was making about it.'

'Well, now it's gone – back with Spencer, where it belongs – and we have more important things to worry about than packages,' said Ma. 'For these lines are not even half finished yet. Maggie, you'll need to get on to them soon as you can, for if they are unfinished, it will be the workhouse at Eskmills for the lot of us.'

However, I had more important things to worry about than fishing lines. So off I trotted on my usual errand of buying the day's groceries at the market on the harbour. But instead of dawdling and gawping at the milliner's stall and the draper's stand, I dawdled at the Mussel Inn. I made sure to do this before I bought my groceries, for there would have been nothing less alluring that me hanging around with a turnip and a cabbage in my creel.

The Mussel Inn was a big, bustling building on the waterfront where travelling folk would spend the night, and where most of the business of the burgh was conducted. The fishermen, like Da, drank in the back bar, and strangers were not welcomed there. The building had an open courtyard in the middle, with two storeys of galleries around it, with rooms off them, including a big assembly room and a couple of parlours, and smaller meeting rooms and the like. It also had a stable and storage sheds, and even an adjoining bakery and a general-goods store and a barber shop, so there was always a toing and froing of folk.

I decided to linger around the general-goods store, which sold a miscellany of pots and pans and pegs and cheap prints, pamphlets and ballads. I must say at this point I did not know exactly what I wanted to happen, should I bump into Spencer. All I knew was that I was feeling the sense of something new and different. I suppose, if there was a word for it, that word would be 'possibility'.

Mibbie Spencer sensed me too, for I was only in the general store five minutes when he sauntered through the door, whistling a jaunty song, which I now know to be a bawdy one about a lusty lady and a tradesman. I stiffened, a cake of Castile soap in my hand. He raised his eyebrows when he saw me and tipped his hat, giving a small bow.

'Well, aren't you a welcome sight this morning, Maggie Dickson?' he said. 'But I've had a sleepless night, sharing a room with a sailor who has not washed in a month, and I could do with a cup of strong coffee. What say you join me?'

My heart raced at that, for, apart from Da, I had never heard a man talk about his bed or washing, or strong cups of anything. I frowned, wondering if Spencer was too fast for me, and if it all got back to Da that I was seen with him, I would be whipped and sent to bed.

'Please don't fret,' he went on. 'I'm a respectable gent. We can take a table in the good front parlour and look out at the boats and be served the finest coffee in a silver pot.'

'Just quickly then,' I replied, and he took the Castile soap from my hand and put it down on the shelf. His fingernails were clean and shiny as pink buttons and I felt self-conscious of my own: short and weak from salt-water. But he paid no heed to them and nodded, instead, at the soap. 'Cheap and oily,' he declared of the pile of creamy white squares. 'And no scent at all. Now I will tell you about the scents and fine fragrances in London, and I may even have a scent for you to try, if you like.'

Well, that got my attention. I followed him out of the store and back into the courtyard, noticing how his greatcoat hung so well from his shoulders. In his wake, I smoothed my braids and wiped my nose and mouth. Then we climbed up the stairs to the parlour at the front, which was the nicer of the two upstairs rooms and was hung with red curtains and had polished wooden floors and sturdy tables laid for dining. He sat me down in a velvet-upholstered chair by the window and went off to find a serving girl, and I took in the view. It is not often that I saw my own town from a second-storey window, for there was no reason for us ever to come and take coffee or tea, or anything, from the Mussel Inn. Except for Da, of course, but thankfully his boat was amongst those bobbing out in the bay.

Fisherrow Harbour stretched before me, its boats docked far and wide. Nets lay drying on walls, and women plodded up and down from the mussel beds with huge creels on their backs. Gulls swooped and fought over every scrap left on the ground. The sky hung low, a grey-green wash full of golden cloud. Men fished and women sold their catch. And that's the way it would go, on and on, sure as the turn of the tide and the wax and wane of the moon.

Spencer returned after a few minutes with a silver tray, set with a coffee pot and two cups and a saucer of scones.

'Now,' he said, 'do you like jam on your scones or a touch of whipped cream, or both?'

Well, I had never had anything on a scone apart from a scrape of butter, and I piled my scone high and proceeded to devour it. He watched, amused.

'I see you prefer the high life to the fishing life,' he observed, the mischievous grin flashing away. He poured the coffee and lit his pipe. 'But I don't think you live the high life now.'

Well, what could I do but shake my head?

'Your folks have you skivvying, do they? I bet you can bait a line in no time and gut a fish in the blink of an eye. Break a chicken's neck and have it in a pot quick as anything. I bet you can set a fire better than any London maid, and darn a sock neat as any seamstress could. I bet you can command the best price for your fish at that market.'

He had me to a tee.

'But you don't want any of that, do you? You want a fine house and a serving girl or two of your own.'

'Mibbie,' I replied. 'But I hardly know you enough to talk about what I want and don't want.'

He chuckled, but without much mirth, then changed tack.

'So your old ma and da have some connections, eh?' he went on, and I feared he might start asking questions about all of that. I already had a response, which was what we were to say to anyone who started asking questions about their side-line.

'I don't know anything about that,' I answered. 'But they are honest as the day is long and have sold fish for five generations at least.'

'Five generations at least,' he repeated. 'Well, never mind all of that for a minute. Look, here.' He pushed a small brown-paper packet across the table and nodded at me to unwrap it. He watched as I dabbed my mouth with my kerchief and wiped my hands before picking it up.

'Wait! Don't open it yet. Inhale its scent first.'

His voice was low now, conspiratorially so, and I swear his eyes and freckles got flashier; and I even declare that the room darkened, such was the drama of the moment. I put the packet to my lips, gently, and sniffed, trying to do so in a ladylike fashion, but of course I had never had to do anything in a ladylike fashion before, so it may have been a rather amateur attempt. But oh, the scent!

'Perfume ingredients,' he said. 'Exquisite, too. Musk and ambergris and cinnamon and civet and myrrh. The perfumiers of London are clamouring for them. For gents' wig-powders and ladies' gloves. In fact all the upper crust is desperate for the most expensive scents; and the ladies of Covent Garden, and the opera-goers and the blue-bloods. Perfumes and potions and eaux de cologne.'

Perfumed gloves! What would Ma make of that? 'So, you are a trader,' I said.

'Indeed, Mistress Dickson, I am. But I keep that a bit of a secret, you see, as I have a man in the port of Gothenburg who passes me some very precious goods that are vital items in perfume receipts, and in turn I have set up a buyer in London, who is a man with a shop that makes bespoke perfumes for his clients. But neither I nor he is minded to pay the high prices on the open market or the import taxes, if you catch my drift, which I am sure you will, as your own ma and da make their spare pennies from folk like me. The tea men,' he added, when I pretended to look puzzled. 'Except that the difference between the tea men and myself is that there is more money to be made in a pouch of perfume ingredients than there is in a sack of tea. For whilst tea soothes the soul, perfume is medicinal.'

He paused to sip his coffee, making sure I was listening, intent, which I most certainly was.

'It is,' he went on, 'I do believe, a *magical* potion that can turn a gent's head and make a plain lady quite alluring, or make an unwashed gent smell clean. Some say it can purify a room of disease.' He stopped here, aware that he had got a bit carried away with himself, but nonetheless I saw it all. I did! I saw the brassy door-plates of the perfumiers' shops. I saw the glassy bottles on the ladies' dressing tables. I saw their maids sneak a dab or two as they dusted and cleaned, unable to help themselves. In short, I saw the London of my own dreams, and this time I could smell it too. It smelled not of dank, sulphurous Thames water or beggars' grot. Not of reeking rush candles or billowing chimneys, or armpit sweat or rat piss, as Joan declared it would. Not of the mussel bait or stale whitefish that hung in the air of Fisherrow. It smelled of perfume and riches and romance.

I didn't take the perfume packet home with me that morning. Spencer tried to press it on me, but I was not about to be caught with that in my scrapbook, for it would no doubt match the unique scent of Spencer's parcel and Joan would be on to me straight away; or, worse, Da. Instead I savoured two cups of strong coffee and both scones and declared myself fit to burst. Buzzing from the drinks, I sat back in my chair and listened to Patrick Spencer.

'I shall be around for another day or two, but then I am back to London, to sell my parcel and obtain monies for the next few,' he said confidently. 'My buyer was assured by a packet just like this one, and I want to shift things as quick as I can. But I shall be back and I do hope we might meet again, Mistress Dickson? You see I don't often meet someone who I think shares my kind of ambition in life, and I believe you might.'

He looked nervous then and ran his fingers though his hair. Nervous, waiting to hear what I would say.

'We could have coffee here again, I suppose,' I replied.

He smiled and leaned forward.

'I am glad you'd like to do this again. I must confess, Mistress Dickson, that I find myself quite taken with you.'

Quite taken! I was quite taken myself. For the first time in my life, I felt a connection with a man.

'Thank you, Mr Spencer,' I said. 'It's been a most charming morning.'

'It certainly has,' he replied.

When I bade him goodbye, he stood up and showed me to the parlour door. He bowed and put out his hand. I took it, feeling the firm touch of his fingers. Slowly, his eyes fixed on mine all the while, he lifted my hand to his lips and kissed it.

It was only the brush of his lips on the back of my hand, but it lit up my entire body.

Chapter Six

Fisherrow
November 1723

W hen Spencer returned, another month had slipped by and winter had set in, but even a Firth of Forth gale could not make me shudder or grit my teeth.

Even Da, embittered by the storms, with the waters unassailable, could not upset me with his temper. For my body still sparked and fizzed from that kiss on the hand. London was calling, and Spencer and I would go.

It had been an agonizing wait, but I had known he would come back. And he did, with three larger parcels this time, straight to our cottage. On this occasion he walked in with no mischief about him, but an air of certainty. It was a Friday. Ma and Da were home, and Da was asleep in his chair. Ma was on one side of the table, having a dram, and Joan and me were playing dominoes at the other – a lazy game, if I am honest, and I was letting her win, for it was always easier; she hummed gently as she played, fishing-folk songs that she had learned at choir, and whenever I tried to join in with the songs, Joan glared at me and stopped singing and said, 'No, Maggie, your voice is flat and you drone.'

There was a sharp rap at the door, and I knew it was Spencer. As I have said before, there were often folk coming and going from our house with parcels and the like, but there was a confidence in that rap. *Tap-tap, a gentleman caller.*

He came in and, when he took off his hat, I could see shadows under his eyes from all the travelling. But I did not mind that, for my heart was thumping so hard in my chest that I thought it might burst out. Joan was blushing again and tidied up the dominoes, and Ma put away the takings. They sat around the table where the rush-light was best. I was sent to fetch the whisky.

'I've a drouth you wouldn't believe after all my travels,' Spencer said, winking at me, and I nearly died because of course Joan noticed and frowned.

'I see you have even more stash for me to store,' said Da, clearing his throat. 'There'll be thrice the price on that lot, I'm afeared, sir.'

'Happy to pay it, my good friend,' replied Spencer. 'For I would like to ask your permission to take your delightful daughter Maggie here out for Sunday lunch with me this weekend, if she would like to come with me.'

I studied my hands on my lap, for I could not bear to see the stares, but they were still on everyone's faces when I looked back up. Da was glowering and his jaw was set in a harrumph. Joan looked like she had been stung by a wasp.

'Maggie is too busy to be spared for Sunday lunch,' Ma said.

'I can do my chores before kirk,' I offered, trying not to sound overly keen.

'Where would you be taking her?' asked Da.

'I'll book us into the parlour at the Mussel Inn,' Spencer answered, casting a knowing look in my direction. 'There's one with mighty fine views across the coast.'

'Maggie can't go gallivanting out like that,' said Ma firmly, folding her arms across her bosom. 'Not to a public parlour.

There's salted beef in the pantry and plenty to go round. You shall come here for Sunday lunch, Patrick Spencer, and we can all get to know you first, before you haul my *delightful* daughter out to inns.'

'I declare I haven't had a home-cooked meal for weeks. I shall bring a bottle of rum that I picked up on my travels,' Spencer replied.

And with that, Ma poured him a very large dram. Joan spent the entire time gawping at him and me.

That night in bed, Joan poked me in the back as soon as Ma and Da had begun to snore. Her sharp little finger felt like a knife.

'Are you sweet on Patrick Spencer?' she whispered.

'Of course not,' I lied, edging away from her as far as I could. 'I've no idea why he asked me out for Sunday lunch.'

'He only fancies you because you're older,' she said. 'If I was your age, he'd fancy me. It's not fair. You're nowhere near as bonnie as me and you are certainly not delightful. Your hair's got nice and shiny recently, but your face is square-shaped and one of your eyebrows is higher than the other.'

Neither of these was true, but Joan was jealous, and I understood that. For I had always been jealous of her. Ma and Da liked her more, anyone could tell that. Ma often made jellies, even though I hated them, just because she knew Joan would eat jelly, whatever the flavour. Spiced jelly. Lemon jelly. Oh, they would make my stomach turn, but Joan slurped them down. And whenever she said she was tired of putting bait on lines, she got to go off and do whatever she pleased.

But there was no jelly in sight that Sunday, thank goodness, when Spencer came a-calling again and we all sat down to a slice of salted beef each, with boiled turnips on the side, and we all tried a finger of rum, which was foreign fire in the belly. The room was thick with turnip-steam and pipe fumes as Spencer gamely handled questions from Ma, such as where he was from and who were his folks, and the like.

'Well over the Scottish border,' he said. 'Near a town in the Middle of England. My folks are in farming, but that's not the life for me.'

Oh, it was all quite exotic, a man from the Middle of England taking an interest in me. I wanted to ask which town and see if I had noticed it on my map, but I felt embarrassed to ask anything like that in front of my family.

Little Paws miaowed at our feet and took a piece of beef from my fingers. Her tongue scratched and I suddenly wondered what Spencer's tongue would feel like. He poured us all another taste of rum and, when he got to my cup, he glanced at me and bit his lip and I wondered if he'd had the same kind of thoughts, and when I drank that rum the fire in my belly surged.

'We have never left Fisherrow,' Ma said. 'We can trace our line back years and years. All the fishergirls married fisherboys. That's how it's always been done, you see. It's in the blood.'

Spencer nodded, understanding that Ma was not exactly warning him off, but letting him know that our entertaining him like this was unorthodox and she was doing him a favour; and mibbie if she let him do it again, she'd be doing him another favour. Ma collected favours like a beachcomber does treasures. I knew he wouldn't care, though. He was *quite taken* with me. Why else would he have come all the way back?

Ma asked nothing about what was in those parcels and if Spencer would get me and him into trouble with it all.

Da said little but sat in quiet thought. He was not used to

there being another man at the table. I liked the fact that Spencer made Da quiet. It made me feel safe. Da did not make his usual complaints that the turnips were stringy or the beef gristly. Mibbie he was wondering if this turn of events might be favourable and what Spencer's connections were, but he didn't ask.

Joan said precisely nothing. She chewed her beef and stared at her plate and would not laugh at Spencer's jokes, and she left the table as soon as she could. I felt guilty. But it wasn't my fault he liked me.

When it was time for him to go, I stood up and walked him to the door. When it was just the two of us – me on the doorstep, and Spencer on the street – he looked serious and reached for my hand.

'It was important for me to get to know your folks, Maggie. I hope I did all right.'

'Shall we see each other again soon?' I could not help but blurt it out.

'As soon as I am back,' he promised. He squeezed my hand and leaned into me. Our bodies met. He kissed me, on the lips this time, and it was the most magical experience I'd ever had.

Joan went sourer still in the days that followed.

Spencer was off, but he had left something behind. Parcels, for there were always parcels, but this time he also left an atmosphere. Joan withdrew from me as much as she could, with us all living under the same roof. She became diligent, doing chores without being asked, and would take herself off for walks and to choir practice and come back looking miserable.

Ma and Da saw how Joan was behaving, for how could they

not? Ma took me to one side as we washed the pots together one night.

'It's time you were married,' she said in a low voice, for the other two were only a few feet away. 'Don't think the thought hasn't crossed my mind. But is there no local lad who's ever caught your eye?'

I shook my head and felt my fingers wrinkle in the cold, greasy pot water. I had never had my head turned by a local lad. Not by one of the fishing boys at any rate.

'Mibbie this Patrick Spencer might be a good bet for you, even if he's not from around here. He seems to be doing well, with whatever his line of business is,' Ma pondered.

'Joan's jealous,' I said. 'She should like to be married to a nice gent and never have to lift a finger again, and have maids all around her.'

'Her turn will come,' replied Ma. 'She will have her pick of boys. Do not let her spoil this for you.'

That was one of the nicest things my ma had ever said to me.

I spent the time waiting for Spencer, growing more and more aware of how unfair things were at home. Da never raised his hand to me after that Sunday-lunch visit, and Ma ceased her threats of the workhouse at Eskmills. I think they were waiting too, to see if he would propose. But the air of their discontent hung over us. I suspect they would have been all too happy to give up their fishing life, despite their claims that it was all we knew. The only other life they knew was criminal, and they were feared to get more involved in that. Occasionally there'd be hushed talk of tax officers and port officers and sheriffs and jails between Ma and Da, and these tales drew Ma's lips into a thin line for hours afterwards.

Spencer came straight to the house a couple of weeks later, as soon as he was back. November had slipped into December.

It was late one evening when we were all dozing by the fire, but I knew Spencer's rap at the door and rushed to see if it was him.

It was, stubbled and wind-beaten and grinning from ear to ear. I leapt into his arms. I couldn't help it.

'I told you I'd be back, he whispered into my ear. 'I don't need my parcel yet, but I needed to see you, Maggie.' He smelled of the sea and his particular magical perfume scent. I breathed him in and pressed my lips to his neck. 'Come and meet me tomorrow at the Mussel Inn.'

We drank coffee again in the upstairs parlour, thick and humming like a witch's brew. He talked of Gothenburg and London again and I listened, agog. After the coffee he asked me to his room, on the pretext of showing me more of his perfumes.

'My chamber's only up one more flight of stairs.' He tipped his head towards the door. 'We could nip up, if you like. I'm not sharing with anyone this time. Got the room all to myself. And I want to ask you something in private.'

I was shocked. After the gentle kisses on the doorstep, this was another turn altogether.

'If you want that kind of visit, there are lassies downstairs in the lushery who might join you for a few pennies,' I retorted.

He laughed gently.

'I knew you would refuse me,' he said. 'Truth be told, I am not interested in those types of girls.' He wiped his hand across his chin, it was cleanly shaved, and I guessed he had likely visited the barber first thing, on my account. I wanted to touch it, to kiss him, but I dared not, for I knew that if I did I would want to go to his room. 'In fact I was going to ask you a certain question,' he went on. 'See, I have something here that I should like you to have.'

With the flourish of a conjurer he produced, as if from nowhere, a golden ring set with twinkly gems that looked just like diamonds.

I gasped and took it and put it on my finger, and it fitted an absolute treat. Spencer watched, chuckling as I turned it in the light.

'Are they real gems?' I asked, for it did look a sparkler but I couldn't imagine he could have afforded diamonds that size, not even with all the perfume he sold.

'Real enough,' he replied. 'I got it for a song, as I was in a rush to put something on your finger. But that's another story for another day. When we are in London I shall take you to a jeweller and get you a proper ring with a real diamond – how does that sound?'

It sounded marvellous.

'So we are engaged to be married now, Maggie Dickson. Let's set up home here in town for a while, then get ourselves off to London when I've saved us enough money. What do you say? I'll need a base here in Musselburgh for another year or so, whilst I establish myself, and it's the best location for my line of work. One day I'll have trusted men in my employ, who can do all the hard work. We'll set up a perfume shop of our own in London, and you can serve the ladies and I can serve the gents. Does that suit you?'

It didn't just suit me, it was the most thrilling thing ever. It was an unexpected turn. It was a rush of love. It was my ticket out of town. How many times had I dreamed of London; pored over my map and imagined being a London girl? Well, now I could be.

I went home to announce my engagement, my head a-whirr with coffee and promises.

Chapter Seven

Fisherrow
December 1723

'Those gems are too big to be real. They must be paste,' declared Joan, after eyeing the ring like a hawk, her face green with envy. 'The whores that hang around the Mussel Inn wear big sparkly glass gems like that. Spencer has probably bought it off one of the whores, and no doubt fugged her too.'

Da clipped her for that, quick as a flash, and I was glad. She sat at the table with a red cheek, tears spilling from her eyes, her jaw set in a firm line.

But it was me that Da was really furious with. I was not daft enough to tell them about our London plans, for they would have asked too many questions about Spencer's trade and I was sworn to secrecy. But I told them we were to be married.

'And I shall be Spencer's wife, not a fishwife,' I said nervously. 'For he wants me to keep house for him.'

'Patrick Spencer is a blaggard and this is just a dalliance,' Da replied. 'I've a mind to clip you too. You come from a long line of fisher folk and you are to marry a local boy, not shame us by marrying some Englishman who will drag you away from your calling and forbid you from doing the work you were raised to do.'

Fishing was not *my* calling, but I said nothing.

'And as for you, Joan Dickson, if I hear you use words like *whore* and *fugged* again, I shall whip your arse good and proper.'

I gathered myself, feeling brave, now that I had a ring on my finger.

'If you hit me, I shall tell Spencer,' I warned my da. I said nothing in Joan's defence and she glowered.

'Are you with child?' Da asked. 'I take it the two of you have been at the capers? Is that what all this is about?'

I reddened and shook my head, mortified at the way the conversation had turned.

'He's a sort,' continued Da. 'No one knows who Spencer is. The tea men don't trust him. He seems to have appeared one day with mystery packages and all sorts of claims about making a fortune.'

'I know everything I need to know,' I replied. And who were the tea men to say who should be trusted and who should not be trusted?

'We should calm down and have a pot of tea,' said Ma, standing up. She knew how I felt. She knew this was my chance. She knew how to handle Da. 'And I take it Spencer is planning on sticking around for a while this time?' she asked gently.

He was planning on sticking around for a while. He was not going to attempt to travel again until after the worst of the winter weather was over. That meant there was time for a wedding and to find us somewhere to live.

Spencer organized the lodgings. It didn't take him long to find somewhere decent in Musselburgh town itself. It was a house with two rooms. More spacious than my own home. Not grand, as such, but a step up in the world. The fact of the matter was that Spencer had the cash to afford it. He

moved in straight away, desperate to be out of the Mussel Inn.
I took Ma and Joan to visit my soon-to-be home. Da refused
to come.

'Well, this will suit you nicely,' said Ma as we stood in the
parlour, taking in the smooth stone walls and the scrubbed
floors laid with new woollen rugs. It was unlived-in and cold,
but was nice and clean, and I had already decided where I
would one day put jars of daffodils, and where a gleaming
looking glass ought to hang.

'This is not the best end of town,' sneered Joan with an
exaggerated shiver. 'It feels damp this close to the river. I'd
have thought Spencer would fancy himself further away, where
the mill owners live.'

'It does not feel damp,' I snapped. ''Tis the fact no one has
lived here a while and it is frosty outside. Once we've had the
fire on and bought some tapestry wall-hangings and thick
blankets, it will be cosy as anything.'

'You pair would bicker about anything,' sighed Ma. 'I am glad
I won't have to put up with it for much longer. You have outgrown
the nest, Maggie, with your talk of tapestry wall-hangings,
though I dare say Spencer would know how to get one.'

But mibbie we might not have time for such things because,
as Spencer had said, we would soon be off to London. 'This
place will do us for a year or so, just enough time so that I
can establish myself and you can keep house and whatnot –
look after the stash and look after me,' he had winked as he'd
shown me around. 'You don't mind moving off Fisherrow and
into the town, do you?'

He knew the answer to that.

*

We were married in St Michael's Kirk on Boxing Day. Imagine it: wed barely more than three months after our first meeting, and a chap from the Middle of England too. Fisherrow buzzed with the gossip. It gave everyone something to talk about as the winter waves chopped at the harbour, stopping the boats from going out.

Ma baked a plum cake and we gave everyone a piece in the kirk hall afterwards, with plenty of tea. Spencer did not ask his folks to come, but said we would go and visit them once we had settled down a bit. He said they might not like him marrying out of farming.

I could understand that – of course I could.

Da said that was off, and how did we believe anything Spencer told us if we didn't meet his folks? But as we were not about to travel to England to meet them, and the Spencers had no notion of what was happening in Musselburgh, that was the end of it.

I wore a new dress that Spencer had a seamstress make for me, and it was a glorious navy and grey striped silk. It was the same dress they hanged me in. Lost now, of course, for as I learned when they cut me down and put me in my burial shroud under the scaffold, there was all manner of a kerfuffle, and my body near snatched altogether. The anatomists were scurrying around me like rats.

But let's away from the gallows for now, though my hanging haunts me day and night, and back to the lodgings on Musselburgh High Street.

We had a large parlour with an adjoining kitchen at the front and one large bedroom at the back, although I must admit, grudgingly, that Joan was correct and there were mornings when I woke up thinking that room was a bit damp. The privy was in the back close, and there was a water well not too far from the gate. Spencer kept his stash of perfume parcels and money in a secure cabinet in the bedroom. Unsurprisingly, he was obsessed with the safekeeping of his stash and had a smith come and fit new locks to the doors and windows. He had the place like a little vault. I don't suppose I really knew, at first, how much he had stashed away, but we never went without meat, and Spencer never went without rum.

The cottage was of solid-feeling stone that was grey and cold in the morning and would warm up gently to become golden in the afternoons and, as I was soon to learn, that was just like Spencer himself.

First, those golden afternoons. Oh, he was never more glorious than when he sat in the parlour, nestling a cup in the palm of his hand, swirling his rum as tales flitted from his lips. He talked little of his early life, steering his stories away from his own childhood, but his thoughts meandered off to the foreign ports that he visited and to London Town, where we were eventually headed.

Gothenburg was the place he sailed to, a port in the Swedish empire. I knew it from the tea men. Sweden had been at war for years, but there was hope it would become a new centre of global trade. Merchants were trying to set up deals there, to import spices and silk and furniture from the East.

'One day Gothenburg will be magnificent. But now it's no place for a lady,' he declared. 'Destroyed by sieges and pirates and rogues. You've got to have your wits about you over there.'

'Are you not frightened to return?' I whispered with a shudder.

'I know who to bribe,' he said. 'For where there's war there's impoverishment, and where there's impoverishment there's *desperation*. Gents with nothing left to their name but their connections. Refugees. These are the kinds of gents who will do anything when they hear there's money to be made from London merchants.'

Ma, Da and Joan were only down the road and around the corner, yet they lived in another world from my new one. I had thought that Joan and I would never be close again, but instead she thawed. She started to pay me visits, to get away from Ma and Da. She came over sometimes when Spencer was out. He liked to visit the Mussel Inn and go for long walks when there was a break in the weather, and I supposed he was restless to get on with his trading. I let him go out without nagging him about where he was going or what he'd been up to, for I had seen what happened when Ma did that to Da, and it never ended well.

Joan and I became more sisterly, now that we were not living in stifling proximity. She needed out of the cottage and to talk freely without Ma listening. She confessed as much one evening a few weeks into my marriage. Spencer was down at the Mussel Inn, where he had started to get in with Da's crowd, and Joan had brought her knitting over so that we could do our chores and gab. She'd brought a bit of seed-cake on one of Ma's second-best plates and I had poured us a small cup of coffee each.

'Ma was all for coming along with me tonight, but I said you wouldn't like it,' Joan told me, her knitting flopped on her lap, barely a stitch done.

'Why would you say a thing like that?' I asked. Honestly, Joan was a wench sometimes.

'Well, you wouldn't like it.' Joan shrugged. 'She would only harrumph at Spencer not being here and say that he leaves you on your own too much.'

'But Da is the same, is he not? Going away all the time. Or is that different because he's in the fishing trade?'

Joan shrugged again.

'Ma is getting used to it,' I said. 'Me marrying out.'

'Well, she needs to get used to it. For I shan't marry a fisherman, either,' said Joan. 'Not now you've shown it can be done so easily and you can end up living as cosily as this.' She looked around at the pristine fireplace, shirts pegged neatly in front of it. The vase of dried lavender on the windowsill. My map of Great Britain now unfolded and pinned to the wall. The room had the scent of clean washing.

'Oh, Joan,' I sighed, 'Ma likely has her hopes resting on you to carry on the Dickson line of proud fishing folk.'

'Then she'll be sorely disappointed,' Joan retorted.

'But you're her favourite, you've always been her favourite and that means you must do the right thing by her,' I warned.

Joan took a deep breath. 'You are right,' she said. 'I knew Ma preferred me – Da too. And I was never nice to you. In fact I took full advantage and I was a right bitch about it sometimes, wasn't I?'

'You were a spoiled cow,' I told her.

'But I was feared, Maggie,' she said, whispering as though they might hear. 'I was feared they would start liking you more, and I would be the one getting into trouble. No chance of that now, not now you've married out.'

That took a lot from Joan, for she's proud and not given to self-criticism. I respected her for that and we sat together a while longer, knitting needles clicking gently, saying little, but content in each other's company.

Spencer came home not long after that and kissed me on

the lips right in front of poor Joan and she looked away, embarrassed.

'I shall be on my way then,' she said, standing up and putting her needles in her creel.

'Don't suck the fun out of our evening, Joan,' said Spencer, 'it's not bedtime yet. Stay and have a nightcap with us.'

She hesitated, but only for a moment, and Spencer dispensed rum into three clean cups.

'Joan here is saying she will marry out of the fishing trade, just like I did,' I told him. Joan went red, but Spencer looked unruffled.

'No shame in that,' he said. 'Plenty of other things to do in life, and plenty of other ways to make a living. Besides, you'll have your choice of young men, Joan.' There was an awkward pause then and I thought Spencer ought not to say things like that. 'But you will have to be a sight less lazy and a bit more ladylike, Joan Dickson. You come on a bit strong, if you want my opinion,' he added.

'You rude bugger,' she shrieked.

'But it's true,' he said. 'When it comes to marrying, a fellow wants a wife who will look after him, like Maggie here. She looks after me good and proper. A fellow doesn't want to be worrying about his wife's moods or getting nagged, or having to cook his own bacon in the mornings, and I reckon you'd be a lazybones of a wife and ask too many questions as well.'

'Spencer, I shall slap you if you don't shut up,' Joan squawked, looking mortified.

He laughed and said he was only teasing, and I said that was plenty from both of them. I'd had enough of her company by then. I yawned, saying it was time for bed and we were keeping Joan up too late. I told Spencer to walk her round the corner and make sure she got home safe, and not to fall out with her on the way.

I washed, then waited for him to come to bed, and I was happy to wait too, for he had introduced me to the marriage act in a way Ma would no doubt say was wanton. Our nights ran into the soft hours. I know not how long we lay together; all I remember is the grey, gritty feeling of not getting enough sleep because of all the things we were doing. Feeling quite thrilled about it all. Spencer seemed to know his way around my body in a way I had not even known myself. I was sure he must have lain with a dozen women before me, to know such things. Before my marriage, a bed was a place for sleeping and snoring and the poking of ribs. Where unwashed bodies sweated, and blankets stank. Now my bed was a place of pleasure and clean, fresh sheets that I had washed and perfumed with the packets that Spencer gave me. It was a place of nakedness and lust.

'Did you learn your ways in a whorehouse in Gothenburg?' I asked him one night, half joking, but half serious because I was jealous of all the other women who might've been before me.

'Of course not. I am just finding out as I go, same as you,' he said. 'But there's no shame in the pleasure, is there?'

But we both knew he was sparing me the details. I tried to put the thought of these other women out of my mind, but it unsettled me to know that there were girls in London or Sweden with feathers in their hats and white silk gloves, whom he had admired and bedded. I did not like that feeling at all.

Another thing Spencer had no shame about was the physic preparations that he gave me to take, now I was a married woman. They came in packets and were a concoction of powders, which he assured me was perfectly safe, but would stop us from becoming a ma and da ourselves just yet. On this we were in agreement. I was as averse to becoming a mother as I was to becoming a fishwife. I had never forgotten the blood on the bed when Ma had her miscarriage, or the look in her eye when she talked of her lost babes, or the worn-out state of her as Joan and I bickered.

Motherhood. I never said as much to anyone, but the word left me cold. I did not want to end up with a babe hanging from me. In fishing folk, the women are not long in their confinement. A week or two perhaps, or longer if they are older and have other bairns to deal with. Then it's back to work, but with double the toil. Feeding and changing and fussing. Nights of no sleep and days of colicky cries. Or worrying over a sick babe and, worse, mourning ones who did not survive. I wanted none of it. Some would call me selfish for that. Unwomanly. Perhaps I was.

So it came as a huge relief when Spencer brought me a physic preparation on the morning after our wedding night. I'd never seen anything like it. Not in all the tinctures Ma and Da had taken over the years for headaches and knee aches and poxes. The packet was in the shape of a neat square and there was writing on the front, two words that I could not decipher, even though I had some limited knowledge of written words; and a sketch of a fine lady with a secretive-looking smile on her face.

'The writing says *Women's Tonic*,' Spencer explained. 'Except it's written in Swedish. It's the most popular one in Gothenburg. All the courtesans use it, so I have heard. Take one dose every morning stirred into fresh water. Just like this.' He emptied the packet into a cup of water and stirred it with a spoon, then offered it to me. It fizzed for a moment or two and, when it had settled, he beckoned me to drink it. I sipped it gingerly. I didn't like the salty taste. I didn't like his easy use of the word *courtesan*.

'Every morning? How will I ever get used to that?'

'Drink up,' he said. 'You'll get used to it soon enough. It's the only way to stop a baby, for if we carry on like we did last night, a baby will come soon enough.'

That was enough to frighten me. I swallowed the drink. I did not ask Spencer how he knew so much about the habits of the courtesans.

Grey mornings, though. That was the other side of living with Spencer. You wouldn't wake him before ten of the clock. I learned that in the first week. He was not rough like Da, nothing like that, with fists flying, but he had a flash of temper to him that made me go quiet. It was on the fourth day of our marriage I found that out. I had been tidying up the bedroom and he had been lying in bed like a stone. I had never seen anyone take a lie-in before, unless they were sick. I went to wake him up, gently touching his shoulder, but he rolled over to face me and out came a hand from the blanket and he jabbed his finger to my face. I flinched.

'Never wake me up when I'm sleeping,' he said.

'I was only going to offer you a bit of bacon,' I replied.

'Well, don't,' he retorted. 'I'll come and get my bacon when I'm ready.'

And so that was me told.

Regardless of things like that, for I had had far worse, I did think myself absolutely in love with Spencer. I was in awe of him. I was certainly in love with his plans to make a pile of money in Musselburgh first, then get to London quick as we could. He said we'd need to save and that living up here was a sight cheaper than living down there, but once we had enough money saved, we would take a coach down south and secure some smart lodgings. He would still have to do his business, of course, obtaining his products. But we would set ourselves up on a splendid row of lavish shops, with cabinets filled with dark bottles: *Patrick Spencer's Perfume Emporium*.

Until then, we passed the worst of the winter in our snug home.

I would cook and clean. He would praise my stews and soups and cleanliness. Sometimes Joan would come and they would bicker a bit, and I would send her home when it all got too much. Twice a week, when Joan was at choir practice and Da was out drinking, I would go and see Ma and we would sit and blether, but not about anything important. Ma and I found it easier to talk about trivial things, like how to spice a plum cake, than the big things, like why I had married out and what would become of Joan, and if there would even be any more generations of fishing Dicksons.

But anyhow that life – that delicate new life I was fleshing out for myself as a newly-wed – came crashing to a halt one afternoon. Spencer had been down at the Mussel Inn again. I was paying Ma and Da a visit when a man came running up to our cottage, saying a press gang had burst into the inn and dragged three men away, and one of them was Patrick Spencer.

A press gang. Navy men.

Spencer was gone. Vanished. Taken off to sea.

Chapter Eight

Musselburgh
January 1724

The thing about the sea is that oftentimes there is no body to bury when it claims a soul. A drowned sailor will sink to the bottom of the great abyss. St Michael's Kirk has seen many a coffinless funeral. But at least there is a finality in death. When the press gang took Spencer, I did not know whether I would ever see him again. Da said the news was that he and two merchant sailors had been taken by members of the Royal Navy Impress Service, who had burst into the downstairs ale room and told everyone to stay in their chairs and not dare to make a run for the door. When they had made their way to Spencer, he had tried to bribe them to leave him be, but these brutes had refused the bribe and warned him that the punishment for not going with them was hanging. They had rowed him off to Leith Port, where the Navy ship was docked. Not even allowed to say goodbye.

The week that followed was terrible. Hours ached on and on, and night rolled into day and into night again, none of it with news. At first I sat in our lodgings and waited for Spencer to walk through the door. I say 'sat', but I slumped on the good chair and lolled on the bed in great despair. I had never felt as bleak. I couldn't eat or sleep, and I finished the rum and would sit in the small hours of the night imagining him rolling at the bottom of the ocean or whipped by a merciless captain or, worse, whoring in a far-off port. It was the worst of the winter. I imagined ice storms and frozen lands. Ma, Da and Joan came and went with pots of soup and tried to keep my spirits up with tales of pressed men who'd returned.

Da was rattled to the core by it all.

'He'll be back in a few months,' he would say, over and over again, for he hardly knew what else to say. 'He'll find a way. He's a bit of a chancer, Spencer, and that's what'll work for him.'

I was not so sure. Da looked more disturbed in those first bleak days of Spencer's disappearance than I had ever seen him. But he wasn't worried so much about Spencer as about himself. He was thinking, *That could've been me press-ganged.* He sent word to all his pals to find out where Spencer might be, but also to find out if the press gang would come back for more recruits. He even kept away from the Mussel Inn.

Da asked if I might want to come back home to Ma and help her and Joan out. Things had not been the same since I left.

I said I would not. I had a new home now.

And the final question, typical of Da: had Spencer left anything of value behind?

I shrugged at that and did not answer it one way or another, but that was a bit dishonest of me.

There were two keys to Spencer's locked perfume cabinet, and we had one each. He trusted me like that, although mibbie he ought not to have done. I let a second week crawl by with no further news. Then, finally, I opened the cabinet. I needed to. I'd had enough cash in my purse to last me that long, but one morning there wasn't enough money in it for a trip to the market.

The cabinet was of a dark wood and had an engraving of a
serpent on it. Whence it had come, I know not, but it had the
grainy feel of a foreign country and the scent of cologne. I had
always kept my key at my side of the bed and so, on a melancholy morning with an empty pantry, I took it and opened the
cabinet. It sprung open – *click* – unleashing a breath of scent,
and inside was a packet of cash. Thank God! If there had only
been perfume, I would not have known know what to do with
it. But cash it was, and although it was not the fortune I had
hoped for, it was enough. I took it out and counted it. Enough
for me to live on for a few months.

Or enough to get me to London.

I couldn't do that, though, could I? What if Spencer came
back and we missed each other entirely? That would be a
disaster. I pushed the thought out of my head altogether and
went up to Ma and Da's and let Ma serve me her hen broth,
and I did not tell them about the stash of money. I knew I
had four months left in the lodgings, for Spencer had bragged
of a long lease when he got the keys. I was all right for a few
months, but if I didn't want to return to baiting lines, then I
had to sort out a plan.

In the end, though, a plan sorted itself out.

One evening, Joan sat at her broth, dipping her bread in and
saying very little, and then afterwards she sat silently by the
fire as I helped Ma wash up. Then she said she would walk
me home.

'I am capable of walking myself,' I told her.

'Let Joan walk you,' said Ma. 'It will do her good to get a
stretch of her legs.'

So we put on our shawls and Ma put together a package of

bread and butter and milk for me, not knowing about my stash of money of course, and we headed straight into the icy wind and the roar of the choppy waters. I was desperate to get out of the gale and reach home as fast as I could, but Joan gripped my hand.

'I can't live with Da a minute longer,' she said. 'You'll need to let me come and stay with you a while, Maggie. Say you will.' The wind almost took her words, but I heard them good and proper. My heart sank. I shook her off.

'But I am a married woman now,' I replied. 'Spencer will come back, I know he will. You can't just take his place.'

'And when he comes back I'll move home again, I promise,' Joan said, 'And he will come back – we know that. But give me a few weeks. I'm at my wits' end.' She looked desperate.

'Has something happened?' I asked. 'Has he hit you again?'

She looked away, but her grip on my hand tightened.

'He pushed me,' she said. 'It happened this morning. He put his hand on my chest and pushed me out of the way. Nothing happened really, but it scared me. He'd calmed down a bit since your wedding, and I thought mibbie having another man in the family meant Da might be feared of getting a punch himself from Spencer, if he stepped out of line.'

'But Spencer's gone now,' I said. I started walking again, to get round the corner and into town. I felt sick thinking of Da, then even sicker thinking of poor Spencer out there, at the mercy of the sea.

'Please don't turn me away, Sister,' pleaded Joan.

I suppose it came to this: that, bicker and bitch as we might, I would not turn my sister away.

'All right, you can stay,' I agreed. 'But I am not running around looking after you, Joan Dickson. You will have to do chores. I am not soft on you, like Ma. And you'll do as you're told, for I am mistress of my own house. Do you promise?'

But she barely gave me 'til the end of the sentence, for as soon as she saw that I had relented she stopped in her tracks and squeezed me tight in a most uncharacteristic hug, and I ended up finishing my speech into her shawl.

'I shall go now and get my bits and pieces,' she said. 'Have you plenty of rum or shall I bring a tot of whisky?' But she was off anyway, skirts flapping in the wind, all the way back to the house to gather her things. I followed her and stood at the door as she packed. I could hear Ma pleading, and nothing from Da. Mibbie he would be happier now, with both of us gone.

But where was Spencer? Would I get a knock on the door one day to say he had died at sea? Would they even tell me, if he did?

The weight of his disappearance felt like an anchor. A water-logged gown. I felt like it would never go away and I was destined to spend my days with the pain of it. I had barely known the man, yet he had come into my life in a flash of light. Spencer had shown me a glimpse of something better.

I watched and waited in the narrow street. It was empty of life. The sky and the sea were a blur of desolate grey, whipped to bits by the weather.

Joan's bits and pieces filled two creels. Two nightgowns, two day-gowns, one Sunday gown, sundry worn linens and shawls, a cup, bowl and spoon as well as her scrapbook and bits of unfinished knitting. When I had left home, my belongings had filled just one creel. She also had a fancy tapestry purse with a tasselled edge, and two paste brooches to fasten her shawls. Market trinkets. Indulgences from Ma.

She moved in with me as easy as a foot slides into a familiar boot. All her belongings were tidied into cupboards and tucked onto shelves. Her half-tangle of knitting rested on Spencer's chair. She was to spend her days with Ma, helping with the lines or selling at the market, and then she could spend her evenings with me. I supposed that sooner or later I would end up back working with them too.

'Let's have some of your rum,' Joan said, as we sat in the parlour having our first evening together.

'You're up first thing, remember, salting fish with Ma,' I warned.

'What about a song then, or a tale? Tell me a story of married life. Tell me what I need to do to get a decent man like Spencer to marry me.'

This kind of talk was not like Joan. She looked downcast, yet her eyes still danced in the rush-light. Joan was bonnie. She had fair hair and a face shaped like a love-heart. She was cherub-like.

'You know you are a fine-looking lass. Why are you worried you won't get a decent husband?'

She shrugged. 'Spencer said I'm a lazybones and a nag,' she replied. 'Mibbie chaps might find me bonnie, but they won't want to marry me – not a moneyed gent anyway. Mibbie I'll end up like the girls at the Mussel Inn. Fine to look at, but not much more than a man's plaything.'

'Oh, Joan, where are you getting these notions from? Do you not have your eye on a lad?'

She pulled a face and shook her head. 'The lads around here are all stocky and stupid. I want a real man.'

Poor Joan. She had spent so much of her life being pleased with her looks that Spencer's words had truly shocked her.

'Well, you won't find many moneyed gents around here,' I

said. 'Get yourself off to Edinburgh, or London.' What good
had it done me? At least she wasn't nursing a broken heart.

'I might well do that,' she replied, looking serious. 'I do fancy
married life, Maggie. There's a passion in me.'

I ignored her and eyed the fire. It could do with another
log and had Spencer been here, I'd have put one on, but I
would rather have an early night than listen to Joan talking
twaddle.

'You stay here and have a rum, if you like,' I said. 'I'm off
to bed.'

Her eyes lit up at that, and I left her and went into the
bedroom. I would have an hour or so to myself before she
came in and joined me. An hour to lie still and think, without
small-talk or trifles. To let my mind wander, uninterrupted:
*Where is Spencer now? Has he escaped from his ship yet? Or is
he becoming used to life at sea?*

I brushed my braids out and put on my nightgown, shivering.
The damp seemed worse, the smell of it hanging in the room.
Perhaps I was as well giving up the lease when the time came.
I could hear Joan singing to herself, a song about creelers and
brine, and it gave me a sadness to hear it sung so sweetly by
my sister, despite the fact that she wanted nothing to do with
creelers or brine. For these were the things she really knew.

I clambered into bed, shivering even more under the cold
blankets. I should have put a hot brick in, but I was becoming
bad at being organized. Joan had already put her nightgown
on Spencer's side – I could see it under the pillow. It was a
nice one too. I lifted the pillow to take a look at it and saw
her scrapbook tucked there.

I had always peeked at Joan's scrapbook; it was natural to
me. Sisters cannot help but pry into each other's secrets. So
I looked again, bracing myself for more sketches of men's

bulging breeches, or worse. The pocket at the back was fastened, so I quickly popped the button open and had a look inside. This time there was something new, which I hadn't seen before. A small folded paper. I pulled it out and gasped at the familiar white packet, although this one was quite empty. The enigmatic smiling woman. Physic powder. Spencer's *Women's Tonic*.

Chapter Nine

Joan came to bed as the town clock struck midnight and the wind finally died down. She slipped under the sheets, smelling of rum. I lay like a rock, breathing deep, pretending to be asleep, for I was so bewildered and furious that I did not trust myself to open my mouth.

Had she taken the powder from my supplies? That was my first thought, but no, my supplies were hidden away and there were no packets ever left lying around. I hadn't even taken it, these past days. It was risky to have such a substance in the house. If I was ever discovered trying to prevent a pregnancy there would be trouble. Imagine what Ma would say. So had Joan got the powders from an apothecary? No, for I had never seen such a packet in Musselburgh. Not at the market and not in any of the shops, not even at the grocer's store at the Mussel Inn. Besides, I dare say if she was at the capers with a man, she would have told me, the blabbermouth that she is. Except if that man was Spencer.

Besides, the writing on the packet was the same. The same strange words written in a foreign language.

'Are you awake?' Joan whispered, turning to me. I could hear her getting comfy on Spencer's pillow. Was she trying to get close to him again? Was she missing him?

'Not really,' I mumbled. *Where had they done it? In this bed? How had they ever had the opportunity?* My mind raced. They were never alone together, apart from the times Spencer would walk her home from here. They would hardly have been at the capers together in the middle of a winter storm.

Then I knew: the nights I went to sit with Ma whilst Joan had choir practice. Twice a week, Tuesdays and Thursdays. I bet she'd skipped it and had come here instead.

I turned over to face her, but I kept my eyes closed. Our breathing rhythm settled into itself. We were so used to sleeping together that we had a way of moving in harmony, even when we'd been at loggerheads all our waking hours. I could tell she was settling in to sleep by the way she clicked her jaw and sniffed. By and by, Joan's breathing deepened, but I was wide awake. I opened my eyes and watched her face in the rush-light.

Fine to look at, but not much more than a man's plaything. Spencer knew that, of the two sisters, I would be the easier wife. He knew I would keep his secrets locked in a safe. He knew I would not stray or be tempted by another man when he was away. He knew I was ambitious for London and would work hard to get us there.

Joan shuddered then, as if she could hear my thoughts, and her eyes flew open. 'You're watching me,' she cried.

'You woke me up,' I said.

She tucked the blanket under her chin and fidgeted for a moment or two.

'Did something happen between you and Spencer?' I asked.

The blanket went very still.

'Did you fug him?' I went on. Now that it was out, it was out. 'Here in this bed?'

'Don't be daft, hen,' she said, but there was a catch in her voice.

'Did he give you something to take, afterwards?'

A pause of three or four heartbeats and then she sat up.

'Have you been looking in my scrapbook?' she asked. I could feel her glare more than see it, so dark was the room. I did not admit such a thing, but I knew then, and she knew that I had gone peeking. But, worse, Joan had gone fugging with my husband.

'You couldn't just let me have my happiness, could you? You had to go and ruin my marriage when it was barely even begun.'

She burst into tears, then got up, taking her scrapbook with her, and shut the bedroom door. And I could not have cared where she went, but in fact she went through to the parlour because she was more afeared of Da than she was of me, and if she had turned up back home at midnight he would have had something to say about it and would likely have belted her for arguing with me, and then again for leaving him and Ma in the first place.

I lay in bed, but did not sleep. I could hear Joan weeping through the wall, as though she were the victim in all of it. As the rush burned, and the wind toyed with the rafters and the window shutters, I watched the shadowy walls, the wardrobe, the curtains at the window, the blanket and the bedspread. All the fine things that Spencer had furnished our rooms with. The blue china vase where I would have put daffodils, had the time come. But what use was any of it now? Even if he came back on the dawn tide, what kind of marriage would we have? Imagine if I had found this out and Spencer hadn't been press-ganged?

Eventually Joan's weeping subsided, and I was grateful for that.

As the sun crept up, I knew that I would be out of Musselburgh on a morning coach. It was midwinter and a bad time to travel. Spencer had avoided winter journeys altogether. But I had to go now. 'Tis a terrible achy feeling to realize you are leaving everything behind. But with a tingle of wonder too. For had I not often yearned for London, and could I not recite the route southwards in my head?

I got out of bed, placing my feet firmly on the cold floor, and quickly packed a creel. I used one of Joan's too, the cow; I even packed some of her better clothes in it, for I had more need of them in London than she would have here. I put the money from the safe into Joan's nice tapestry purse, for I had nothing of that size myself and I would need to take that as well. I felt bad for a minute, pockling her things like that, but think of what she had done!

I passed through the parlour light like a ghost and stood, a moment, watching Joan sleeping soundly on the chair, under a blanket. Mibbie she would live here until the next rent was due. I would not put it past her at all. Mibbie Spencer would come back and they could be together. I checked myself in the looking glass. I looked as I felt: washed out, with bleary eyes. I tied my bonnet and pulled my plaits firmly over my shoulders.

I had never left Musselburgh before. Some of the fishwives took a cart to Edinburgh each day, up to Fishmarket Close, to sell their wares. But Ma said the two-hour journey there and back was a needless bother, even though you could get better prices. And the customers there were innkeepers and paid cooks and ladies' maids and the like, who would sniff and tap and inspect everything and look down their noses at us and ask for the *juiciest* mussels and the *most succulent* oysters, and so on. It was more of a bother than it was worth for Ma and Da, who also had their side-line in looking after smuggled tea.

But even though I'd never left the Honest Toun, folk came and went all the time, and the hub of all things in and out was the courtyard at the Mussel Inn. So that was where I went, carrying a weighty creel on my back. When I arrived, the kirk clock had only struck seven, but already there were carts being loaded with goods and drivers, and passengers eager to be on their way. I had decided the best way to go about my business was not to talk to anyone I recognized, for that would raise significant questions and they might not even let me go, without permission from my da. And if that seems strange for a married woman, my da was not a man you would cross. So I pulled my bonnet over my face as far as it would go and kept my head down, looking only at the hay-strewn mud below my feet and occasionally glancing up.

I soon spied a small fellow readying a coach and I made my way over to him.

'Good morning, sir,' I began, and he barely even stopped what he was doing, continuing to make sure everything was roped into place.

'If you're looking for a hitch, I'm off in half an hour and it's London I'm headed to, by way of Carlisle as I've mail to drop there. Three shillings up front.'

Drivers like him must see runaways all the time.

'I never rush, especially not in this weather, and I'm doing overnight stops at the inns at Lauder and Kelso, and wherever else I might need to stop after that for the sake of the horses,' he said. 'And a lass like you will need to look after yourself too, for I'm only a driver, not your guardian. I'm almost full today. Two gentlemen passengers and a load of salted herring at the back, not to mention the mail. They are the priority, not daft lassies. Are you in a rush to get anywhere?'

I shook my head.

'The Great North Road is quicker, but no-one is headed down that way this morning,' he went on. 'And the Carlisle route is safer, if you ask me. For you're more likely to be robbed over that way, it being busier.'

I had not even thought of being robbed and I must have looked alarmed, for he softened then and stopped fiddling with the ropes and stood up.

'Don't fret,' he added. 'I've never been robbed yet, and I carry a knife on me, just in case. You're as well to do the same, a young lass like you, and you can get one in that general store.' He ran his eyes up and down me, but not in a lewd way, more to check me over. 'And you don't look it, but if you happen to be with child, don't even think about getting on this coach, for I'm no midwife.' I shook my head, horrified at his frank talk. 'Oh, that's happened before.' He shrugged. 'And by the way, I'm not one for helping maids escape who've got into a fix by capering with their masters. Too much trouble. So if either of those categories applies to you, then you'll need to wait for the next coach south.'

Neither of those categories applied to me. I shook my head even more vigorously, feeling solemn.

'All right then, come back in twenty minutes, and I shall need those three shillings,' he continued.

I walked round to the general store. I had a decent feeling about the driver. I like a plain talker, for I'm a plain talker too. He had a soft accent that sounded a bit like Spencer's, but he was much older and his clothes were the most crumpled I had ever seen. The young lassie behind the counter in the store barely nodded as I asked for a sharp knife, and when she offered me a selection, laid out on a linen cloth, I chose something small and neat – enough to peel and core an apple, or stick into a highwayman, should one come along. Then I bought a small bottle of whisky, to keep out the cold, and I must confess I went into a panic to ensure I did not suffer any inconveniences on the journey and bought a sewing kit, some Castile soap, some powder to keep my armpits fresh and two pies, one meat and one fruit. Then a water can, of course, for I had forgotten one; and by the time I piled all of these into my creel, I was glad I was only walking back to the courtyard. All in all, it was more money than I had ever spent before in one go. But it kept my mind off the betrayal. It kept me moving forward.

When I returned to the coach, the courtyard had thronged into even more of a hubbub and I was truly feared now that someone would recognize me, so I marched as fast as I could, head down, and handed the driver his three shillings before he could change his mind.

'You sit facing the rear,' he instructed, 'for the gents are to face the direction of travel. And if you think you are going to be travel-sick, or need any attention for anything, knock sharp on the side.'

I nodded, but he didn't see that as he was too busy pocketing his fare and taking my creel to store under my seat. Then he stood aside to let me on, and I made myself as comfortable as I could, relieved that I was finally out of sight. Not long afterwards I heard the driver greet the two gents and then murmur something to them, which I supposed was his way of letting them know there was another passenger, then they boarded too, bidding me a polite good morning.

Well, I could tell straight away they were not real gents, of course. Aside from the fact that real gents would have their own private carriage, this pair of young men were traders, I could tell, as they had boxes to store; and one of them pulled out a parchment and they proceeded to go over it as soon as they were seated. So they would be boring company, which was just as well, for as the carriage pulled out and began its long, swaying, lurching trek, it dawned on me good and proper that I was leaving. Leaving Ma and Da and poor Little Paws, who was grey-whiskered now and I would likely never see her again. Leaving the gulls and their forlorn cries.

A fishing song ran through my head – 'Weel may the boatie row' – and that was me now: rowing off on a strange sea. I had seen enough of silvery shores and skies. I wanted gold. I thought of Joan, waking up and yawning and stretching her arms, all stiff from a night on a chair, and then realizing I'd vanished. I wondered if she would feel bad, or worried for me. I thought of Spencer, in the full and certain knowledge now that he would be in the arms of a port whore. I swigged my whisky.

My heart, my breath, the taste of fire – for that is what I had become now. Shrunken to the essence of myself. As Musselburgh flashed by, I was no longer part of it. Not of the kirk, nor the mills, nor the whitewashed houses nor the grassy fields. My past was falling away from me. I was shedding it as a snake sheds its skin. I was facing backwards, hurtling forwards. As the men pored over their papers, I closed my eyes and hoped I would never see the Honest Toun again.

Chapter Ten

Kelso, Roxburghshire
February 1724

We arrived at the River Inn, Kelso after two gruelling days on the road. I was freezing cold and bumped and bruised and bashed to bits, I cannot lie. I had managed not to be travel-sick, but only just. Mibbie if I had been out on boats more, like the fisherboys, I might've had a better stomach for travelling.

The first night we had stopped a few hours in the tiny village of Lauder, but that had been brief, and now we rode towards Kelso, slow and quiet as the sun rose. The sky was the colour of violets. Ice glowed over the countryside. Our breath hung in clouds. Oh, I was traversing the roads on my very own map. I was making my way down the route I had dreamed of. I could scarcely believe it was happening. I wished now that I had crept in and unpinned the map from the parlour wall and brought it with me, but that would have woken Joan. Instead I took it all in, all of the scenery and scents, until we arrived some hours later at the River Inn, a handsome hostelry on a neat street a little way down from Kelso's market square and near the banks of the Tweed.

It was late afternoon by the time we got there and the world had warmed up a bit. As the driver handed the horses over to the ostler, and the gents got out and sorted their boxes, I stretched my legs to get the blood back into them. I had caught glimpses of the market town on our way in and I wanted to see it now. It reminded me of Musselburgh, with its riverbanks and white cottages, but was more dignified, without the screech of gulls overhead. The innkeeper's wife assigned me to the attic where the ladies were put, and gave me the key to a small room with two beds.

I made my way up three flights of rickety stairs, past paintings of swans and ducks and men catching trout. When I got to the top I was puffed out. The other bed was occupied, but whoever my room-companion was, she was out when I arrived. This lady had left a gold-coloured cloak on the stand, which I thought an extremely bold bit of colour, and a collection of pots on the table filled with face-paints. At this gaudiness and finery I panicked again at whether I had everything I needed for London. After inspecting myself in the dusty looking glass above the washstand I concluded that I could not arrive in London in such a dull bonnet as this, and I decided to see if there was a milliner selling decently priced hats. Oh, and this lady's marvellous pots! I examined them. One contained rouge and another was half full of a heavy-looking white paste, and there were two wool pads sitting beside them. Beside all of that was a small brown bottle with a cork stopper and a hand-written label on the side. The ink was faded and thumbed, so even if I could have read, I would not have known what liquid it contained or what to do with it. I did not much like the look of the bottle. It looked powerfully medicinal.

The pots intrigued me, though. I had never worn rouge or face-paint of any kind, merely imagined myself with a spot of it on my cheeks as a London girl. Joan had secretly mixed her own rouge once, in an oyster shell, from some ingredients she had bought from the apothecary in Musselburgh. When she waltzed into the parlour with two bright-pink cheeks, Da had been onto her straight away and taken it out to the midden and said that only whores wear paint. But there I was, in a new town, newly heartbroken, and I supposed I might dab some on to brighten me up, so to speak, and I was sure the lady who owned the rouge would be none the wiser.

The looking glass was of poor quality and had not been dusted for some time, so I had to peer closely, but I brushed the pink wool pad across my cheek. There was not much of a difference on the first dab, but I got the gist of it soon enough and was quickly admiring myself. What a difference a spot of colour made! *Spencer would fancy me like this,* I thought, and then my heart sank with the fresh dismay of all that had happened, and what a shame it was that he would never see me looking pretty like this. For of course in my dreams of London, with Spencer, I was gaudy and glitzy and he quite the dapper gent, but it was all a sham now. *Don't think of it,* I urged myself and put a bit of rouge to my lips this time. But just as I was smacking and pursing my lips and fluttering my eyelashes at myself, the chamber door clattered open and in marched a haughty-looking well-dressed lady. I dropped the rouge pad but, alas, a moment too late. I was caught in the act of stealing her face-paint.

'You little thief,' the lady cried, tossing her hat on her bed and pulling off her gloves. 'Those are my bits and bobs, and I should never have left them out. Mr Baxter said there was a new girl lodging here tonight, but he never said she was a light-fingered little wench.' She stood and glowered at me. She was tall and spectacularly pretty, with white-blonde hair in ringlet curls and eyes like fine blue china saucers.

'I am hardly a thief, miss,' I said. 'I've had a tiring journey

and I was only trying it on to perk up my face.' I've had years
of silly bickers with Joan and, in my experience, they flare up
fast, but then dampen down as quick. But this lady was not
having any of it and was clearly in the temper for a hot fight.
She threw herself on her bed, almost squashing her hat, and
folded her slim little arms crossly.

'What's your name and what's your business in Kelso?' she
demanded.

'I'm Maggie Dickson and I'm only here one night,' I said,
trying to sound reassuring. 'I've come from up north, by the
coast, and I'll be off in the morning. I am bound for London,'
I added, with an air of what I hoped was haughtiness to match
her own.

'And what is your business in London?' she asked, and I
thought her a nosy cow, but I answered anyway, for I did not
want her turning on her sharp little heels and telling this Mr
Baxter I was bad news.

'I am setting up a trade in London, as I have an interest in
perfumes,' I told her. Now this was a lie, for I had no knowledge of Spencer's trade or contacts. But I had remembered
what he'd also said, about apprenticing myself as a seamstress
or milliner, with my knowledge of lines and knots and fast
working hands, and that is what I planned to do. That plan
felt a little too loose, however, to be sharing with strangers and
I wanted this lady to think highly of me.

'Perfumes, you say?' She sounded intrigued, but asked no
more. 'Well, Mistress Dickson, you shall keep your hands off
my belongings and I don't want to be woken before nine,' she
continued. 'I keep late hours and I need my beauty sleep. So
if you're on a morning coach, ready yourself quietly.'

I nodded and she thawed a little and started unlacing her
boots.

'Oh, it's been a long day,' she said. 'And I am peckish already and it's not yet supper time.' She peered towards my creel. 'Goodness that's an unwieldy-looking basket. Is that the fashion by the coast? Do they carry them on their backs? Are the girls there all broad-shouldered like you?'

I nodded, feeling like a hulk.

'Do you have anything decent to eat in it?' she went on. 'I can't bear to go downstairs yet and sit there, with all those men gawping at me and trying to buy me cheap ale.'

I did, as it happened. I had the bottle of whisky, which I brought out and her eyes lit up at, and I had a big piece of gingerbread, which I had bought in Lauder and not finished, so I let her have the rest of that and a tot of whisky and that appeased her greatly. She sat and nibbled away at it all, quite delicately, and I hovered around, not knowing whether to go and get that new bonnet or stay and become acquainted, for I was not well versed in the ways of travelling women.

After a few moments I asked her what her name was and what her business was and why she was in Kelso. I asked in a friendly way, but she did not like the questions much.

'I am Mrs Rose, a widow,' she said. 'I have an uncle who lives here in Kelso – a physician as it happens, a widower himself – and I am visiting him.' She frowned. 'And he likes me to visit him at his cottage, but not stay the night, for he does not have the space for a guest. He is a kindly man, my uncle, and I am his favourite niece.'

Well, that was an odd story, but I let her carry on with it.

'My uncle is a doctor, Dr McTavish. He is often up north, in Edinburgh, as he has a medical practice there, but he lives the rest of the time in his little cottage further up this road,' she went on. 'I join him for lunch, and I usually stay a while. We play dominoes actually, and then I am back here for supper.'

The tale sounded tall, and a cover story for something far saucier going on between the two of them, especially given her rouge collection. She had the decency to blush as she told it, but I took in her beautifully tailored gown, the moody blue of a stormy sea, and her fine boots, polished to a squeak, and I thought there was clearly money to be made playing dominoes in Kelso.

'I love dominoes,' I declared. 'Do you have a set here?'

She looked a little horrified at that.

'Sadly and, unfortunately, no. Dr McTavish keeps his dominoes in a brass tin at his home,' she declared.

Of course there were whores at the Mussel Inn, but I never really saw them and, from what anyone said, they hung around the bar and would do anything for a penny or two. This whore had the air of a real lady, aged around five-and-twenty, I would guess, so a little older and a great deal edgier than me. I wondered how many customers she had, or if she was solely mistress to this Dr McTavish.

'Are you in Kelso long?' I enquired.

'I'm here for the foreseeable,' she said. 'Dr McTavish visits Edinburgh every six weeks or so, to see his patients, and he is only just back.'

He must be keeping her well, but I am sure she would prefer to be in her own rooms, which was mibbie why she was so put out at my arrival. Well, that was hardly my fault, was it? So I told her I was heading out on an errand and I would leave her to rest and she seemed appeased at that, settling herself down on her bed and seizing upon her little brown bottle with a sniff of anticipation, which I was now sure contained something potent, given to her by her doctor friend.

I took the tapestry purse from where it was tucked in the bottom of my creel and off I went to Kelso square. The shops and the market were almost closing for the day, but I managed to find a small hat shop that sold very fine bonnets and, after much deliberation, I settled on a navy one with a delicately frilled edge. I'm sure it's something I could have sewn myself, but I did not have the time nor the inclination. I spent a while browsing the baskets in the market to see if there was something less like a fishwife's creel, but although there were plenty, none were as sturdy, and I needed mine for the journey. When I got to London I might find something and, at this thought, my heart fluttered a bit with nerves. I was almost out of Scotland now. I was about to cross the great divide.

I knew absolutely no one in London. I knew nothing about it except what I'd heard from Spencer and the tea men. I knew it was a place where you could make your fortune, but I also feared it could be a place of grave danger. Of rogues and thieves, and worse. Mibbie it was full of Spencers. I shuddered at that. I now felt guilty at the fact that I'd just bought the bonnet and nearly took it back there and then. Spencer had left a fair bit of money, but what if I couldn't get an apprenticeship? I fancied learning something frivolous, like how to add feathers to caps or how to sew frills on bodices, but what if these seamstresses looked at me the same way Mrs Rose did and declared me too *broad-shouldered* to sit in their elegant workshops? I vowed there and then not to spend another penny, except on food and ale, until I was safely in lodgings and had employment, even if I had to start off my London life as a Thames fishergirl.

I returned to the River Inn in time for supper and, after I had freshened up and put my bonnet in my creel, I sat at a dining table opposite Mrs Rose, who was eyed heartily by the two gents I was travelling with. But she paid no heed to them and must have been well used to men measuring her up all the time, for she tucked into her fried trout quite hungrily.

How did she manage it? To eat calmly whilst all were agog; and to sell herself for fine gowns. When I had lain with Spencer I had loved him with my body and soul. Mibbie Joan had too. Had Mrs Rose decided to become a whore for fur cloaks and the best leather boots? Or had she no choice?

I did not dare ask her. She sipped a straw-coloured liquor from a thin glass and regarded me.

'It's French wine. Mr Baxter keeps a bottle behind the counter for me. You can go and fetch yourself a glass if you like,' she offered. 'In fact fetch the bottle.'

I did, not quite sure whether I felt like a sophisticate or a courtesan asking Mr Baxter for the French wine. He gave nothing of his thoughts away and I sat with my glass, the bottle between Mrs Rose and I, listening to the chatter and song. For the first time in a while I felt merry. Mrs Rose relaxed too, cradling her glass in her hand. She wore pretty rings, nicer than my glass one, and I thought mibbie there is something to be said for women having enough of their own cash to buy rings and French wine and not giving their love away to men, like I had.

'Sip it slowly, for wine is halfway between ale and rum in strength and far nicer in flavour, but it goes to your head quick enough,' Mrs Rose urged me. She did the same, taking dainty sips and dabbing her lips with a red lace kerchief each time. Red to match her rouge. I warmed up.

'Tell me more about this perfume trade,' she said.

My heart sank. But I did not want to be caught out in a web of lies, for I was enjoying the evening. 'Perfume is a marvellous thing,' I said, repeating the kind of things Spencer had said. 'It can make an ordinary gent smell most alluring, and it can make ladies lose their minds and spend a fortune on something in a tiny bottle.'

She sniffed the air. 'I adore fine scents. *Adore* them. But I do not detect any fine scent on you, Mistress Dickson. In fact I detect the smell of horses and carts and armpits.'

I shot her an awful glare at that, the kind of look that Joan would have got for saying something rude. 'I am surprised you can smell anything,' I said. 'With your nose jammed in that brown bottle so often.'

Mrs Rose blinked. I dare say she was not used to talk like that. For a split second I regretted my outburst. But then she laughed.

'Oh, you are a funny little thing, my dear,' she said. 'Here, have a little top-up of my wine. Just a tot. Oh, I dare say you might be right. But if you have not had the pleasure of laudanum, then you have not had pleasure at all.'

'I should not like to try laudanum,' I replied. That was a word I had heard before, from the tea men. It was a word uttered in whispers and shudders and with shakings of heads. You could grow to depend on it. 'I do not like the idea of relying on bottles and potions to get through the day.'

Mrs Rose grew solemn at that. 'You are wise,' she said. 'But that's my weakness.'

By and by, some of the more refined folk retired to their rooms, including my fellow coach gents, and the songs got a little more raucous. One man stood up and tapped Mrs Rose on the shoulder and whispered something into her ear. She listened most intently, at first shaking her head, then after more whispering she nodded.

The man disappeared upstairs and Mrs Rose turned to me again, her voice thick and sweet with wine.

'I shall retire now, but do not come to the room for another hour, if you don't mind, and in return for keeping your-self out of my way, you may have another glass of my nice French wine,' she told me. 'In fact you might as well finish the bottle.'

I knew exactly what all this was about. She meant to enter-tain the man in our room. She had likely had a decent offer for an hour of her time. I did not like to be any party to this kind of caper. But what could I do? I was persuaded by the promise of the wine, and poured myself the rest and watched the clock. It was a fine evening all right, with singing filled with *diddle-diddles* and *fair maids* and *petticoats*, and bellowed guffaws erupting around the room. But when Mrs Rose's man returned after almost an hour, I decided I'd had enough wine and wanted nothing more than to lie down and get a decent night's sleep. I set down my glass and thanked the innkeeper's wife, who was bustling around the place looking exhausted, and I made my way up the rickety stairs and past all the paintings of the fish and fowl.

Mrs Rose was wiping off her face-paint and seemed pleased enough with herself, humming a ditty as she went about her ablutions. *Is it really that easy? Is this what becomes of women who travel alone?* I stripped to my nightgown, feeling plain in her company, and got under the covers, brushing my hair and watching her as I let the blankets warm me up. She was pretty enough not to need any cosmetics, I thought, and she didn't half admire herself, prancing around the room in her creamy corset and silky drawers. Her skin was the colour of sunshine and her shoulders were freckled. I felt frowzy, lying there in my musty nightie, for what was I but a wide-shouldered, stout thing good for hoicking creels and not much else besides.

'How long have you been widowed?' I asked her, wondering if this part of her story was even true.

'Two years,' she replied. 'My husband was a sailor and he died in a sea storm.'

Well, that smarted, and my face fell and she noticed, pausing to see what I would say. Mibbie Mrs Rose would understand something of affairs of the heart.

'I lost my husband to the sea too. I was married, quite recently, but my husband was taken by a press gang,' I told her.

Her eyes widened. 'You poor soul,' she said. 'And him too, abducted like that. How cruel. Did you love him dearly?'

'I did,' I replied. 'With all of my heart, but the worst of it was that I then found out that he'd betrayed me with my own sister.'

'Oh!' she cried, aghast. 'What a calamity.' She perched on the edge of my bed and took my hand. Her hand was cool; mine warm. Her blue eyes searched mine. Her lashes were thick and long, her brows two perfect arches. I was reminded of a doll we used to play with, Joan and I, with a drawn-on face.

'When I discovered their affair, I got on the first coach out of town,' I admitted. 'I took all his savings and I'm going to make a success of my life, I swear it.'

'Oh, you shall,' she said. 'Men are beasts. *Beasts*. They only want one thing. My Dr McTavish . . .' Here she paused, thinking of how to phrase it. 'My Dr McTavish, he's a dreadful man. Old and nasty and he thinks he can rule me just because he pays me an allowance and gives me laudanum. But I'm the same as you, Mistress Dickson, I want to make my own mark in the world. I can't wait to get out of this horrible little inn and have my own place – imagine that! – and not have to answer to anyone.'

I nodded, knowing how she felt.

She squeezed my hand.

'And it gets worse,' she went on. The last of the fire sizzled in the grate and the candles flickered. I knew she was about to disclose some great horror. 'Dr McTavish has me at his mercy,' she whispered. 'For what you said before is right: I am heavily reliant on the laudanum. It keeps my nerves in balance. It's the only thing that'll do it. Dr McTavish gives me a bottle a week. On top of the allowance. But I do not trust the man. Not as far as I could throw him. Do you remember I told you he was widowed? Well, I suspect he got rid of his wife.' She paused and stared at me, most theatrically.

'Got rid of her how?' I asked.

'Well, he is a doctor, so it could have been any potion or poison. But Mrs McTavish was alive and well until twelve months or so ago, about the time I met him. I met him here, in this very inn, one night when I was passing through; and I was on my uppers because my husband had left me barely anything and I'd been evicted from our lodgings. I was travelling, looking for work. Anyway he complained about Mrs McTavish constantly. Kitty, that was her name, the poor dear. After a day or so of taking me for lunches and walks and so on, he declared himself most in love with me.' She fluttered her eyelashes at this. 'Most devastatingly in love with me. And how different I was from Kitty, who was a monstrous nag. And his marriage was chaste and miserable. He begged me to stay awhile here, in Kelso, and not venture any further in search of work. He gave me my first dose of laudanum, which he said would help my nerves; said he would reward me for my company, from time to time. Any price. Well, a few weeks later Kitty died.'

'Oh, goodness,' I breathed.

'She had dropped dead, just like that. It was the talk of the inn for a while. Poor Kitty. One morning she was fossicking through her orchards for cherries and apples, and by lunch she was clean dead. They said it was her heart. Well, Dr McTavish said it was her heart. But I do not think there was anything wrong with her heart, for she was only a woman of thirty-five.' Mrs Rose drew a deep breath, and I could see her pulse quivering at her throat. Her skin was goosepimpled. 'He poisoned her. I am sure of it. To get her out of the way.'

'If you suspect him of such wickedness, why do you associate with him?' But I could barely believe this tale. Mrs Rose was the most melodramatic person I had ever met.

'You are right,' she replied. 'I should not associate with him at all. But he is my best source of income for now, and I will move on when I have saved up enough to live on.'

It sounded awful. I was relieved I was not this pretty little thing, terrified of the man she relied upon. She reminded me, suddenly, of my own ma. And although you could not find any two women who were less alike, they both had the fear of a man about them. It shrinks a woman, that fear. Diminishes her to a shell.

'But never mind me,' Mrs Rose continued, suddenly remembering my tale of woe. 'Never mind my silly stories, and my suspicions. You have been through the wars, Mistress Dickson. And a young thing like you.' I nodded again, feeling sorrier for myself by the minute. 'You deserve good fortune and I know you'll get it in London, with your perfume business.'

'Thank you,' I replied, although I did not admit that I actually had no connections in the perfume trade in London and had rather exaggerated my situation to impress her. 'And I am sorry for trying on your face-paint earlier, only I had never worn it before and I was trying to make myself feel a bit better.'

'Well, as we are being honest, Mistress Dickson, I will admit that I think you suited that rouge. It made you look pretty as a berry.'

Goodness, I blushed at that. For I did not see myself as pretty at all, but I did decide to buy a pot of rouge for myself, once I got to London.

Mrs Rose made soothing sounds then, and rose off the bed and carried on her ablutions, but this time she flashed me occasional glances, making sure I was all right.

She blew out most of the candles, leaving one on the side-table, and we snuggled down under our bedspreads in unison. I felt my eyes grow heavy and I knew I would fall fast asleep soon.

'Goodnight, Mrs Rose,' I whispered. 'I shall be quiet as a mouse in the morning, but it was good to make your acquaintance.'

'Goodnight, Mistress Dickson,' she said. 'And good luck on your adventures.'

And with that, I fell into a dreamless sleep, for which I was very grateful.

I woke abruptly the next morning to the clatter of the horses being tied to their carts in the courtyard. The sun was shining crisp and bright through the small attic window, warming up my bed, and I swung myself up and out, braced for the next stage in my journey. Tiptoeing at first, so as not to wake Mrs Rose, I was astonished to see that she was already up and gone. Her bed lay empty, the bedspread tossed to one side. I turned back to my own bed and pulled out my creel, ready to dress for the day, but it was in a terrible mess – all my bits and pieces dishevelled.

I realized at once, of course, what had happened, but I still tore through my belongings looking for the tapestry purse. It was not there. The new bonnet gone too. Mrs Rose had upped and taken them, and her cloak and her own fine dress and all of my money, save for a few pennies that were lying at the bottom of the creel.

But she had not taken everything. She had left my clothes and the rest of my things, and two items on the washstand: her rouge and face-paint pots. Mibbie it was an oversight. Mibbie it was her horrible way of trying to make up for what she had done.

Chapter Eleven

I panicked all over the inn, going into all the downstairs rooms to see if there was any trace of Mrs Rose. I found the innkeeper's wife and her cook taking the morning rolls out of the oven and, when I told them what had happened, the innkeeper's wife sent the cook out to tell my driver what had occurred, then sat me down at the kitchen table and poured me a strong coffee.

'Mrs Rose,' she said, 'I have always been wary of her, but she is well connected in Kelso.' Her hands worried from her hips to her chin to her apron and she shook her head all the while. 'What a bad business. A terrible to-do.'

'She has left me with only pennies.' The coffee was too hot and too thick and too sour, but I sipped it anyway, trying to get my head straight.

'She consorts with the widower Dr McTavish and I have never liked him, but he will be furious she is gone,' Mrs Baxter said. 'He's quite an influential man, Mistress Dickson. I hope he does not blame us for her disappearance. Mibbie she'll see sense and come back.'

'She'll not be back,' I replied bitterly. 'She has my life savings.'

'Oh, hen,' sympathized the woman. 'Shall we fetch the constable?'

I thought hard about that and nearly said yes, but what if they said I ought to return to my own home? And where had the money come from in the first place, for had I not stolen it from Spencer, who had obtained it from smuggled goods?

I shook my head. 'It is gone now,' I said.

There was a knock on the kitchen door and my coach driver stood, looking awkward, folding and unfolding his hat.

'I've heard you've been robbed, Mistress Dickson,' he said. 'Seems Mrs Rose has taken one of the horses too – a decent one at that. Myself and the ostler shall take a couple of horses ourselves and see if she's in the vicinity, and find out if the night watchman saw anything. We can delay our journey by an hour or so, but no more.'

Off he went, and I felt grateful that someone was looking out for me and hoped hard that Mrs Rose had not got very far at all. The cook returned and gave me a morning roll, but it soon became too crowded for the three of us in there, so I went back upstairs to sort out the mess of the room and have a think about what on God's earth I was going to do.

I had already paid my London fare, so I could still travel. I had a few pennies and that might see me all right for food. Mibbie the driver would help too, for he seemed a bit sorry for me. But then I would arrive in London with nothing to my name and nowhere to sleep. *Oh, curse that awful bitch, Mrs Rose. Rose by name: beautiful, but thorned. Is my life blighted that everyone I come across will betray me?* I looked around me at the clothes strewn across the floor, the mess my creel was in, and I could not move a muscle. The only thing I saw fit to do was get back under the bedspread, utterly defeated, and sob my poor heart out. So that is what I did.

A while passed. I felt the sun go behind clouds and come out again. I wept. I caught a whiff of how rancid my armpits had become and cared not a jot about it. Mrs Rose had probably taken my armpit powder too. I heard carts leave and folk creak about the stairs, and I felt so exhausted they would have to carry me out.

Eventually the innkeeper's wife came to my bedside and put her hand on my shoulder.

'There's no trace of Mrs Rose, and your driver must leave soon, for his gents need to be on their way,' she said. 'Are you travelling today? He says he can take you now, or else he will owe you the rest of the journey the next time he calls, but that might be in a month or so.'

I did not answer.

Mrs Baxter sighed and I could sense her looking about the room.

'Listen to me, Mistress Dickson,' she went on. 'You have been hard done by on your way to London. Do not go there without a bit of money behind you. It is not a place to arrive penniless. It will swallow you up.'

My eyes flew open at that, but she did not see, for I was buried under the bedspread.

'Folk think London's a place where fortunes are made, but some of the tales I hear in this inn are grim ones. You'd need somewhere decent to stay, for starters. And somewhere nice. Many of streets are strewn with filth, and there are barefoot urchins in the bad parts, who will rob you quicker than Mrs Rose did.'

'But I have nowhere else to go,' I mumbled.

'Well, you can stay here a while,' she replied. 'Mrs Rose had paid for her bed for a month and she was only here a week. There's plenty of work in Kelso. What line of work are you in?'

'I'm a Fisherrow girl,' I said.

'A Fisherrow fishwife?' she cried. 'All the way down here? Well, never mind that. I don't ask people's business, but your folks are well known as hard workers. Famously so.'

I nodded, still under the blanket, but listening intently now.

'A Fisherrow lass,' she mused. 'Well, I never in all my days thought I would see a Fisherrow lass in my own inn. The hardiest women in Scotland, and one of them right here in the River Inn.'

Are we? I'd had no idea. I'd thought myself ordinary. Ma and Joan too. Now I realized that word of us must travel, for we travel ourselves with our creels as far as the Edinburgh markets, where all sorts of gossip and stories must spread. I felt a flicker of pride in my home town. It surprised me.

'Well, I would take you on myself,' she said with a delighted chortle. 'In the kitchen or serving. Anywhere in fact. I bet you could gut a trout in a flash. I bet you'd show us how it's done.'

I nodded again.

'And carry heavy loads?'

Heavier than some lads could.

'I pay sensible wages too,' she added. 'You could save.'

I pulled the blanket away from my face.

'Kelso's a good place,' she continued. 'Never mind what happened with Mrs Rose. We have a decent trade, and most folks are kind. What do you say?'

What could I say? 'I should be most grateful for that chance,' I told her.

Mrs Baxter looked pleased as could be. Then she hesitated. 'You are a good girl, though, aren't you? You're not a runaway or anything like that?'

'Certainly not,' I lied.

'And I do not mean to pry, but you *are* a maiden, aren't you? And free to make your own decisions. Free to work? There's not a husband who's going to come looking for you, causing all sorts of trouble for us all? It's just that I see you wear a ring, but it looks like a paste one to me.'

'That's right, Mrs Baxter. I'm no one's property but my own,'
I lied. 'I wear the ring to keep men from bothering me.' I dared
not tell her about Spencer and that I didn't even know if my
husband was dead or alive, in case she changed her mind.

She nodded, folding her arms in front of her. She was a
stout woman of forty years or so. Plain-faced with watery eyes
and a chin that sank into her bosom. Her apron was grey, but
pristine. Ma always admired a woman who kept a clean apron.
'A clean apron is like a neat line of laundering hanging in the
back close,' she'd say. 'The mark of a respectable housewife.'

I needed respectable. I needed pristine. I needed a decent
bit of luck now, after all the calamities that had befallen me.
As if she could read my thoughts, Mrs Baxter chewed her lip
and fixed me with a certain stare before saying what came
next.

'Now, Mistress Dickson, I am taking you on trust, for I
believe you to be a decent lass from hard-working folks.'

I opened my mouth to say something, but she carried on
talking over me.

'Mistress Dickson,' she went on, blinking slowly, seeming to
enjoy how my name hissed a little in her mouth. 'The River
Inn is a place where folks come and go, but at the heart of it
are hard-working, honest Kelso folks, who go by our reputations.
On the roads between Scotland and England there are inns,
and there are *inns*, if you catch my drift. Ours is a good inn.
There are always going to be folks like Mrs Rose, and the kind
of gents who enjoy her company. But those are the patrons,
and we are the proprietors. In other words, Mistress Dickson,
we keep an honest household. We must, for the parish officers
come calling quite often and they would like us shut down,
for they think we are a house of loose morals. But if I was to
ban every whore and every thief from this inn, I would likely

close down within a month, so I have to turn a blind eye to much of what goes on downstairs in the public rooms, and often in the bedrooms. But we who work here are above scandal.'

'Of course,' I whispered.

'Any whiff of scandal and I would have to put you out on your arse,' she added. I flinched at her language. 'I've hired maids before, and sometimes it works out and sometimes it doesn't. I had to send the last one home, for she got herself into trouble with a patron. Off she went to the House of Correction, but that's what happens if you don't obey the house-rules.'

'The House of Correction?'

'Oh, you must have seen it on your way into town,' Mrs Baxter replied airily. 'The big house on the outskirts, with the high wall. It's where the parish officers send the vagrants and beggars, and the thieves and whores.'

I frowned at that, but she did not seem to notice. I had not seen any such thing as a House of Correction, but I suppose I didn't really know what one looked like.

'Well, you can start tomorrow,' she said. 'I am pleased we have struck a deal.

My plan hatched, as a creature from an egg. Delicate at first, but then bolder and with all the urgency of new life.

I would stay a while working at the River Inn and save, and then depart for London. I was still desperate to go. It was a dream and I wanted more from life than to be stuck in a market town, but it would have to do for now. The River Inn had the feel of busyness and of being at the heart of the trav-elling route. It was as good a place as any to get myself set up again whilst the rest of the winter passed. The Baxters – the innkeeper and his shrewd wife – ran a tight ship, but I trusted them. As long as I worked hard and lived up to my reputation as a reliable fishergirl, seeking her fortune in the world, they would do me right.

So there I was, for the time being. Nestled amongst thatched cottages and handsome town houses with gardens and orchards and surrounded by peaceful farms. Nice and clean, and not a whiff of sea air nor a speck of sand. Just a market town where the Tweed and Teviot shake hands. A town as sturdy and sure and drab as the brown trout that filled its rivers. And I dare say that would suit hundreds of girls like me. In fact they might even count themselves lucky to have landed on their feet like this, after such a close shave.

But not me. Oh dear, I wish it *was* me, but the yearnings would not stop. I still hankered for London and, when I heard the morning carts roll out of the yard, humming with forward thrust southwards, I vowed that would be me one day soon.

Sometimes I would catch a flash of my ma and Joan. They would come to me in the kitchen, when Cook fried fish, or by the hearth when I washed and dried my stockings and they dangled in rows.

At night, in the very dark and still of it, when nothing moved save the rustle of rats in the courtyard hay, I imagined Spencer whispering to me from a far-off sea. And, despite everything, I imagined these words: *I miss you.*

Mrs Baxter took me on as her assistant, serving the patrons and helping clean the rooms, and that kind of solid work kept the Fisherrow ghosts at bay.

I had nothing to do with the stables or with taking money. Mr

Baxter oversaw all of that himself. Mrs Baxter and her cook made all the meals, but I was an extra pair of hands for running about and washing pots, and she often declared that she did not know what she ever did without me; and now that I was here her life was ten times easier, as I did the work of ten men and was far better than any other of the helps she had ever hired; and it was true what they said about the fishwives of Fisherrow: reliable and hard-working and decent to the very core.

Well, for my part, it was hard work all right and long hours from breakfast to after supper, but all far easier than dealing with bait and lines and cut fingers and stinking fish and heavy creels, and taking up lazy Joan's slack.

But increasingly my thoughts turned to home. To Ma mostly. She would not know whether I was dead or alive. How long would it be before they would all stop talking of me? When would they start to think me gone for ever? When would I become unmentioned?

I soon discovered what Mrs Baxter had meant when she talked of the parish officers and their House of Correction. Late one evening, just as the ales were fizzing down to their dregs, the front door flew open. Two men in high hats stalked in, carrying brass lanterns.

'The parish officers are here,' I heard Mr Baxter call to his wife out back, his voice sounding strangled.

There was a flurry of activity around the room, as if a gust had blasted in. Books were tidied into bags, backs straightened, dice and playing cards pocketed. A man who had been singing a bawdy song about a street called Grope Lane fell silent.

The men walked up to the bar and would not sit down, nor take a drink, even when Mr Baxter tried to insist.

'We do not drink spirits, and we do not take alcohol of any sort in public,' I heard one of them say.

Mr Baxter nodded to me with a look that meant *carry on as you were doing*, so I continued to wipe tables with my damp cloth and pick up empty cups and glasses. The atmosphere was so tense, with no one saying anything at all, that I could not escape into the kitchen fast enough. There Mrs Baxter and Cook stood with their dish rags slung over their shoulders, looking grave.

'They visit once a month or so,' Mrs Baxter said to me in a low voice. 'They are looking for any excuse to shut us down.'

'They think we are an immoral establishment,' observed Cook. 'And ought not to sell any alcohol, nor let women in the door.'

'Utter nonsense,' spat Mrs Baxter. 'It makes me furious that they throw their weight about.'

Cook shifted from one foot to the other. 'We are not careful enough, Mrs Baxter,' she said. 'You know my thoughts on the matter.' She turned to me.

The low rumble of voices at the other side of the kitchen door told me that the parish officers were in conversation with Mr Baxter.

'You are our third kitchen maid in three years, Mistress Dickson,' she continued, with a flourish of her dish rag as she brought it from her shoulder and toyed with it idly. 'The one before you got herself into quite a fix.'

''Tis easy done,' murmured Mrs Baxter.

'There are fellows who will promise you a betrothal if you lie with them,' said Cook. 'And plenty of them come through these doors. Mrs Baxter here had to throw the last girl out for coming to her complaining she had been promised a betrothal, then had woken to find the chap gone and a baby started, didn't you, Mrs Baxter?'

My landlady tutted and nodded her head sadly.

'And where is she now, the last girl?' Cook asked the question, but answered herself, in hushed tones, sucking her teeth as she spoke. 'She was sent to the House of Correction and she gave birth there, and now the babe is under the care of the parish, for she will never be able to take care of it. Wet-nursed at Muir Farm and apprenticed there when it turns fourteen.'

A log cracked in the fire and the cauldron that hung over it sizzled, a teardrop of soup oozing down the side. My armpits prickled.

'The parish officers will not stay long,' said Mrs Baxter, rubbing at the faint bristle on her chin, as if trying to reassure herself more than us. 'Let's busy ourselves with that stock-count of the pantry cupboard. Maggie, see to those pots.'

The pair made their way into the cupboard, their backsides at the door, their apron strings tied in neat loops. As they counted packets of tea and boxes of white pepper, and jars of preserved plums and raspberry jams, I lathered the pots with weak soft soap and tried to give them a decent scrub in the tin bath of tepid water. I could not stop thinking of the woman sent to the House of Correction, beside beggars and vagrants and thieves. Of the baby, dragged up by folk who were not even its kin, and put to work as soon as it was able.

When I went back into the parlour, the parish officers were gone and the mood was lighter. A new game of dice was up. As I put glasses back on shelves, Mr and Mrs Baxter chatted in low, worried voices.

'They checked the visitors' book and seemed satisfied. They had a good look around the place and asked the patrons for their names and their business. They were assured that we were hoarding no highwaymen or prostitutes,' Mr Baxter told his wife.

'It is a good thing Mrs Rose went when she did,' his wife commented. 'They would have had something to say about her.'

'I am sure Dr McTavish would have stepped in and stopped her being thrown out,' said Mr Baxter. 'He knows the parish officers too well.'

'Well, we live to fight another day,' replied Mrs Baxter. 'They would need a good reason to close down this parlour.'

It worried me, talk like that. For I was not protected – not like Mrs Rose. I could not put a foot wrong, not if I was to stay at the inn long enough to save for London.

Chapter Twelve

Kelso
March 1724

O ne evening when I had been in Kelso a month or so, a quietish evening when the inn was only half full, I noticed a gentleman sitting with a parchment and quill, which was a funny sight beside his game pie, so I stopped at his table and asked him if he needed a bigger table.

'I am fine, lass,' he said. 'I am well used to juggling my work and my supper.' It turned out he was a scribe who took payment for writing out folks' messages and got them sent to wherever they needed to be sent, by way of one of the post boys who called at the inn.

'And you can get them sent anywhere?' I asked, curious.

'Tuppence for Scotland, thruppence for England,' he said. 'And you'd need to dictate it to me tonight for I'm off first thing.

I knew it was the right thing to do, even if it cost me some of my hard-earned wages. And if Spencer came back, he'd know where I was. Ma and Da could take the letter to someone at the Mussel Inn and they could read it out to them.

'I've never dictated a letter before,' I said, wiping my hands on my apron and feeling nervous, for it all felt quite official.

'Nothing to it,' he replied reassuringly. 'Just say it as you would if the person was in the room, and I will sort out the rough bits.'

I went to the kitchen and told Mrs Baxter I needed a break to do some business. Pouring myself a glass of French wine for a bit of courage, for I'd become accustomed to the taste, I sat back down opposite the scribe. He was a small man and clever-looking, with round spectacles and a neat grey beard. He nodded to me as I sat, and then took up his quill.

It was a strange thing to be doing, and I took a gulp of my wine and made sure my hair was tidy and my apron straight – not that it mattered, for my folks would not see me, only hear my words – and I focused on the congealing gravy on the scribe's plate in order not to get upset.

Dear Ma and Da [I decided not to include Joan, as I was still furious with her],

I write this letter from the town of Kelso, which, if you happen to have seen my Map of the British Isles, is near the border with England.

I am sorry to have taken off in such haste, but [here I paused, as I was not sure how much to say] *I needed to get away from everyone.*

I did not get much of a start to married life, and I am young yet and feel that I have much to give to the world. Do not think of me in anger, but rather think kindly that I have set off on my own journey. It may not be the life that you imagined for me, and I know that your first thoughts will be angry ones and bad tempers, but this is my life to live. I am headed to London and I shall write from there, once I have got myself organized. Pray, do not shout at one another

over this or blame each other, for surely we have all
had enough of that.
　　Your daughter, Maggie

I left the letter at that and did not add more words, despite
the fact that it would cost me tuppence regardless, for I really
just wanted them to know I was safe. I was embarrassed to
say these things out loud, but the scribe had clearly heard far
worse and simply wrote it all down, then read it back to me
as I had another drink of wine. Oh, the wine tasted suddenly
sour. My mouth watered, the way it does when I might be
sick. Mibbie it was all too much. I could not even look at the
scribe's leftover gravy now.

'Are you all right, Mistress?' he asked, noticing my pallor. I
nodded. 'Often the writing of a letter can be a difficult thing.
Usually I guide a person and give them a bit of advice on their
message,' he went on, considering the parchment with a
furrowed brow. 'But I see there is more of a back-story here
than I would care to ask about.' He glanced at me again. 'Do
you want to write to anyone else? I see you talk of *married life*
here. I could write two letters to the same town – won't cost
you extra.'

I thought hard for a moment or two, swallowing back the
sicky feeling, then nodded. He took out another piece of
parchment and dipped his quill in his ink.

Dear Joan,
　　You have always had the better of me and I hope
you are happy with the way things turned out, even
if it broke my heart. But I shall tell you something. I
shall make a success of my life. I shall show you that
you were wrong about me, that I am not an idiot, nor

*good for nothing much. You might have won everyone's
affections, but they don't know you like I know you.
You shall never leave Fisherrow, but I am making my
way in the world.*

    Maggie

I knew it was childish, but I was so very furious with her,
so I suppose that note was not only for her, but for Spencer
too, explaining exactly why I had upped and left with his
cash – not that he was ever likely to read it. I even wondered
if Joan herself would know what was written in the letter, for
if she wanted to find out she would have to take it to someone
who could read it for her. I thought she probably would.
Curiosity would get the better of her.

The scribe finished the letter off with a flourish, sat back
in his chair and looked at me.

'Is it too much?' I asked, fearful it might be the wine talking
now, and that he would think me a spiteful cow.

'It's not the worst message I've passed on,' he replied. 'Your
husband ran off with this Joan, did he?' I must have looked
aghast, but he went on, with all the air of an expert in matters
of the heart, 'You are only a young thing, look at you. There's
always more fish in the sea, and p'raps you might be best
learning a lesson from whatever's happened to you. Now are
you sure you want to write to this Joan, and not your own
husband? For he will be worried about you.'

'He's at sea, and no one knows where,' I replied, not wanting
to go into the whole story.

The scribe shook his head and scratched his beard. 'A sorry
mess then,' he said.

'I shall never trust anyone again,' I told him. I had drunk
too much wine.

'Oh, don't be theatrical,' he said gently. 'You just have to learn who to trust. Folks have got to earn your trust. That's something that only happens bit by bit.'

He was right. I had thrown myself at Spencer without really knowing him at all. I had never met his family, and Da had been wary, but I had ploughed on regardless. Then I had shared too much of my story with Mrs Rose. I had lain myself open to them.

'How long will it take for the letters to arrive?' I asked.

'A week or two,' he said. 'The post boy will have a few deliveries, I expect.'

I went and got my tuppence from where I safely stored my earnings, a locked drawer in my room. I hadn't even noticed the locked drawer that first day, so green was I. The key I kept about me all the time, on a string around my neck. When I had finished my business with the scribe I went back to my chores, scraping gristle from plates and trying not to feel sick again, closing my ears to the bawdy songs that the patrons sang when they had had a fill of ale.

Often I had to dodge a wandering hand or avert my eyes to a lewd wink, or ignore cries and catcalls that made vulgarities of my unfortunate name – *Mistress Dickson, Mistress Dick, I have my own Dick right here.* I knew I could have any of them too, just like Mrs Rose had. And I knew it happened and that no one batted much of an eye, except when the parish officers were around.

Mr Baxter kept a gentlemen's store under the bar, which was a wooden box from which could be purchased things like Castile soap and tooth powder, and something the patrons referred to as 'implements of safety', which I never saw, but were apparently skins that a gentleman put on his nethers to stop the pox, should he be getting intimate with someone.

Sometimes a local girl or a lady would happen into the River Inn and become friendly with a patron and accept a drink from him, and they would disappear off for a while. I knew exactly what they were up to.

When night falls in a market-town inn there is a sense that anything can happen, and it won't matter in the morning when the carts pull away to other corners of the country. By the end of supper time the world outside has fallen to a dark standstill. But under its thatched roof and oak beams, the River Inn glowed – a lantern to all who roamed the roads of the countryside, who navigated its rutted and dangerous ways. Those who had arrived safely and had avoided the highwaymen and rain and wind were assured of a bed and a hot meal. Which gave way to a devil-may-care atmosphere.

I'd meant what I said in my letter to Joan: I would make something of myself. But when I counted my pennies, I could have wept at how few there were, compared to the coins I'd had stolen from me. It would take months to even get close to having a decent bit of money set aside, enough for lodgings and a bit to keep me going.

But I still hankered and hankered to go.

If I had heard tales of London from the tea men, they were nothing compared to the tales told in the parlour of the River Inn. London was on the up and up. Anyone could do anything there. Why, every patron seemed to know a man who had arrived there barefoot and within twelve months he had quite turned his fortunes around. Imagine it! Imagine coming back to Fisherrow in a few years wearing a fur cloak and a velvet hat. *Only a brief visit, Ma, for I cannot leave the servants too long, they will get lazy. Oh, you must all come down and visit.*

Every man who was headed south from the River Inn went off neatly groomed and cleanly shaved by Mr Jackson, the barber, who kept a chair in a room near the scullery. I would watch them go, passing them on my way back, and heading from the kitchen door to the grocery man's cart, which was piled high with sacks of flour and carrots. The men all smelled high and bright, of Mr Jackson's scent-bottle, a spiced concoction that sang of foreign shores. Of morning rainfall. Of open roads. *Look how well you've done,* Joan would say, when they came to visit me in London, in that dreamy future I'd concocted. *Oh, Maggie. We had our differences, did we not? But you have turned your life around.* And Ma would hug me and whisper, *I am proud of you, hen.*

A few days after the scribe departed, two well-heeled women arrived on their way back to Scotland from London. I trusted no one, of course, and they slept in the twin beds in the other attic room. But I lingered over them for a while after supper, as I liked the company of women as a change from the male patrons, and they were polite but distant. When I asked their whereabouts in London, they said they resided – *resided!* – in a magnificent street in Mayfair. I believed them too, for their coach had caused a stir when it arrived, with its velvet padded seats and matching curtains, and a man kept a watch on it overnight.

'I should like to go to London myself one day,' I told them, keeping it vague and giving no details about any savings, in case they should decide to rob me in the night. 'Men come and go all the time, but I hear mixed opinions about whether it is a good place for a woman to seek her fortune.'

One of the women paused to consider the question most carefully. She wore no face-paint and her gown, though perfectly tailored, was a dowdy twill, so I presumed she was not a whore. She had the pinched Presbyterian look of a kirk minister's wife. She glanced at her companion, who was younger but had a similar air.

'A woman ought not to *seek her fortune* anywhere,' she replied. 'She should leave that to her husband. But there are certainly opportunities. And more so than here,' she added. 'So I suppose if you are minded to work all the hours God sends, then London is a better place than Scotland. There are certainly umpteen inns, aren't there, Mistress Penman?'

'Dozens of inns,' this Mistress Penman said. 'You would not be short of inn work.'

'And apprenticeships, do you suppose?' I asked. 'In the ladies' clothing trade or somesuch?'

'Oh, there are apprentices all over the place,' said Mistress Penman. 'London is full of them. Our milliner has three girls working for him. Don't you remember, Mistress Marshall? One of them had spectacles that were smeared thick with her own fingerprints, and you wondered how she ever saw out of them, never mind how she ever sewed a straight line.'

'Dreadful,' said Mistress Marshall. 'Oh, there are more apprentices than anyone knows what to do with. You can't get the service in some places, for there are too many apprentices. Young men and women like yourself. All seeming to do very well for themselves, and spending their wages like there is no tomorrow, wouldn't you agree, Mistress Penman? On entertainments and frivolities. I should say the theatres are not what they used to be at all. Full of working folk. Quite *filling* the stalls at the Theatre Royal. Cheap hats and paste jewels as far as the eye can see.'

I stroked the edge of my own glass ring. I was not put off by these two snobs, not at all. Their tales of the new London were music to my ears. Music fit to fill a hundred theatres.

But then there was a new problem to deal with. Worse than any I had dealt with before.

Chapter Thirteen

Kelso
April 1724

F inally the day came when I had to admit to myself that I was with child.

It was a dawning suspicion that had crept up on me, week by week. Think of the snake, the serpent – how he comes upon Eve – and that is how my pregnancy came upon me. Hidden at first, in plain sight. For I'd eaten heartily, now that I had a glut of treats I had never eaten before, like roasted turkey of a Sunday or date-pie, although I did not seem to savour the taste of these things so much as the food at home. *Mibbie it's not salted enough,* I'd thought.

And the night I dictated my letters to the scribe I had felt nauseous, but it passed. At some stage into my first weeks at Kelso my belly swelled and my apron strings had to be tied looser, which was to be expected, I suppose, what with all the wholesome food. But on some days I would have a queer spell and feel out of sorts, and I could not face anything but cold water. It was a mild, off-colour feeling that was neither one thing nor another. It was not like the stories the fishwives told of their pregnancies: wild and roaring, and full of vomit pails; the reek of morning fish guts fit to make their ears ring. It did not *feel* like I thought a pregnancy ought and, truth be told, pregnancy was the furthest thing from my mind. I had assumed that Spencer's *Women's Tonic* had worked. That my taking of the powders had been the end of such matters and that, once taken, the draught did its job. It had certainly tasted potent enough.

But eventually, after a couple of weeks of feeling off-sorts, one morning I could not shift my bones. Mrs Baxter thought I was sickening for something.

'You are off-colour,' she said, appearing at the door when I had not come down that morning.

'Mibbie I have caught an ague,' I said.

She disappeared and came back up again, bringing me warm wine infused with sage and leaving it at the door, along with a small bell. 'I don't like sickness, I shall not come too close, but ring this bell if you need anything.'

I did not ring the bell. In fact I slept without fever or chills, but the dreams were vivid and unlike anything I had dreamed before.

I dreamed of a snake. I think that was my first snake dream, certainly the first I can remember, and this particular snake was colourless, but firm and slippery like a trout. Iridescent beneath the water.

When I woke up, I tried to drink the wine, but it tasted of vinegar and I realized that the taste of foods had changed too much for it to be just Cook's methods. It was only when I lay back and wondered if my aches were to do with my monthly visitor that I puzzled and frowned, then realized I had mibbie skipped my last monthly visitor. Even the one before that had been scant. In fact I had not bled properly and heavily since mibbie December, before Spencer and I were married. And that was four full months ago.

I staggered out of bed and tried to see myself properly in

the looking glass. I had to stand on a chair to do so, but I managed. And there I was in full glory. Gone was the girl I had always been, with broad shoulders, but a thin waist. I was thicker in the belly.

I was back in bed, sitting bolt upright and panicking, when Mrs Baxter came back with an egg and some bread and butter. She stood in the doorway.

'Mibbie if you're still poorly tomorrow we can ask Dr McTavish to see you,' she said.

'Oh, there is no need. I am feeling better,' I declared. 'I think a good bit of rest was all I was in want of.'

'I am relieved to hear that, Mistress Dickson,' she said. 'I hate to see anyone abed, let alone a healthy girl like you. It reminds me of when I lost my babies. Four beautiful babies they were — all gone to be with the angels.'

I felt dreadfully sorry for her then and wondered if they had all died at once or one after the other, and if it had been a fever that swept the town or they had not survived the birth, like my own ma's other bairns. But I didn't ask. *Will mine slip away too, wither in the womb? Would that not be for the best, for what could I offer a child?* I had no real home, no husband and no family around me. Instead, I said I should be back at my kitchen duties in the morning.

'Eat up your egg then, before it gets cold. You'll need your strength,' Mrs Baxter went on, bustling into the room and putting the tray by the bed. She paused then, appraising me in a funny way. Mibbie it was the shock on my face that I was trying to hide. But she said nothing, just bustled out again and went back to her pastry-rolling.

*

I spent the rest of the day panicking and racking my mind for a plan. I knew a pregnancy lasted nine months or so, if it was to come to term. That meant I would be having a babe in the autumn. And if I did not come to term, I would be having something else, for pregnancies failed and bairns died all the time. The ones who survived were the little miracles. Except that I did not feel this was a miracle at all.

It was a disaster.

As far as I could see, I had three options. The first was to go home. I could not afford to continue the lease on our cottage for too long, so that meant I'd have to go back to Ma and Da. Or rent something cheaper, like a bed in a shared room, perhaps with another family or with a married couple, like many folk did. I could work until the babe was born, then try to get some more work afterwards. But I couldn't bear the thought of going home. It felt like being dragged back by a current. I did not want the pity of the fishwives, making sympathetic noises when they saw my growing belly and asking if I had heard anything from Spencer yet. I did not want everyone to see me as a failure. The lass who tried to make a better life for herself, but failed.

The second option was to come clean and throw myself at the mercy of the Baxters. But the thought of that was just as bad. Mrs Baxter would put me out on my arse or, worse, the parish officers would hear of it and I would be sent to the House of Correction. I'd told Mrs Baxter I was unmarried! I couldn't tell her I had lied. She would not even believe me. And I would be confined with nursing. I would be no use to her, and an embarrassment. She would send me back to Fisherrow for my honest, hard-working kin to look after me.

That left me with only one real option. Carry on as I had been.

I could travel to London before the baby was born and find lodgings and settle in. I was counting my wages every week.

I simply did not have enough money now, but if I saved for a couple more months or so, I could do it. But I needed to make my journey before everyone guessed, or risk my decisions being made for me. If I played it right, I would arrive in London in good time, with the story that I was a recent widow. I could find a woman to help me with the birth, and from then I would work from home, as the fishwives did, taking in whatever work I could get. Sewing, fishing lines – it did not matter. Mrs Baxter's eagerness at hiring me had made me see myself in a new light. I would not struggle.

Oh, but the shock of it. I had never wanted a baby. Had not factored it into any of my plans. I was not maternal. Mibbie one day. Not yet.

It was expected of me that I would bring forth children, as my mother had done, and her mother before her. But I had seen what it did to them, the way it changed their bodies and their minds. The mourning of the ones that didn't survive. The drudge of caring for the ones that lived. Babies changed their mothers. Ma swore she lost a tooth for each one of her pregnancies, as they sucked the very essence from her. Babies scared me. The birth of them. The death of them. I did not hate them or even dislike them.

I just knew I did not want one. Not here, in Kelso – and, if I was being honest with myself, then certainly not in London when I was trying to get myself established.

There was talk, in Fisherrow, of a neighbour who had grown weary of baby-carrying and, at the first sign of her tenth pregnancy, had tried another option. I was a girl when I overheard this story. We were cleaning and gutting in a huddle on the harbour, and my hands were near numb from the cold. As I dipped my hands into the basin of catch, the low gasp in my ma's voice caught my attention as the story unravelled. I can't remember the details; didn't really understand them. But one woman said, 'She tried to bring it down before the quickening'; and another said, 'She visited a house in Edinburgh'; and the first said, 'She nearly bled to death – they used an iron skewer' and there were more gasps and shudders. My gutting knife nearly slipped out of my fingers. The icy water burned my skin. Another woman said, 'Did she not douche after the conjugals?'; and yet another said, 'Shh, the youngsters will hear.'

I did not know what a douche was, although I have figured it out now, and mibbie someone should have told me to douche after my conjugals with Spencer if I did not want a babe, but no one did.

I knew what an iron skewer was, as we kept two by the kitchen fire and we put chickens on them to roast. I knew they pierced flesh.

Fear came to me that morning on the harbour, as I slid my knife into the bellies of fish after fish and spilled their guts onto the slab. If you try to stop a babe once it has started, you might bleed to death. You are better off abandoning it and leaving it at the mercy of the parish. Mibbie that would be the best thing. But I needed the anonymity of London to do that, for if I did it in Kelso, folk might guess it was mine.

Fear came to me again that day in the River Inn when I looked at myself in the mirror and saw the bulge of my stomach.

Fear, slithering and sliding relentlessly. It swam up the Tweed like a water snake. I dared not try to stop the baby coming. It would be too dangerous. I must let nature take its course. I must get to London. Then, once it was born, I would decide what to do. I would know what to do for the best.

*

The next morning I rose early and drank half a cup of water. I dabbed Mrs Rose's leftover rouge onto my cheeks for a spot of brightness. I tied my apron loosely and went downstairs to the kitchen. Cook was stirring a batch of porridge over the fire and she handed me the ladle, so that she could get on with the bread rolls.

'It's a relief to see you,' she said. 'But you look like you've barely slept. Pull your cap down over your hair – it's everywhere this morning.'

I tucked my hair into my cap. I would get through the next few weeks. Then I would be on my way south.

Chapter Fourteen

Kelso
May 1724

M rs Baxter decided I needed much more fresh air and exercise after my spell in my sickbed and took to sending me out on errands and walks. I was thankful of the break and the time alone, so that I could think.

I would walk the length of Kelso, past the blooming gardens and apple orchards and the rush of the rivers. I walked and I planned. I ventured as far as the outskirts of the town and came upon a secretive-looking place with high walls all around. I knew at once it must be the House of Correction, for there were locked gates.

I did not go back there again. It gave me the shudders to think of who might be kept behind those gates. How easy it was to slip from the civilized world to the dark corners of a prison. All it takes is one bad move.

On weekday mornings I was amongst the first at market, with a list in my head of all the items the grocery boy had forgotten, and whatever fresh fish we needed. On Sundays I had to go with the Baxters to kirk. We had to look respectable. The parish officials were always there, in their black capes and with their silver-topped canes, and would glower at us as if they were looking for a reason to throw us out. Mrs Baxter held her head high and listened intently to the sermon and would nudge me to do the same if she could tell my mind was wandering by my stifled yawns. I would not go so far as to say that she was overly kind, rather that she saw me as her charge.

She gave me money for cloth, to sew into a work smock more suitable than my own clothes. I was grateful for that, for I felt I would burst out of my own gown soon enough. I bought a thick bolt in a charcoal grey that reminded me of the dull cloth they make at Eskmills. Dull enough to hide behind. I stuffed my fantasies of the London life behind the sack-like smock: the fashionable stocks of goods piled high in the haberdasher's, the goldsmiths, the fortune-tellers and theatrical plays. How would I ever manage any of that with a babe wailing at my breast? I could hardly leave it alone and go out on the town. I would not be able to afford nice things if I was paying for its keep.

Kelso's Friday market was the busiest, just like home. It had the same feel of wildness about it, of coming to the end of the working week. The flesher's stall would be a flurry of blood amidst the petrified shrieks of animals, as the wealthier families would often bring him a fattened pig to butcher. At the other end of the market, hides and fleeces were strung out on lines. A fiddler played for thrown pennies, dogs barked incessantly, and pedlars sold everything from buttons to bottles of cough cure. The place was thick with dung, and the muck would cling to your boots so that, even after the market, you stank of it.

That morning I was out with a list of three things in my head. A nice fresh trout, of course, the biggest one I could get, although Cook bulked out the trout pies with so much milk and flour that the patrons were lucky to get a piece of real fish in a slice at all. A length of fine black lace for Mrs Baxter's best cape, for she had seen her neighbour with a lace trim on hers and decided she could not be upstaged at kirk. I was not to tell Mr Baxter of this, for he would likely not notice, and I was to sew it for her myself, if that was all right. And, finally, a packet of tea. The Baxters loved their tea and there was a small emporium off the market square that stocked it, alongside other luxuries like snuff, rum and chocolate. The tea that the grocer sold was cheap and was bulked out, like Cook's trout pie, I thought, with sawdust or dried dung or somesuch, but the Baxters were not tea experts and swallowed it down, oblivious.

The tea-seller knew me by name and always greeted me well, as I had been a couple of times now and inspected his tea leaves with more scrutiny than most of his customers.

'Mistress Dickson, I was expecting you,' he called. 'Come for the Baxters' usual. I tell you what: I have a nice new blend here that Mr Baxter might like. Shall I put some in a bag for him to try? You too? Here, put your grocery basket down on the counter – you look worn out.'

I nodded as he busied himself with measuring out the leaves. My sicky feeling came back and my head pounded. The smoky smells of the tea leaves were overpowering. Worst of all, I felt a fluttering inside me. Like a moth batting at a window. It was the baby stirring.

'Is everything all right, Mistress Dickson?' The tea-seller looked worried.

'I just need a chair for a moment or two,' I replied, sounding weak.

He put me in his chair and brought me a draught of something in a cup and handed it to me, watching me carefully.

'Now you drink this, Mistress Dickson, and it will perk you up a bit. You look a bit off-colour, if you don't mind me saying so. Is anything the matter?'

'Not at all,' I lied. 'I think I've been working a bit too hard, that's all.'

He frowned. He did not look like he believed me, but he didn't ask any more questions. I sipped the draught he had given me. He went back to his shelves and let me sit for a while. Slowly my sense of normality returned. The sicky feeling subsided and my heart calmed down.

'I'm all right now,' I told him. 'I'd best take my tea and get back to the inn.'

'Well, if you're sure,' he said, surveying me a little. He was a small man, with three or four days of grey bristle spreading from his cheeks down his neck, but otherwise was neatly turned out in a dark tunic and breeches. I imagined, if I got close enough, his bristle would smell of tea leaves – of the box Da kept under our bed.

I stood up. 'I'm sure I am well again,' I replied, and he bade me goodbye.

Had he guessed I was in the family way? He was a purveyor of many exotic goods, and I wondered if he sold women's tonics or drinks to help with the morning sickness and knew exactly what a woman looked like when she was pregnant.

I could not have anyone guessing. I took a deep breath and stood on the doorstep, looking onto the market. The sky was low with cloud, and a spring rain was just hanging off, which gave everything an air of urgency. Folks were piled with parcels or carrying sacks over their shoulders. A boy who'd been peeing earnestly a few minutes earlier was now playing with a stick at the side of the road, wielding it like a sword.

I picked my way back as quickly as I could between heaps of dung and damp straw and dirt. I arrived at the inn as spots of rain started to dot around me. I went in through the kitchen door, past the stables, which were quiet now, and handed out the goods.

'You took a while,' noted Mrs Baxter with a pinch of disapproval in her frown, examining the length of lace.

'There's a new tea blend to try,' I told her, and she cheered up at that.

'Nothing like a pot of tea to calm the nerves,' she answered, taking the packets from me and sniffing them.

But I disagreed. Tea had never calmed my nerves.

That night, after a long shift dealing with the excesses of the Friday market – the drunk and overfed patrons, who got rowdier the later it got – I was desperate to reach the peace and quiet of my room.

I stood at my window, looking out at the dark street. I put my hand to my belly as if to stop the baby from fluttering again, for I did not want to feel it. It wasn't simply the presence of the babe. It was the absence of Spencer – what might have been.

If only it wasn't this bare room in a town I hardly knew; if it wasn't even London. If only it was our little place in Musselburgh High Street, his shirts drying by the fire. Mibbie Spencer would be smoking his pipe and looking at me, unable to help himself fall in love with me even more, now that I was with his child. *Well, we didn't plan it, but we shall make the best of it, Maggie, what do you say?* Then, when the babe was here and she was swaddled in a soft blanket in her crib, he'd look down on her and declare, *She is your image, my love, she will set London alight. She is brighter than the moon and stars.*

But it was none of those things. It was this. There was no moon or stars to see; the cloud had stayed low. The only light came from the windows of other houses, faint and yellowy, and from the line of glass lanterns that glowed sporadically up and down the road. I shivered. The darkness bellowed at me, *Pull yourself together, girl. You're in this alone. And you must decide what to do for the best.*

Chapter Fifteen

Kelso

June 1724

I began to move slowly through the weeks, as if through wet sand. I startled at sudden noises or even when my name was called.

Eventually, after a few attempts, I sewed Mrs Baxter's new lace trim onto her best cape. It took a long while, for I would go to bed exhausted each night – a new exhaustion that threatened to sink me to the floor. The baby whirred and buzzed inside me, on and off, but I felt no great love or bond, only fear. My stomach grew and I was sure I would be found out any day. I counted the days and months, back and forth, and calculated that I must leave Kelso by the end of July or the beginning of August, for I would be due to give birth around the second or third week of September.

My sewing was as haphazard as my thoughts. Mrs Baxter did not like the way the cape sat on her shoulders when she tried it on. It was a Saturday morning and she was keen to look her best at kirk the following day, as she and Mr Baxter were hosting a Sunday lunch. The parlour was to be closed to anyone but those invited. The guest list included the minister and his wife and some of the finer folks of Kelso. The Baxters were always keen to show everyone that the River Inn was a place of good repute. We were in my room.

'Unpick this lace,' she said, scowling at herself in my looking glass. 'It's too frilly. I can't go to kirk like this.' Then, alas, she spied my rouge pot. 'What whoreish ointment is this?' she cried. She towered over me, grasping my face and looking for traces of whoreish ointment. Mercifully there were none, as I had not been out that day.

'It's not mine, it was left by Mrs Rose,' I replied truthfully.

'Have you ever entertained a patron in this room?' she demanded, looking about her as if there might be more traces of whoreishness.

'Never,' I declared. 'And I never will, Mrs Baxter. For my ma always said men bring nothing but trouble.'

She gave a tight little nod of her head and ran her eyes up and down the length of me. I clenched everything, hoping she would not notice the swelling around my middle. Her eyes lingered there, but she said nothing.

'Men do bring trouble,' she went on. 'But only if you let them. Practise your psalms. You will find all the teachings there that you need. And unpick that lace.'

Kirk was dull and I knew all the psalms. Fisher folk are God-fearing folk. There is not much that will put the fear of death into you more than watching a tide swell under a black sky, waiting for your menfolk to come home safe. So there are not many psalms I'm unfamiliar with, and Mrs Baxter seemed appeased by that.

Afterwards we rushed home at a quick trot to get lunch laid out. Cook had already boiled a ham 'til it was falling off the bone and she only needed to do the cabbage. By the time the guests filed in, glorious in their states of grace and ravenous for their roast, the parlour had been swept of pipe ash and dropped dice and aired out, and the tables were assembled together and scoured of any stale ale. I was to serve, not sit, and in return I was to be given my own plate in my room for a quiet lunch, which suited me. Truth is, I hardly got any time on my own and I needed thinking-time. Thinking was precious to me. It was the time when I could run through my worries and, most importantly, plan.

But first I was to dish out buttered cabbage and pleasantries.

A pompous-looking gentleman sat near the top of the table, next to the minister. I noticed him straight away, for he was the tallest man in the room, with shiny silvery hair and sharp shoulders. He carried his chin at a high tilt and looked down his nose at everyone. When it came time for me to pour him his water, he fixed me with a cold, unblinking stare and his eyes followed my bosom as I leaned over, saying nothing.

Well, what can you do about that? Not much, so I glared at him and when I went back into the kitchen, I made sure my apron was as high as it could be and I was showing no hint of flesh.

Cook sent me out again with the wine bottle, and of course the silver-haired fellow's eyes lit up at that.

'Pour me a generous splash,' he murmured when I got round to him. I kept my eyes on the bottle, but I felt his bore into me. 'I've seen you around Kelso, from time to time,' he said. 'My name is Dr William McTavish.'

McTavish! The wicked Mrs Rose's so-called uncle? The man she feared had murdered his own wife?

He held out his glass and pursed his lips. He wore a jet-black ring that gleamed lavishly. His hands were slender, with the longest fingers I had ever seen.

A chill raced through me. *It must be him.* A lewder grin I had never seen; it practically salivated. The Baxters must be turning some blind eye to his antics, to have him at their Sunday table.

'A pleasure to meet you, sir,' I lied, 'I am Mistress Maggie Dickson.'

'And you are the Baxters' new maid, eh? Come all the way down here from the fishing ports or somesuch, is that right?' he asked, a curve of amusement on his lips, his tongue flickering between them. He sipped his wine and put his glass down, readying himself for an answer.

'I am indeed, sir, from Fisherrow,' I replied meekly, for I did not want to upset this gent and end up poisoned, even though I was desperate to find out if he had any news of the wicked Mrs Rose.

'A bleak place, I've heard,' he mused. 'Although the oysters are second to none. I have rooms in Edinburgh very near Fishmarket Close. I do like to choose my own seafood. Selecting shellfish is not a job I would trust to a servant.'

'And you are a physician,' I said, for I was thinking in the back of my mind that although I would not like to trust this man with my life, one day I might have to, if there was a problem with the birth.

'I practise regularly in Edinburgh,' he observed, 'for the monies are better there. Anyway, enough of this small talk, for I believe that we have a mutual friend.'

'Mrs Rose,' I said. 'But she was not my friend, for she stole all my money, and all the town knows it.'

His eyes darted about the room to see if we were being overheard, but the minister was deep in conversation with Mrs Baxter.

'Tell me, have you heard anything of her since?' he asked.

'Not a word,' I told him. 'But I am keen for news.'

'Well, that makes two of us – you and me both – for I am most keen for news of her. And if you do hear of her, I would like you to tell me, would you do that?'

I assured him I would, although I did not fancy Mrs Rose's chances if he ever caught her. Mibbie he would poison her, like his poor wife Kitty. Good.

His lewdness had shrunk away now, leaving something else – a look of bitterness. I knew, then, that whatever Mrs Rose had done to me, she had infuriated the doctor. 'Well, Mistress Dickson, if you are ever in need of any tinctures or sleeping draughts, pay me a visit. Mrs Rose swore by laudanum for her nerves; ladies often do, and I do not charge a fortune for it.'

I hoped I would never need his attentions and I did not want him staring at me any more, for if he was any sort of doctor, he might realize I was with child. By now, the rest of the table were rattling for their wine, so I excused myself and went to fill their cups, making sure my apron hung nice and loose over me.

But my hands shook. He had frightened me, this gent. There was something off about him. I could just see him slipping his inconvenient wife a draught of something deadly. *Here you go, Kitty, this will help your nerves.* I was not surprised, now, that Mrs Rose had run away from him. If I was her, I would have done the same. I could not forgive her for taking my money, but mibbie she was running for her life.

When I went back into the kitchen, Cook asked if I was all right and I said I was perfectly well, but I did not like the look of Dr McTavish.

Cook surveyed the kitchen door to make sure she would not be overheard. 'Stay clear of him,' she warned. 'There are all sorts of rumours about him. It's hard to tell what's true and what's made up.'

'Don't I know it,' I replied.

Where is Mrs Rose? I wondered. In London most likely, in lodgings I ought to have been in, living the life I ought to be living right now. I tried not to feel bitter about it all, but much later on, when lunch was scoffed and the guests stuffed full and sent home, and the dishes done, I sat on my narrow little bed, eating a cold plate of ham and cabbage leftovers. I could not help a wave of fury about the women who had betrayed me. My own sister, and the whore Mrs Rose.

What was to become of me?

It was early summertime now. A cool, greeny summer when the days were growing to their longest.

I had a pile of coins, for Mrs Baxter paid me every week, and it was growing too. By the end of July it would be enough.

I also had one pair of boots, in need of minor repairs. Two shawls. One bonnet. Four gowns, including my navy wedding gown, all of which had been let out. Assorted petticoats and knickers, in various states of rag.

I had bought things for the birth too. Things I would need. Linens, for I knew there would be blood. And the baby would need to be dressed, whether I kept it or left it on a church doorstep. So I had bought another bolt that could be cut up for tail-clouts and swaddling, and a box of pins. There was something else, also. A little baby bonnet in pure white wool with creamy silk ribbons. I had seen it at the market and could not stop myself from handing over a penny and slipping it into my creel.

*

The next morning, Monday, brought silver cloud and a bold gust of wind about it. I rose with it. I stole downstairs, out into the stables, and asked Jack the ostler for a quiet word.

Jack was a shy fellow, small and wiry, who never said much to anyone, not even to Mr Baxter, for I often heard him bemoan the fact. 'Jack chats away to the horses all day long, but all I get from him are grunts,' he would rumble. Mrs Baxter would soothe him and say it did not matter, for Jack was hired for his gentleness with beasts, not for his conversational skills.

Jack looked uneasy at the prospect of a quiet word with me. He rested his weight on his sweeping brush, seeming not to know which hand to hold it in.

'I need you to keep a secret,' I said. The stables were bustling. A cart was being loaded up for the road.

Jack nodded, looking even more uneasy.

'The coach driver, the one who brought me here,' I went on. 'How often does he come here, would you say?'

Jack sucked his teeth and passed his sweeping brush from one hand to the other a few more times.

'I would say he comes here once every few weeks or so,' he finally declared.

'And have you seen him recently?' I asked. 'For I haven't, but I might have missed him.'

'He's not been back awhile,' said Jack. 'Are you looking for him?'

'I am indeed,' I replied. 'Only to have a word. So when he does next come back, can you be sure and find me and let me know?'

Jack nodded.

'And is he a regular, would you say? Are you certain he will call again in the next few weeks?'

'Come to think of it, I would,' said Jack. 'He always likes to have a full coach, whether it be passengers or mail or parcels, so he might be holding off to make his journey worth the while, but he has passed through here for many years now, as long as I've worked here.'

I thought Jack chatted very well indeed, and wondered if mibbie Mr Baxter just did not know what to ask him to get a decent bit of conversation out of him.

'Thank you, Jack. Now this is our secret, do you understand?'

He nodded again, firmly this time. 'Well, if that will be all, Mistress Dickson, I have a lot of hay to sweep this morning and horses to feed,' he replied.

That was all. I was back to the scullery before anyone could miss me, to launder bed sheets, a job that would make my arms ache, but never mind. That coach driver had said he would still take me to London. I would hold him to his word.

I was pegging the bed sheets onto the washing line and they were looking as clean as I could really get them, these being the sheets of a travellers' inn where dirty feet and unwashed bodies leave unfortunate grime, when Mrs Baxter came to find me and send me out on yet another errand.

'We're at the end of the salt packet,' she said. 'And the grocery boy is not due. We can't do a stew without salt. Can you go and find some? There's usually a salt-seller on the south corner of the market.'

Off I went, drying my hands on my skirts. I could not carry on like this, though. I ached. I longed for a confinement. Imagine it, lounging on a bed all day.

I dragged myself up the street towards the salt-seller. But I did not make it that far. For just a few feet from the market square, as I was passing the dark mouth of an alleyway, a hand reached out and grabbed my arm.

Chapter Sixteen

We stood facing each other. It had been almost half a year and so much had happened, and it had changed us both. Joan wore her hair scraped tight under her bonnet. There were dark circles under her eyes and her dress sleeves were grubby. Her skin was rough. She was thinner. She was not the old, proud Joan that I knew.

'I should never have written to you,' I said. 'It was not an invitation for you to come and find me.'

'Sister, I am sorry,' she replied, the words rushing out. 'I know I'm the last person you want to see, but I had to come. Much has happened.'

Something bad. I could tell by the way she spoke, rapid and breathless. Was it Spencer? Had he returned? Or had Da hurt Ma? *I should never have left.*

'Tell me now,' I urged her.

'You have ruined our mother and father with your disappearing act,' she said, tears springing to her eyes. 'We are the talk of the tea men. There were rumours you'd run off to find Spencer and stolen some money from Da's stash. Folk were calling on Da at all times of the day and night to check nothing had been taken. Now they are saying Ma and Da are not to be trusted, if they can't keep their own daughter in check. Marrying out of fishing, to a rogue like Spencer, then both of you disappearing altogether. Smuggling is all about trust, Maggie. They don't trust us any more. Da's getting the cold shoulder from everyone in the Mussel Inn, and now he's either out on that boat or sitting in his chair, drinking. Ma thinks he'll come a cropper at sea if he doesn't stop and she will end up having to work at Eskmills. I came to find you, in desperation.' Joan pulled a kerchief from her sleeve and wiped her eyes and nose. The kerchief was as grubby as her sleeves, and I felt the most terrible pity for her. And the most terrible guilt.

'I ran away because of you,' I told her.

'I know it, and I felt awful that morning when I woke up and you were gone. I've been a bad sister. I did the worst thing a sister can do.'

'So when you say *I* have ruined Ma and Da, what you mean is *we* have ruined Ma and Da,' I retorted. 'And I don't even care if I have ruined Da, for he is rotten already. But you, Joan Dickson, ruined my marriage.' I folded my arms.

'I am a wicked girl,' she sobbed.

'Why Spencer? Of all the men in Musselburgh, why my very own husband?' I started to cry myself, I couldn't help it – all the emotions I had forced away were here now, pouring from me. It was the sight of her. The sound of her, the way she clicked her jaw and sniffed.

'I think I was taken by great passions,' she heaved out. 'Of anger and lust and greed. I am weak, Maggie. I have all the wicked traits they preach against in kirk.'

I shook my head at this truly sorry sight.

Then she lifted her head. 'But don't blame me for everything,' she begged. 'I did not send you packing; you decided to go. You alone. And I had to go back home and tell Ma and Da and pretend I had no idea why.'

I took a deep breath and gathered myself together to ask the dreaded question. Deep in my belly, the babe flickered in anticipation.

'Has there been any word from Spencer?' I asked. 'Anything from the sailors. Rumours even?'

'Folks say he was taken onto a big ship that was headed south to help fight a war,' she said. 'Far south. Spain.'

Oh! The babe kicked at that.

'Spencer cannot fight a war,' I cried. 'Spencer can't fire guns or defend himself from navy men. He will die. He will drown.'

'You still love him then,' Joan said.

I had not thought so, until these last days. I had thought I hated him. But I carried his child. His kicking child. Both sailing their own waters now, miles from each other.

'I am Spencer's wife,' I said.

Joan stuffed her kerchief back into her dress sleeve.

'And you had a caper with him in my bed, didn't you? When you were supposed to be at choir.'

She nodded.

'And he told you all sorts of stories about the ladies in Gothenburg and how fancy and sophisticated they are.'

'He did, and it made me feel fancy and sophisticated too, and it was exactly what I needed to hear. Oh but, Maggie, it was just what you needed to hear too. You were mibbie a bit green to believe he would stay true to you.'

Oh, I had been green all right. Perhaps I ought to forget all about him. But then what would I tell the baby when it asked about its da? A hero lost at sea? Or that one day Daddy might be back. *Any day now.*

'You are doing well for yourself now, Maggie, aren't you, though?' Joan interrupted my thoughts, as she'd always had a habit of doing. 'To afford a letter sent by post.'

'I am doing all right,' I agreed.

She screwed up her face.

'There's something new about you, though. You look well. Wholesome. It must be the change in the air.'

Oh God, she will guess, she will guess. 'I am the same as I ever was,' I huffed, pulling my shawl about me.

But Joan was undeterred. She came closer – so close I could feel her breath on my face. She smelled like home: of old smoke and old fishing lines. I must have smelled the same once. She put her finger on my chin and tilted my face up.

'Oh, you are wearing rouge, you wench!' she shrieked. 'Rouge right there, on your cheeks. 'Are you a whore, Maggie? Is that what's become of you in Kelso?'

'I am not a whore, you cheeky cow,' I told her. 'I found some rouge lying around, left by another patron at the inn where I live. And how long have you been in Kelso anyway?'

She blushed. 'A couple of days,' she admitted. 'I arrived at the River Inn, but I couldn't face speaking to you.'

'So where have you been sleeping?'

'Two nights under the stars,' she said. 'When I told Ma I was coming to find you, she gave me ten shillings, but I did not want to waste them.'

'Oh, for heaven's sake.' Joan was impossible. 'Anything could have happened to you. Men are passing in and out of this town all the time. Thieves and runaways, and all sorts. And besides all that, there are parish officers who police the town for immoral behaviour, and there's a House of Correction down the road where you'd be sent as a vagrant.'

'Well, I'm a vagrant no more,' she replied firmly. 'I've found you. So we can be together now, can't we? You and I. Sisters again.' She took my hands in hers then and squeezed them.

My sister had betrayed me, but it was far more Spencer's fault than Joan's. She had been an idiot, but her trip to find me was her way of trying to make things right. I could not turn her away. I could not risk the silly girl being picked up by the parish. She would not last a night in a jail. I would have to take her into my room with me. Even if it was only for a few days. Then I would send Joan home and get on my way to London.

But how I would hide my pregnancy from her, and avoid being dragged home to have the baby and live with Ma and Da for the rest of my days, I did not know.

I took Joan back to the River Inn and she was welcomed into the bosom of the place, for no one knew my history with her and they thought her a devoted sister indeed who had come to join me. Joan gave Mrs Baxter one of her shillings and that was her booked in for the week, and I was determined she would be on her way back up the road after that. I knew Ma's motives – Joan's too – were not for my welfare, but because they needed to show everyone that I was safely returned. I hadn't thought it through, hadn't really cared about the conse-quences of my running away. But they had been severe.

Joan did not take to life at the River Inn as I had. She did not like the rough edge of the men in the parlour, for they leered at her in a way she had not been leered at before, and far more than they leered at me. Back home, Da's reputation ensured that local lads did not really mess us about. Here, we were only really under the protection of the Baxters. And the patrons were not handsome charmers like Spencer. They were men of the road, some of them running from gambling debts or the law, and others desperate for the sight of a woman.

Joan would spend her days aimlessly wandering the market, coming back talking of lengths of cotton chintz, candlesticks, china cups and buttons, but only in a half-hearted way, as she knew she had no hope of affording such goods. Ma's shillings were emergency monies, not to be frittered.

I did not give her a glimpse of the key around my neck or make any mention of the locked drawer that stood between our beds. I did not quite trust my own sister not to bolt with my savings, back home or to London, or anywhere.

Joan spent her evenings sitting edgily in the parlour for only as long as it took to finish a small plate of supper, before heading back to our room. At night she would lie in her bed and I in mine, and we would talk. The dark made us honest.

'I do not much fancy it here.' That was her favourite thing to say.

'Are you not enjoying seeing the world a bit?' I finally asked. 'You always told me you'd marry a man of the world. You won't find many of them in Fisherrow.'

'I do want a fine man,' she said. 'A mill owner or a land-owner's son. The men I've seen so far here all seem to be on the make. Heading south to make a fortune, or trading this and trading that. I want the sort of man who is already made or has a decent job. And mibbie there aren't any in Fisherrow, but there are one or two in Musselburgh.'

Ah, Joan had finally set her sights on someone back home. That explained her restlessness. I did not probe her more, but it made sense. Her talk was all of going home and making sure Ma was all right. Of how we would all have to stick together and look after Ma, for she was feared Da would knock her black and blue one of these days. Each time Joan opened her mouth, my heart sank. I felt myself being pulled back to Fisherrow, helplessly fighting the drag. It was the drone of her voice, the catch in her throat. As I drifted off to sleep I was there in the box-bed. I was five, or twelve, or fifteen again. Then I was back in my marriage bed, with Spencer – only Joan had spoiled it for us.

Then there was a snake. It would coil up from under the bed, tongue flickering, tasting the air. I would wake up with a start, my hand on my throat, trying to pull the serpent off me. Drenched in sweat.

'You are talking in your sleep,' Joan would murmur. 'Why have you started doing that?'

I kept my secret from her for no more than a couple of weeks.

I had been down in the stables, talking to Jack the ostler again, begging him for any news of my coachman. 'Have any of the other drivers seen him, or heard news of where he may be?' I asked.

'I will enquire,' Jack promised, looking wary. 'But if you're planning on leaving, you'd better tell the Baxters first. You're a good pair of hands to them.'

He had thrown me, truth be told, with that remark. I didn't want to tell anyone any of my plans, for it never bode well for me. I nodded, folding my arms in front of me. Absent-mindedly I must have stroked or patted my belly. Upstairs, Joan had been watching me from the window, wondering, no doubt, why I was talking to the stable boy.

When I got back to the room she stood, hands clenched at her sides. She had been through my belongings. She had pulled my creel from under my bed and had gone through it. The linen bolt, pure white and clean, now lay spread across my bed. The box of pins opened. The bonnet beside it.

She regarded me with fresh eyes, narrow and suspicious, resting on my belly.

'You are fat,' she said. 'Fat with a child.'

'That's no one's business but mine,' I replied.

'Let me see,' she insisted, coming towards me and putting her hands on me. She felt me, her hands pressing against me. 'You are far gone,' she gasped, leaping back. She looked scared.

'I am not so far gone,' I told her. 'I am a few months gone, that's all.'

She shook her head and cupped her hands over my stomach again.

'Maggie, you are well gone. That smock hides it, but your breasts are huge and your belly's like a turnip.'

'What do you know about these matters?' I retorted. 'Nothing. You are no midwife. You know nothing of birthing.'

'I've seen plenty of the fishwives at the end of their pregnancies,' she said. 'And that is what you look like. When did you last bleed? We need to work it out.'

'I've another three months to go,' I told her. 'But it must stay a secret. Things are strict here. The Baxters think me unwed. They are under scrutiny from the parish officers, who don't like this inn. The officials think it immoral, with all the comings and goings of folk, and they keep a close eye on all of us. If anyone was to suspect I was with child, it would be disastrous. I can't support the child myself, with no husband. I could be put in the House of Correction, Joan.'

'But you are married,' she said. 'You have done nothing wrong. Simply tell the truth.'

'How could I do that?' I cried. 'I would be whipped for such lies. I have got myself into a bit of mess, that much is true, but I will get myself out of it, just as I have always looked after myself.'

'Well, we need to go home and that is all there is to it.'

'No, Joan. You go home and I am going to London. That is my plan. Your coming here has not changed it one bit.'

'I am going nowhere yet,' she retorted.

I said nothing, but let Joan believe she was taking charge. I let her fuss about me and put me to my bed that night. I confess I let her do all of it with no complaint. I felt exhausted. So I was relieved to lie in bed and let Joan bring me bread soaked in milk. She vowed not to tell the Baxters yet, and I knew she wouldn't, for she felt exactly as I did. We did not want them – or anyone else in Kelso – deciding our fates.

We lived like this, oddly, for a week or so. When I say 'oddly', I mean that we lived side by side as we once had, but with something between us. Not merely the babe. But something unsettled, as though we were back to being enemies again. My exhaustion continued. My feet ached and my belly did too. It would start to tighten, with a dull ache that spread down the length of me; then just as I began to wonder what was causing the ache, it would subside.

Chapter Seventeen

Kelso
July 1724, one night, in the dead of the night

*A*nother snake.
　　This one writhed.
It could not lie still.
It coiled and uncoiled.
It squeezed my guts. I fought it; pushed it away.

I felt wetness. I had only just got to sleep and yet I was being pulled awake. The pain was intense. *I must be dying.* It squeezed again and the cramp gripped me from belly to thigh. I woke up, on the verge of vomiting, but the purge was more than simply vomit. I retched. I cramped. I opened my mouth to scream.

'Oh God, the baby is coming!'

It was not me who spoke, for I could not speak. My mouth was full of pain.

Joan came at me like an apparition, candle and white nightie, floating in the yellow light.

'Maggie, there's blood.'

I do not remember much of what happened, only that it was quick – quicker than I had imagined it would be – and the snake vanished and everything was real and vivid.

My own belly, the candlestick at the bedside, the damp

sheets. I know it was the dead of the night, because the night-candle was fresh and had barely burned. I came in and out of the world and I had a terrible urge to push, but when I did, I felt myself being torn in two, yet my body pushed anyway. All by itself. I know I kept telling Joan to fetch someone: Mrs Baxter, Mr Baxter, Cook, *anyone*; but she was transfixed in shock and did not leave the room.

Joan, my sister, did not leave the room.

She stood and stared as I delivered the baby. It came out in a pop of pale skin and folded limbs. None of them kicking.

It came out purplish and too small.

'It is sickly,' I said. 'It has come too soon.'

'It's a girl. She looks too fragile,' whimpered Joan. 'She does not look right.'

'Fetch a physician,' I wept. I tried to stand up, but my legs trembled. Blood bloomed across the bed. 'There's a Dr McTavish in a cottage down the street. He will help.'

'Put the baby to your breast,' said Joan. 'Swaddle her. She will be all right if you nurse her.'

I told Joan to find my little knife, the one I had bought at the Mussel Inn the day I left, and she cut the cord. I pressed the baby to my breast, and she whimpered and finally started to suckle. It was a piercing feeling of pain and relief, and all at once I wanted to pull the baby away from me, yet sit and stare at her in awe. She lay against me as Joan fetched a linen and wrapped it around me and the baby. It was the only useful thing she had done in that awful hour. Then she fetched a shawl and wrapped it around her own shoulders and sat and shivered.

Then, for many, many minutes, we sat together in shocked silence.

The baby was too early. I knew it from the weight of her

and from the weakness of the suckle. She weighed less than a pair of thick stockings. The candle fizzed and melted down the hours of darkness, the hours of safety when secrets like newborn babies could be kept. She was too early but she was a wonder. Her face was like Spencer's face, his little miniature. I couldn't stop staring at her. She had his ears, tiny seashells, and I had an urge to go home and lie in bed with Ma. She smelled of blood and bodies; oh, she even smelled of the spice of Spencer's locked cabinet. A wave of exhaustion came over me, but I had to fight it with every ounce of my strength.

'What are we to do?' I whispered. 'Joan, what are we to do? Can you go and fetch Mrs Baxter – wake her up and tell her what has happened?'

'We will go home on a morning coach,' replied Joan. 'As you said, we would be shamed if we stayed here, both of us. Those parish officers you talk of will decide what must be done with you. The decision will be taken from you. By the time we could even do something sensible, like fetch Da to come and vouch for you, you'd have been incarcerated. Me as well, most likely.'

'You will have to tell the Baxters what's happened,' I said, ignoring her. 'Get Mrs Baxter on her own and make sure she has had her morning coffee. She is a hag until she's had her morning coffee.'

Joan put her hands to her ears. 'Stop havering, Maggie. These people are not our people. We are not Kelso folks. We are Fisherrow girls, and we need to go back to safety. You will not be looked after here; you are useless now. You are an embarrassment. You and that baby are an expense the parish won't want to take on. Ma will have one look at that bairn and take you back in an instant. Both of you.'

*

I lay back and let it all wash over me. Joan's desperation was really about her own fear. I drifted in and out of sleep. I dreamed of workhouses. Of the story Cook had told, about the previous maid, the one who left the River Inn, in disgrace. 'She was sent to the House of Correction . . . and now the babe is under the care of the parish, for she will never be able to take care of it. Wet-nursed at Muir Farm and apprenticed there when it turns fourteen.'

And that is when I decided it. This babe, this tiny girl, would never be ripped from me or wet-nursed, or apprenticed to a ruddy-faced Kelso farmer to churn butter and feed pigs and weed and mow and sew. I would not let anyone tear us apart. She was mine and I would care for her. She needed me.

There was barely room for me and the babe on the thin bed, but I clasped her in the crook of my arm and drifted, in and out of sleep.

By and by, the light came up. I heard Joan again and her voice had new panic in it. 'Maggie,' she urged. 'The baby does not look right.'

I looked down. She lay still. Too still. There was a greyness to her lips.

'She is gone,' whispered Joan.

'She can't be gone,' I said. I held her up and took her to my breast again, willing her to turn and suckle. I put my finger to her lips, but they did not move. 'Joan, fetch someone,' I panicked.

'We cannot fetch anyone now,' she replied.

I rubbed the babe's lips. Rubbed her cheeks. Pressed on her chest to try to bring her back to life. But she flopped.

Then there was nothing I could do but bury my face in the swaddled, lifeless body.

'Rest her soul, rest her soul,' Joan kept saying.

'She was too weak,' I sobbed.

Then Joan was on full alert. 'Time to bolt,' she urged through her tears. 'We can't stay here now.'

'Fetch Mrs Baxter,' I pleaded again.

'And then what? Physicians and constables and investigations, and all sorts, that's what,' said Joan. 'You will have to explain what has happened and why you kept it all a secret.'

'But I've done nothing wrong,' I replied. 'I loved her the minute I saw her.'

'Oh, but you have done everything wrong,' Joan cried, a terrible strain in her voice. 'For you have brought the worst kind of trouble into the home of strangers.'

The morning light warmed the bed. Soon I ought to be up and about. But my womb bled, and my breasts leaked, and my baby was dead.

'Tell them I am sick, and cover for me today,' I told Joan. 'You will have to do my chores. And tell Mrs Baxter not to bring anything up to the room. If she tries, then you must take it from her and bring it yourself.'

'If you are caught with this dead babe, we will be in terrible trouble,' whimpered Joan.

'I will give the babe my own burial,' I told her. 'I will give her my own private farewell. It is no one's concern but mine. I will take her to the river, and she will wash into the sea, where her father sails.'

Joan did not stop me. She must have thought me mad, feverish, seized by fear, but she did not stop me. She dressed and put on my apron and went downstairs.

As soon as the door clicked behind her, I got up and locked it.

I went back to the bed and lifted my baby up. She was colder and heavier than I had remembered, as if her little, light soul had left and in its place was my awful, awful grief. I swaddled her again and placed her gently into my creel and covered her with a linen, soft and gentle, as if I were tucking her into a cradle for a nap. I was about to put the bonnet on her when I stopped. I could not be parted from it. It was the only thing I would have left to remember her by.

It was mid-morning now. I could tell by the arrival of the grocer's cart. In a few minutes everyone would be in the kitchen and the pantry, putting the delivery away.

I dressed, padding my bleed and my breasts with rags. I picked up the creel and unlocked the door. The landing was silent. I crept downstairs and slipped out of the front door, straight onto the street.

The lane down to the river was deserted, except for the song and bustle of morning birds. I stumbled, for my boots were not laced right and I bled into my rags and my eyes bleared with tears. All the while I talked to the babe, as if she were alive, telling her where we were going and what we were doing and how everything would be all right: *No need to fear the workhouse now. No life of toil for you, my precious soul.* The creel scuffed against my side as though it were a child walking with me, hand-in-hand, not really minding its way and tripping over its feet. *I will always feel like this now, as though I am walking and talking to a child who is nothing but empty air.*

The lane ended. The riverbank opened up before me, damp and cold.

I laid my babe on the riverbank and kneeled down, kissed her head and then I pushed her into the rushing river.

Chapter Eighteen

I stumbled back to the inn and up to my room, the creel knocking at my legs. When I got there, I gathered the bloodied sheets and put them into the creel and put it under my bed. The straw mat underneath me was ruined, but I could replace that. I opened the window to get air in. I was going through the motions in a state of shock and disbelief. I got back into bed. I lay on my side, imagining myself floating down the river with my baby.

Joan came upstairs, with tea and some bread and cheese, and I sent her away for fresh linens. When she came back, I sat up.

'You must go home and tell Ma you have tried your best, but I am not for returning,' I said.

At first Joan protested, but not with much vigour. What she had witnessed had terrified her. 'And you will just carry on as normal, will you? Pretend nothing happened and save up your pennies for London?'

'Things will never be normal,' I told her. 'But I have not come this far, and endured this and lost my own babe, simply to come home again.'

Joan made slow work of putting the cheese on the bread and pouring the tea, for she was in shock too. Finally she said, 'What is it, Maggie, that makes you so determined to keep running, even after this? Tell me.'

I looked down at my hands. They were rough and raw, from

washing and laundering and all those chores. But they looked better than they had looked before, when they spent their days in brine, cut to shreds with fish-hooks and gutting knives.

'If I come back home, I don't think I will ever leave,' I replied. 'I will get caught up in our family's ways, and I will be so distraught at what has happened to me I will be too afraid to try again. And truth be told, Joan, I do not like how Ma and Da favour you. I will have made that even worse by running away.'

'Then I will not ask you again,' she said. 'But I will go back. The world past Fisherrow is a frightening place, with its Houses of Correction and highwaymen, and all sorts. And Ma needs me, and we need to show the tea men that we are trustworthy in some ways.'

'You must never speak of what happened with the babe to anyone,' I warned her. I did not ask if she had her eyes on a sweetheart mill owner or somesuch, for I truly did not care.

'I never want to think of last night again,' she said. 'It was worse than anything Ma spoke of when she talked of losing her children, but I know I will never get the sight of the poor babe out of my mind.'

On that, we were agreed.

I walked Joan down to the stables the next morning and made sure she got on the right coach. Then she drifted off, huddled in her best shawl, her face paler and more worried than it had even been when she arrived.

'She was not for staying long, was she, hen?' Mrs Baxter joined me in the yard. She smelled of pastry and apples and spice, and I had a terrible urge of longing for the baby, to smell her damp head again. 'My dear, you are quite ashen. Did the pair of you fight?'

'We always fight,' I replied sadly.

'Just as well she's gone then,' mused Mrs Baxter. 'For she was no use covering your shift. Thank goodness you're back on your feet. Now, come inside and get these pies before they burn.'

And that was the way it went, for a day or so, a sense of normality closing in on me despite the fact that my world had collapsed. For how could there be joy in the taste of an apple pie, when my baby had gone? How could the patrons hoot and screech and talk of saucy girls, when the world was so cruel? How could they drink ale? How could anyone do anything?

That was the way it went.

And then someone found the baby. I knew by the shriek in the kitchen.

It was Cook's shriek, and Cook was not a woman prone to shrillness or outbursts, but a fisherman had come in, around mid-morning, and said he had been at the river when he had noticed something downstream that did not look right, not right at all, amongst a crop of rocks, and he had gone to have a look. 'I thought it was a drowned animal,' he kept saying, shaking his head and sounding quite bemused. He'd not known what to do with the baby. 'If I laid it out on the riverbank, a fox might've got it.' He was talking and talking. 'Wouldn't 've been right to leave it.'

And so he had put the baby in his creel and brought it to the first place he could think of – the nearest place really – which was here, and had come in the kitchen door, not wanting to disturb the patrons, and had lifted the lid of his creel, and that was what made Cook scream. The baby in the creel on the table in the kitchen, beside her good knives.

His creel wasn't like mine; it was much smaller than mine.

I remember thinking, *He mustn't be much of a fisherman if he only needs a small creel*, but I suppose it was big enough. Big enough for a tiny baby.

The hullabaloo carried into the parlour and everyone cleared a space and, when I realized what all the shrieking was about and that my dead baby was in the basket on the table, I screamed too – screamed at everyone to leave her alone.

I dropped the bag of washing I had been carrying, and I went over to the basket and I would not let anyone near her.

And that was how they knew it was my baby.

They put my story together, piece by piece, like bait strung on a line, as the fisherman's nerves were calmed with a large whisky. The constable came, then the parish officials.

A runaway, a glass ring, a pallor. A sister who came and went, saying little. A fishwife who'd abandoned the trade. They'd had high hopes I'd be as hard-working as my reputation, but on second thoughts mibbie they'd also thought there was something strange about me.

Had I killed the baby? Had I left it there to die, or smothered it? Well, if it had been born dead, why not alert the Baxters? Why had I not employed a midwife? Where was my sister now?

Then an urgent letter was written to the sheriffs in Edinburgh and the rider told to leave immediately. The constables took the baby away and I shrieked again, and one of the parish men slapped me and his ring caught my skin and it bled. My face bled and my womb bled.

'What will you do with her?' Mrs Baxter asked the constable. By then it was the middle of the afternoon and there had been no lunch served, as the parlour was now taken up with important men and their scribes. *The chicken will spoil, for it is on its last day,* I thought. Then someone went upstairs and dug in my creel and found the bloodied linens and there were more shrieks. Mrs Baxter said nothing about the patrons milling at the parlour door, nor the fact that Cook was not fit to work for the rest of her shift. Shame had been brought on the River Inn.

'Mistress Dickson will need to be kept securely,' a constable said.

'She cannot remain here,' said a parish man. 'She would escape. This is already a house of immorality. Did you not suspect she was with child?'

'She told me she was a maiden,' replied Mrs Baxter.

The parish man turned to me and spoke very slowly, as though he thought me a simpleton. 'Mistress Dickson,' he declared, 'the deliberate concealment of a pregnancy is a grave matter indeed.'

Well, I had not known that. I thought it was my own private business, the things that were happening inside my womb. But this man appeared to have an authority over my body, even its most secret parts.

'I was saving to go to London and have the baby there,' I told him.

No one liked that. Mrs Baxter shook her head.

'Maggie, girl, why did you not just tell me?'

'Indeed, Mistress Dickson, why did you not ask the parish for help?'

They made it sound so simple, as though me telling them would have made everything all right. But that was all pretence and lies, to stop any blame being laid at their own door.

They took me to the House of Correction. They carried me on an open cart and by the time they had got that together, the main street was lined with folk, all come to see the girl who left her baby on the riverbank. They did not shout or throw cabbages or stones, or any of that kind of mob hysteria, but they did pull their bonnets and caps and shawls tight about themselves and stare. Man, woman, child. The tea merchant, who looked at me like a puzzle that now made sense. The boy I'd seen peeing in the market. I wanted to stand up and tell them what had happened, that the baby had died and I had given it my own farewell, that's all, but two of the parish officers sat with me and I knew that if I moved, they would pull me back down. I was not bound or put in chains or called names or anything like that, not yet, but they looked at me like they thought I was the worst mother that ever lived.

Mibbie I was.

Chapter Nineteen

I was taken to a vast high-ceilinged dormitory that had three tall windows on each side and no curtains. Thin bed-mats lay in neat rows, occupied by a dozen girls and women of all ages, whom I came to learn had been incarcerated after being caught on the roads and villages between Scotland and England in various displays of immoral behaviour, such as vagrancy and prostitution and idleness.

Some of them wore fine clothes with laces and trimmings, and I was reminded of Mrs Rose and even wondered if she might have spent time here, but there was no sign of her. I wondered if the last maid was still here, the one who got pregnant and was kicked out of the Baxters' inn, but mibbie she was long gone now that her babe had been born. We were overseen by wardens and watchmen, and by a matron who was a stout spinster in a pristine cap, who sucked comfits and smelled of ginger. They all carried canes.

We slept in that room upstairs and spent our days in a workshop downstairs, beating hemp with mallets. I did not know the purpose of the job, merely assumed it had something to do with rope-making. There were three men, rough-looking sorts, but we were not allowed to talk to them at all and they slept in another part of the house altogether, with night-watchmen and locked gates keeping us apart. I would not have wanted to talk to those men even if we had been allowed. They looked menacing and brought an air of edginess to the workshop. I knew without a doubt that were it not for the watchmen guarding their every move, canes at the ready, those men would do something.

I had begged for a rest, but was told I must go to the workshop for two hours every morning.

'This is a House of Correction, not a lying-in chamber,' Matron clipped. 'I will attend to you as required, but you must earn your keep. The other women are in the workshop eight hours a day.'

I was to remain here until an agreement had been reached about what to do with me next.

No one came and interrogated me or came to support me, so I was left with my fears and the awful words uttered by the officials ringing in my head.

I thought no more of Joan, or Ma or Da or Spencer, only of the soul who had lived inside me and died a few hours after her birth. I did not know grief could hurt like this. My breasts swelled wickedly red and tight. Matron brought bandages and bound me, saying I was to tell her if I felt feverish, but it did not come to that. I wished for the fever, though. I wished for death.

I did not sleep more than a few minutes at a stretch. When I did, my dreams were vivid and wretched and every one of them ended the same: with the baby floating down the Tweed, wailing for me. Sometimes I dreamed of snakes curling round her little body. I woke up startled, clawing at the bandages, but Matron would not let me take them off. 'Not yet, girl, and try not to think of the baby or the milk will not stop.'

On the first night, as we lay on our mats under the sunset, one of the women asked me why I was here. It was after Matron had bound me and given me a caudle of wine and egg and honey, which she said would give me my strength back. I drank it as she watched, and then she took the cup away.

The room was silent for a while and I thought everyone was drifting off to sleep. But the woman, the oldest one of us, asked me loudly and I could hear the blanket-rustle of everyone lifting their heads to hear the answer.

'You've had a baby, but where is it?' she asked.

'She died,' I said. 'She was weak.'

'And why have they brought you in here?' she went on. 'Have you no man to support you?' Her voice was harsh with shame-less curiosity.

Then Matron came back. 'No talking after bedtime,' she scolded. Her cane clicked against the floor. I had not seen her hit anyone with it, but had no doubt that she would. She paused at my bed. I could smell her ginger-breath and the soapy scent of her skin. 'Mistress Dickson is here as her baby was found on the banks of the Tweed,' she said.

There was a sucking of air, a sitting-up in bed, an outburst of cries at that.

Matron's voice rose above it, sing-song and sharp. 'The circumstances are not clear and the matter is being investigated, so I will thank all of you to ask no more questions of Mistress Dickson as she must save her answers for the constables.'

No one spoke to me after that, except things like 'Pass the porridge pot' or 'Move your arse' as they squeezed past me in the narrow halls. They wanted nothing to do with me. They turned away from me and wouldn't meet my eye. Now, as I look back on it, I am trying to remember if I even cared.

I think I would have been most upset, had it not been for the fact that all I thought of was the baby. Day and night I would yearn and, most of all, wonder where her poor body was now.

I think I had a couple of weeks of this before I was called to the office with news. A parish official sat behind the desk and the constable stood next to him. Matron stood beside me and, though there was a chair and I was exhausted, I was not invited to sit in it.

'You will be removed to Edinburgh,' the parish official said. 'A coach is being readied as we speak.' There was a parchment in front of him, lying on the desk, and he kept pointing to it with his gloved fingers. It was crammed full of looped writing.

'What does that note say?' I asked. 'Who's it from?'

He looked surprised, as if he did not expect me to be so curious about my own fate.

'It is from the clerk of the High Court of Justiciary in Edinburgh,' he said. 'In response to the letter sent by the constables of Kelso. It requires that you are brought to the court to have your case heard there. It says,' here he frowned as though reading something distasteful, 'that the accusation of concealment of pregnancy is a grievous one and must heard in the capital, *not the shires*, so that it can be given due scrutiny by learned judges.'

'The child's body is already in Edinburgh,' added the constable. 'At the Incorporation of Surgeons and Barbers. They are conducting post-mortem tests on it, to try to determine its cause of death.'

Bile rose in my throat, and I thought I might vomit. I staggered. Matron put her hand on my back. They all stared.

'Someone ought to inform your kin,' said the parish official. 'If you give details, we will have a letter drawn up. The constable will take it; he is accompanying you. Your family will have to make preparations for you to be admitted to the jail next to the courthouse. You'll need suitable clothing and blankets, and food sent.'

I was hot, too hot, as though a fever was coming. My armpits and the back of my neck erupted in sweat. 'But my ma and da can't read,' I gasped, 'and it will come as a terrible shock to them. They will need the letter read out to them, and my sister too, although Joan knows full well the baby was born alive. She was there. You will need to find Joan.' Everything felt like it was galloping at me, and I had to grip onto the chair to steady myself.

'Careful with what you say to her,' admonished the constable to the parish official. 'She is nervous and agitated. But I'll keep a note of this Joan and will make sure she is questioned.'

'We will send her up to Edinburgh with blankets and an extra shawl,' said Matron, 'or she will perish on the journey and that will be the fault of us in the shires.'

Everyone agreed to that, with a round of reluctant grunts.

'And she will need bandages and linens – plenty of them,' added Matron tightly. 'For the lactation and the lochia. She still leaks.'

The parish man winced, as though he had been smacked with Matron's cane, and scowled at me as though I were cattle.

The carriage was large and severe-looking with black curtains at the windows. As well as the driver, there was the constable and two other men hired as guards, in case of highwaymen. They tied me to the constable with a piece of rope.

When I look back on that journey, I do not think of it as a singular line, the kind of line you see on a map. I think of it in jolts. Of the stories the men told to pass the time: of the Jacobites and their wars, and whether they would ever put the Stuarts on the throne, which they all hoped would happen, but you had to be careful who you said that to. Or whether it might be better to emigrate on one of the ships going out to the Americas or Canada and go fortune-hunting.

But mostly I remember how that journey unfolded in my own self. Of seeing my creel packed neat with the rest of the luggage and thinking Mrs Baxter would have done that, and realizing that my savings would likely still be in the locked drawer. Of a cheese pie they gave me, which I tried to eat before I saw mould on the pastry shell. Of travel sickness and vomiting on the constable's lap, and the way they all stood up to wipe him down and left me heaving. Of the linens growing warm and wet between my legs and the smell of my own lochia and stale vomit, and the men catching the scent of me and putting their kerchiefs to their noses. Sometimes I would think I could hear the sea, but it was just the wind and rain. Often I had questions that I dared not ask and they died on my dried lips.

Would they bury the baby in an Edinburgh kirkyard or put it in a jar on a mortuary shelf? What would the surgeons find when they cut it apart? Would they say I tried to kill it?

What was the punishment for concealment of a pregnancy?

Chapter Twenty

Edinburgh
August 1724

The fishwives told tales of Edinburgh and said it was crammed tighter with folk than pebbles on a beach. They spoke of Fishmarket Close, which you could smell before you got to it and hear the cries of 'Fresh fish' soar to the skies like gulls. They spoke of buildings ten storeys tall. They said it was a town in layers, where the rich lived on the top floors and the poor in the cellars, and all manner in between. But regardless of whether you were a chimney sweep or a scholar, everyone rubbed shoulders with everyone else on account of how narrow the streets and stairs were.

There were societies for this and societies for that. Servants of some of the high ladies would buy the cheapest fish to be distributed to the poor, and servants of other high folk would order buckets of oysters for balls. There were gin shops and medicine shops and fortune-tellers and whores. Cock-fights and fiddle players who'd pass caps for coins. Amongst it all scurried scores of caddies: men and boys in blue aprons, who ran errands and carted water and cried the news and sold pamphlets. The fishwives and the salt-sellers were similar kin, all coming into town each morning on rickety carts from the edges of the Forth, and they were looked down upon by those who lived in the closes and sold linens and wines and jewels.

My Edinburgh had none of this florid life and colour. My

Edinburgh was a cell high up in the tolbooth, bleak and dark, and filled with wretched women like me and those I had met in the House of Correction.

The oldest was so old she died in her sleep two days after I arrived and was found slumped at dawn. The youngest was a pickpocket, aged no older than twelve when she was flung in beside us, although she did not know the year of her birth and we all sat with her and helped her guess her age by the size of her and the whiteness of her teeth, and the fact that she had not bled yet and was very attached to a cloth doll. She was set for a public whipping and said, with bravado, that she was more than ready for it.

On my third day a young man came to visit me and said he had been appointed by the court. He sat in the chair on the other side of the barred gate that fenced us in. Men in wigs and capes would come and go from this chair, speaking in sombre tones to the women whose names they called out. He looked no older than me, with a patch of hair at his lip that might one day become a moustache. He spoke in whispers, as though he was embarrassed to be there. His name was Mr Suttie and he was my advocate.

'I have no money for an advocate, sir,' I warned him.

He waved his hands vaguely. 'The court pays the advocate's fee in cases like this,' he said.

I watched his hands come to a rest on his knees. 'Cases like what?'

According to the surgeons who had plucked my baby's lungs from her chest, she had breathed before she had died. They had set the lungs in a basin of water apparently, and they had floated. Like sponges.

'That is correct,' I replied. 'She took some breaths and suckled but then she fell asleep and died.'

'The fact is that if the lungs had no air in them, it would have been ascertained that the child was stillborn,' he said. 'But she was not.'

'I never said she was,' I told him.

He waved his hands again. 'The court is simply establishing the facts,' he went on. 'The baby was a weakling, but with no apparent disease, and the court is concerned with the matter of your deliberate concealment of the pregnancy and the fact that you attempted to dispose of the child. Those two irrefutable facts mean a jury could be directed by a judge to find you guilty of infanticide.'

The words he used were official-sounding and complicated, but I knew from the way he whispered them exactly what he meant.

'I did not murder my baby,' I told him.

'I am afraid the facts suggest otherwise,' he said. 'And concealment is a grave offence. Was the child illegitimate?'

'No,' I said. 'My husband was taken by a press gang.'

He raised his eyebrows at that.

'Concealment usually involves an illegitimate child,' he explained. 'So we might argue on that point.'

'I didn't conceal the pregnancy, I just hadn't got round to telling people yet,' I said. 'My sister Joan guessed.'

'She will be called as a witness,' he told me. 'But even then, it would have been expected that you would at least have spoken to those you were living with – your landlady, for example – and told her of your situation and begun preparations for the birth and motherhood. Or returned home to your family and told them. Instead you attempted to hide all evidence that you were with child. And the fact of the matter is that you did attempt to dispose of the child in the River Tweed.'

'But I didn't know that was so wrong,' I said. 'I didn't want the parish officials involved, for they might have put me away.'

'But what has happened, Mistress Dickson, is far worse,'
Mr Suttie said, 'for it is a capital crime, with the death-penalty
if you are found guilty. You might face the hangman.' And with
that, he lowered his eyes to his hands.

There are only eight Hanging Days a year in Edinburgh, to
ensure enough of a spectacle – enough anticipation. I learned
this after Mr Suttie had gone, listening to the women talk
about who was up in court next.

I sat and listened to them chitter and chatter about this, as
my blood and milk finally tapered off and I felt myself drying
up; my last connection with my daughter withering to nothing.
Somewhere not too far away, over the spires and tenements,
her little body was stored with the anatomists, and I retched
when I thought of that. But I had barely eaten, so it was an
empty retch, and I had become so used to grieving silently
that none of the women noticed.

I thought of the hangman's noose in a detached way, as
though it lay at the end of a corridor and that corridor was a
long and arduous one, filled with so many obstacles – such as
standing up in a courtroom and seeing Ma and Da again, and
listening to Joan on the witness stand – that I could not even
worry yet about the destination. Denial, I suppose. And mibbie
I even welcomed the notion, for I was in the depths of some
despair that I had never even known. Not even after what had
happened between Joan and Spencer.

The grief for my child was a world of despair. I had spent
my pregnancy fearing her birth. But when I had held her in
my arms, I had fallen in love with her.

There were no condemned prisoners in the women's room;

these unfortunate souls, once sentence was pronounced, were taken to another part of the jail and put in a holding cell called the Iron Room, in a passage that went between the prison and St Giles's Kirk, where they were taken to pray on Sundays. Every time these folks shuffled from their death-cell to the kirk or the gibbet, they did so as one pitiful group, surrounded by guards with pikes, so the chatter went. There were always far more condemned men than women. And whilst the women were generally coiners or thieves or the occasional murderess, many of the men were hanged for crimes against the Government or the Crown.

Most of the women in my cell were not headed for the gallows, though. Most, once their case was called, expected to be whipped or fined or transported or simply dismissed. I suppose that's why their talk often turned to the gruesome aspect of our jail, which appeared to me to be more of a factory of death and misery than anything else, where oat pottage was slopped out from a cauldron onto battered tin plates twice a day, and those who had the funds supplemented the gruel with baskets of bread and meat sent from home, and we all fought over the tepid water in the washpail every day.

The turnkeys were a variety of men whose names I never learned, but they patrolled the gate day and night. One or two did more keenly, studying us. Sometimes a woman would detach herself from the huddle and stand at the gate, and she and a turnkey would engage in some form of close activity through the bars. This happened with a few of the women with a few of the men, but most often with one woman, Molly, and one particular turnkey who did a shift in the afternoons.

For this, he would put out the lantern-light in the corridor, so their lewdness happened in darkness. Later Molly would be seen with a flask of liquor, but I had also seen these women with bottles of laudanum or pocket mirrors or combs or cheap scents, all bought with a fumble.

'He can get you anything,' Molly said to me one afternoon after she had done her trick at the gate with the turnkey and the lantern had been re-lit.

She offered me a sip of her flask and I took it, and it was rum, and it tasted like being in bed with Spencer.

She sat down beside me on the stone bench. 'That turnkey there, he likes you,' she went on. 'He told me he's been watching you and he likes your ankles. He sees them when you lift your skirts at the piss pail.' I gasped and she laughed, a juicy laugh that sounded like pipe smoke and bawdy jokes. I clutched my shawl. She lowered her voice. 'He says you're in for baby murder, but I've not told the girls that. They'd kill you with their bare hands if they knew.'

'I did no such thing,' I told her.

Her eyes were huge and gleaming. She had taken something more than rum, that was for sure.

'You'd best tell the turnkey that,' she said. 'And sweeten the message with something nice.' She grabbed my arm, a grip that was shockingly firm. 'You'd best do it before he starts gabbling to all the girls, my dear. He's told me to tell you that directly. Now if you will excuse me, I do not like to sit with baby murderers.'

She stood up and went to her mat. As she lay back, her stockinged legs akimbo, so that all the world might view her skinny white thighs if they wished, I rose shakily and made my way to the gate.

The turnkey was there, sitting on the chair. He stood up.

'In need of anything in particular?' he asked, coming close. He was bald and short and had the hollowed look of a man who had mibbie spent a spell in a cell himself.

'I am not a baby murderer,' I said, keeping my voice as quiet as I could.

'Tell that to the judge,' he replied. 'But in the meantime, what's your tipple? What are you missing, from the outside? A spot of whisky? A nice bit of beef steak? Rosewater? There must be something?'

'I don't want anything,' I said.

'I'll tell you what,' he continued, 'give me a flash of what you keep up those skirts of yours and I'll make sure no one hears what you're charged with.'

I wondered, as I lifted the front of my skirts and watched him stare at me down there, what kind of man would want to see such a thing, for I had only recently given birth. I wondered if this was how Mrs Rose felt to have that horrible Dr McTavish look at her nakedness and take advantage of her. And if there is a place that women might go to in their minds when they are forced to submit to a man, to shut him out. I tried to find it, through my breaths and the flicker of my closed eyes, but I did not.

I would need that place, if I was to stay here.

And if they hanged me, I would need to find it on the gallows.

He dismissed me after a few long moments and I could tell by the look on his face he had enjoyed my discomfort. I went back and sat on the bench feeling violated, even though he had not touched me. I did not want anything he could procure. I wanted desperately to hear from Ma, though, but nothing arrived for me. No message, no basket of fish, no visitors.

In any case I did not have long to wait and wonder at the silence. I was not called back to show my naked parts to the turnkey again. For after a few short days Mr Suttie returned and told me that my sister had been located and my case would be heard in court without delay.

Chapter Twenty-One

My case was heard by a judge called Sheriff McAllister and half of Edinburgh town, for the courtroom was filled with all manner of life by the time I was marched up to the dock. They spilled from the balcony and the back benches: some in robes, some in rags, some with parchments and quills, and some in their cups, for the stink of liquor and pipe smoke made me feel high as a bird.

I was put on a stool and told to stand when Sheriff McAllister entered and only to sit down when he did. Downstairs, before the trial, a young clerk with spindly hands had brought me my creel and told me to put on my best gown, then stood and watched and cracked his fingers as I stripped and put it on, unembarrassed to stare.

We had to wait half an hour for Sheriff McAllister, and I spent it watching the time tick past nine of the clock on a brass lantern clock that hung on a wood-panelled wall, and searching the assembled mass for my family.

I could hear what was being said about me loud and clear, for no one seemed to care if they spoke too loudly in my presence.

'She has the broad shoulders of a fishwife, look – she would have crushed that baby to death quite easily!'

'No wonder the husband joined the Navy; look how she scowls, imagine the temper on her!'

'The hangman's work will be cut out for him, for she will kick like a mule on the rope, mark my words!'

And then the chuckles and the guffaws, and the passing of hip flasks and the sniff of snuff-taking, and the crunch of comfits and the scraping of quills as the hand of the clock dragged itself forward, inch by inch.

I could not see Ma or Da or anyone else amongst the spectators. My dress itched and stank of damp. My young advocate, Mr Suttie, kept himself deep in conversation with the man next to him, but would constantly wipe his hands on his breeches, which made me think he was nervous. Finally Sheriff McAllister appeared.

'Bring in the witnesses,' he said, and at that a man opened a door and out poured everyone I knew. The Baxters, Cook, Ma, Da, Joan and even the fisherman who had found the baby. Ma wore a black gown I had never seen before, so it must have been new, and a pair of black gloves. She looked more sombre than I had ever seen her, as though in mourning for me already. Da looked bedraggled, as though he had just got off the boat. Joan trembled. Ma looked about the room, searching for me, and when she found me her face collapsed like wet sand. She buckled and Da had to grip her arm and make her stand up properly, and a murmur swept around the room that sounded like 'Shame, shame'.

That was when I really understood how awful it all was.

They put Da on the stand first. He looked sober and scared. A man called Lord Leith led the prosecution, which is to say that he probed around, looking to make me out to be a baby-killer, and occasionally Mr Suttie would stand up and object.

'We are trying to establish a picture of Mistress Dickson's life and background,' announced Lord Leith. 'What sort of a daughter would you say she was?'

'She was a good girl, she was brought up to be decent and law-abiding and God-fearing,' said Da, his voice weak and gravelly compared to the strident tones of the other men. 'Until she met a man called Patrick Spencer and it all went downhill from there.'

Lord Leith liked that. I could tell by the way the colour bloomed in his cheeks.

'Downhill, eh? Would you say your daughter was easily led, sir? Weak-minded? Frail?'

Mr Suttie rose to object, but the sheriff nodded at Da to answer.

'I know your instinct will be to protect your daughter. But remember you are under oath, Mr Dickson,' he warned.

Da looked scared. 'Perhaps not weak-minded, no. Perhaps too strong-minded, I'd say,' he mumbled.

Lord Leith liked that even more.

They did not call Ma, for it was decided, after a huddle with the sheriff that, as head of the household, Da's views were enough to establish my background and character.

'Frankly,' Mr Suttie told me when he returned from the huddle, 'I am not sure your mother would help your case. Mothers have a tendency to cave under questioning, and a mother's testimony tends not to be taken as seriously.'

I looked over at Ma but she wasn't looking in my direction. She was surveying the courtroom, her eyes darting in fear. Mibbie Mr Suttie was right.

There's not much to say about the evidence the Baxters gave, for it was all factual. Neither had guessed my state of pregnancy, nor had I given any inclination or even asked for extra meat or milk, or shown an unusual appetite for sweet or strange foods.

'Some might say,' pondered Lord Leith to Mrs Baxter, 'that you cannot be a very observant landlady if you did not notice the gestation of an infant under your own roof.'

'I had no clue,' protested Mrs Baxter. 'Mistress Dickson acted perfectly normally. This has all come as a terrible shock to me. To have a dead infant brought into own kitchen. The inn has become notorious and we have lost our usual patrons, and instead we have folk calling at all times of the day and night asking to see her room, asking for a viewing, as though we are a house of fascinations.'

I heard a ripple through the crowd, then of 'Oh! We must go to Kelso and view it too!'

Joan looked at me constantly and every time I caught her eye, she flinched and looked away.

When the Baxters and the fisherman had taken their turns describing the events, Lord Leith called my sister to the stand. She rose, a small, bewildered slip of a girl, yet somehow still pretty, and the men on the balcony edged forward.

'Your instinct will be to protect your sister,' Lord Leith said. Joan looked wide-eyed at that. 'But you are here to tell the truth of what happened on the day she went into labour and the baby died. First, so that the court is clear – very clear, my dear – did Mistress Dickson know she was with child?'

'Yes, she did,' replied Joan, her voice barely a squeak. 'But she was hiding it from the Baxters.'

'Speak up, girl, for we can barely hear your voice. I am sure you have a nice loud voice, for you are a fishergirl, are you not? Now pretend you are at the market selling your fish and use that loud voice,' Lord Leith told her. 'Now, *hiding it from the Baxters* is what you have just said. Hiding the baby from the Baxters. In other words, concealing it.'

Well, that went down well, and everyone in the room settled down with fresh snuff and confits for the rest. Joan cleared her throat and begged for water and sipped it, holding the cup between two shaking hands. Then she put the cup down and delivered the rest of her testimony, louder this time, gripping the edge of the table in front of her as though she might vomit with fear.

The labour had started shortly after midnight, Joan said. She had guessed at my condition and tried to get me to come home with her, but I had refused, desperate to get to London.

'And what was it about London that so enticed your sister?' pondered Lord Leith. 'For she had few skills for city life. She could gut and sell fish, but clearly she thought she deserved better rewards.'

'She had always yearned for London,' said Joan. 'She had an ambition to go there.'

'And this ambition of hers. Would you say it was all-consuming?'

Joan nodded, looking petrified.

'To the point where she would sacrifice anything? Even her own child?'

The room was silent for a heartbeat or two.

'I cannot say, sir,' stammered Joan. 'I do not think she would have wished ill on the little mite. It was a darling little thing.' Her eyes welled with tears and she bent her head down, almost folding herself over the table.

'Straighten up, we are almost done. A precious little mite, I can imagine.' Lord Leith addressed the crowd. 'I myself am a father of three living children, and of one child who went to be with the angels. There is nothing that shows God in his mercy any clearer than the face of a newborn babe.' His eyes welled with tears too. Everyone's did.

Not mine, though. I was incandescent at the man. I willed Joan to see him for the bully he was and to stand up to him, instead of letting him talk down to her like this.

'And did Mistress Dickson bond with the baby, when it was born? Was she enraptured with it, as mothers usually are?

'I think she was shocked,' said Joan. 'We both were.'

The crowd were hooked on her every word.

'Are you sure – beyond all doubt – that the baby succumbed to its own weakness? Was there ever a point when you turned your back on your sister and she might have smothered the baby? Held her hand over its mouth?'

'I am sure that did not happen,' said Joan.

Of course it did not happen, I willed her to say.

'You did not turn your back on your sister, with this secret child, for one minute?' demanded Mr Leith.

'Well, of course I had to turn my back and tidy up the room and all of that,' said Joan. 'She was in the bed.'

'Ah, but is it possible that your sister could have taken the chance, in that moment, to do a quick but terrible deed? For one swift action would change the course of her fate, and make sure she could get to London and freely live the life she had yearned for, instead of being forced to care for a child.'

Joan! Tell this court I would never kill a child!

'I cannot remember,' Joan stuttered, in floods of tears now, which ran down her face, bloating it.

She stared at me, as though searching for forgiveness, but I had none.

For she had the chance, didn't she? To stand up for me and say that I would never have done such a thing as to murder my own newborn babe. But Joan did not. And whether it was the fear of that petrifying courtroom or the ceaseless interrogation of that devil Lord Leith, my sister did not stand up for me when I most needed her.

When all the drama and the weeping had finally ceased, and my family were back in their chairs, Ma and Da with their arms around my sobbing sister, Lord Leith turned to the sheriff.

He pointed at me with a ringed finger, but did not look in my direction.

'Mistress Dickson is clearly a woman of secretive motives, with no hint of maternal love about her. There is nothing I can say to you other than that the facts of this case speak for themselves. She did wilfully conceal an unwanted pregnancy. Even her own sister only found out by her own guesswork. And it is perfectly clear to me that when that babe was born, Mistress Dickson took her chance to snuff out its life in order that she could fulfil her selfish ambitions.'

He went to his table and picked up a piece of parchment and read from it.

'Under the Act Anent Murthering of Children 1690, if any woman shall conceal her being with child and shall not call for assistance during birth, then if the child is found dead the mother shall be found guilty of the murder of her own child, regardless of whether there is any direct evidence of murder. In such cases as this, when the infant has died, the concealment of the pregnancy is a crime, Sheriff McAllister, and there is no defence.'

The sheriff looked emotionless, and then my counsel, Mr Suttie, stood up and addressed him.

'Mistress Dickson rejects all of these accusations. Her own sister has admitted she was there at the birth. When her sister guessed at the pregnancy Mistress Dickson did not deny it. How could it be described as a concealed pregnancy if she had assistance?'

'Come to the witness stand, Mistress Dickson,' the sheriff said gravely.

I cannot say how the courtroom reacted when I stood up and took the stand, for the world shrank at that moment, until all that was left of it was the high-pitched singing of my blood racing through my head. I wondered, briefly, if I might collapse or forget entirely who I was.

Mr Suttie's young-mannish voice pulled me back.

'Tell us,' he said, 'how you felt when you saw your babe?'

My words fell like husks into the room. 'I fell in love with her,' I replied.

'And had you kept your pregnancy a secret? Or were you just caught by surprise perhaps, and had not gathered your thoughts enough to tell everyone?' I could tell Mr Suttie was offering me a way out – an excuse.

'Caught by surprise, sir,' I told him. 'For I had been off-colour for some months, but did not think for a minute I might be with child, for I had only been married a brief while before my husband was press-ganged.'

The sheriff rapped his hammer on the bench and interrupted us. 'Mistress Dickson, did you not even think for a minute you might be with child? Your belly was swelling and you must have felt movement? Were your gowns not getting tight?'

'Mibbie they were,' I admitted, remembering how I had sat and unpicked the seams, letting them out. 'But I thought it was the fine meals I was getting, and it was not until quite near the end that I guessed.'

Sheriff McAllister exhaled.

'In that case,' he said, 'how might you explain the fact that when your creel was searched by the constables, this item was amongst your possessions – a singular item that suggests, without any doubt, that you did indeed know that you were expecting a child and had known about it for some time?'

And with that, he lifted something up to show the courtroom what he was talking about.

The little white baby bonnet.

There was another huddle with the sheriff and the law men.

I watched the bonnet lying on the sheriff's bench and wondered if I might just reach across and take it back, and I think mibbie I did try, my legs rising up, but two men pulled me back to my chair.

Then I noticed the way the clock had moved, when it all felt like a flash, but somehow it was already twelve of the clock, but I realized time did not really matter now.

Then the sheriff stood up and gave a long speech, but I do remember the most of it, for how could I not?

'Mistress Margaret Dickson of Fisherrow, lately Kelso. I do not believe that you deliberately tried to murder your child, for the bonnet tells us that you planned for its survival. But it also tells us that you did know you were pregnant.

'You confessed your condition to your sister, once she had guessed, but you had not told your wider community – a community who would have offered you and the baby the necessary support. Whether the baby might have lived with the intervention of a physician or midwife is a matter of uncertainty, but the possibility remains. The fact is that you did not give the infant the best chance of survival and, when it sadly succumbed, you tried to hide the entire matter.

'So, on the indictment of the murder of an infant, by concealment of pregnancy, I have no choice but to find you guilty, and that, like murder, is a capital crime for which the punishment is hanging.'

Chapter Twenty-Two

The Iron Room was a cruel place.

It was a full flight of steps underground, low and damp-ceilinged and devoid of light and hope. They called it the Iron Room on account of the fact prisoners here were once held in shackles before their executions, but conditions were better now and we were simply locked in. It was a room of hushed regime and muffled despair. I was taken to the women's side, separated from the men's side by the main corridor. When they pushed me in and closed the gate behind me, the other woman – there was only one – looked up from where she was lying on a bed-mat in the corner and regarded me with mild curiosity, but no great sympathy. She was adrift, in her own world.

A female guard came, who reminded me of the matron at the House of Correction, on account of her gown and cap. She addressed me through the gate, although she might as well have been addressing everyone else, for there was nothing personal about what she said.

'Mondays are bath-days, Tuesdays fresh meat, donated by the kirk and we thank them in our prayers. On Wednesdays there are morning and afternoon religious instructions, specific to your situation. Thursdays are visiting days and Fridays we tidy our cells and wash the floors with vinegar. Weekends are for quiet contemplation, and we all walk to the kirk on Sundays. We are inspected each morning for signs of fever or disease and quarantined, if necessary. In the seven days ahead of a Hanging Day – which is the period in which we find ourselves now – we do all of these as normal, except that visitors are allowed every day and the minister comes each evening.'

The woman in the corner spoke. Her voice sounded like dried earth.

'You are lucky, hen. You've only got few days of this.'

There was a murmur of agreement from the men's side, although I could not see their faces very well, as the lamps were dim.

'So you have missed your bath, as we were all bathed today' – the guard had a jarring habit of using 'we' – 'but I will see what I can do, as we do not wish to go to Our Lord unclean. And we will need to find you a clean smock too, for your clothes are filthy and likely flea-ridden.'

She tutted then, as though I was an additional burden she had been forced to take on when she was already at some great capacity, before putting her lantern up in front of her and making her way out.

In the silence that followed, which was only a moment or two, a rodent scuttled from one corner to another and there was a far-off shout of some sort that came from above and reminded me that we were only a few feet away from people living quite ordinary lives.

The men started up a conversation again, two of them, in low tones and it appeared to be something about cock-fighting, as though they were pals in an ale bar. The other woman patted the mat next to her, for me to come and lie down.

'Have you any gin about you, hen?' she asked, although she must have known as well as I did that you were searched for liquor and knives and poisons before you were taken to the Iron Room.

'Mibbie your family will bring some, if you ask,' I said.

She sniffed. 'They've turned their backs on me,' she replied. 'The next time I see them, they'll be watching me hang, to make sure I'm dead. That's if they bother to turn up at all. And they will leave my body for the anatomists, for they've made no plans to bury me.'

I did not ask why, nor why she was condemned, for I did not want to tell anyone my own shameful conviction. For it was shameful.

But I did not know what I did was such a crime. No one had told me.

It's not as though my ma had taken me to one side as a lass and told me all the things I must never do. I knew it was a crime to steal or forge a coin or call curses in the street, but I had never known it was a crime simply to not tell anyone I was with child. Or to give her my own farewell. And yes, I'd once considered giving her over to the parish, but I would never have harmed her.

I lay on the mat, shattered. It was evening now, and one of the men called over to me and said someone would bring a supper soon. There were more calls like this, and I knew the men were trying to get me into some kind of conversation, but I did not want any of it and I was glad when a turnkey came with trays of food. It was better than the gruel we were given upstairs. I surveyed the plate of chops and peas, which, although dry and tepid, was the only real meal I had been given in days.

'They want us in good health for the gallows,' the woman said to me, picking up her chop with her hands. They don't want us dying of typhus or starvation first. That would disappoint everyone. If you don't fancy that chop, I'll take it.'

I was hungry, but with no appetite, which was a ghastly

combination. I chewed on the chop, and it reminded me of Ma's Sunday lunches. Would they come and visit? Would they come and watch me hang? I had not had the chance to say anything to them in the courtroom. I had been dragged out too quick.

Then the woman guard came back down and called me over to the gate.

'I shall not keep you long from your meal,' she said, 'but I've organized for you to get a bath tomorrow morning.'

I could not have cared whether I was bathed or not and she looked disappointed that I didn't seem grateful. But she ploughed on regardless.

'You'll have a nice bit of soap, and you ought to wash your hair twice too – two soapings to get the grease out properly. I'll make sure the water's hot for you. Afterwards you'll have your appointment with the doctor.'

'And what is that for? Am I to be given medicine?' I asked.

'Oh no, he is not that kind of a doctor,' she said. 'The prison physicians can take care of all of that, and we receive them in the mornings as and when required. No, the doctor is the man who will hang you, my dear. He needs to weigh and measure you, to make sure you hang nice and quick.'

I spent my twenty minutes in the bath – which was scorching hot at first, but quickly cooled – looking at myself. My belly was loose and my nipples browner than they had been before the pregnancy, and there was a dark line running downwards from my navel. The baby had changed me, and I liked that. I liked that she had marked me. I put on the new prison smock. It had such neat and pure stitching that I felt it had likely been stitched by the women parishioners of St Giles's and I imagined them sitting in a circle, a guild or a commission or somesuch, taking honey cake and praying for the poor condemned women beneath their feet, and going to bed that night in their clean beds feeling they had done such a good deed the Lord would surely notice.

After all of that, with my twice-washed hair plaited tight and smelling of soap, and my white smock, I realized I looked like a woman set to hang.

The doctor received the condemned in a small room at the end of the passageway, nearest the kirk. On Hanging Day that's where he stored his clothes, for he wore a cape and a hood when he hanged folk, to keep himself anonymous. There was a weighing platform in the corner of the room and a measuring stick.

'He will inspect you quite fully,' warned the woman guard. 'But do not squirm or refuse him, because you do not want him to get it wrong.'

She left me there and I thought I might vomit, and I had to swallow back the sick and wipe my watering mouth and nose on the sleeve of my clean smock and it left a grey stain.

Presently the doctor arrived. He was not dressed like a hangman, but like a well-to-do gentleman, with a black hat and a silver-topped cane and a good cape. But as he bade me a good morning, my heart almost stopped, for I recognized him at once. He was very tall and sharp-shouldered and had a certain presence about him.

Edinburgh's hangman.

The doctor. It was Dr McTavish, from Kelso.

'I knew I would surprise you,' he said, tossing his hat and cape on the stand. 'But you are not to be afraid. I have hanged one hundred and forty men and women so far in my career, and I consider myself the best in the trade.'

He carried on like this, breezy, as he rolled up his shirt sleeves and examined his pocket watch. 'I am with the Incorporation of Surgeons and Barbers. And of all the men and women I've hanged, I've never had a single complaint from any of them about the quality of my work.'

He looked up at me then, a flash in his eyes, mibbie thinking himself artful.

'Do you try that quip with everyone?' I enquired.

'I try to lighten the mood,' he said. 'This is not the most pleasant job, but it pays the bills on my houses in Edinburgh and Kelso.'

'Do the people in Kelso know what you do?' I asked, for no one had mentioned it, and the River Inn had been a gossiping place.

'Oh no, they would treat me differently if they knew,' he said. 'A hangman wears a hood for a reason. And the folks of Kelso are of a low intelligence and would not understand that hanging is a craft.'

He was truly the most despicable of men. As he took up his measuring stick and proceeded to ask me to stand straight, I imagined he was well capable of poisoning his wife. Poor Kitty.

And that was when it came to me.

'Dr McTavish,' I said, keeping my voice low so that he had to lean in towards me to catch my words, 'have you seen our mutual friend, the dear Mrs Rose, since she absconded?'

'Alas, no,' he replied in a whisper, his lips almost flickering at my neck. 'But if I did see her, I do not know what I would do first: kiss her or hang her for the way she treated me, by running off like that.'

'Mrs Rose did talk quite boldly of you,' I said.

He hesitated, just for a moment, before carrying on in his morbid task.

'Step on the weighing platform,' he instructed.

I did. Now I was taller than him and I stood in front of him, facing the wall whilst he adjusted the weights.

'Mrs Rose told me a funny story – not funny like your quip, Doctor, but a strange tale that made my hair stand up on end, so gory it was. A tale about you.'

This time he did stop.

'And what was this tale?' he hissed.

'Well, I hardly dare tell it, sir, for it paints you in a terrible light, but if you insist,' I answered.

And he stood and listened to what Mrs Rose had said about him: that she thought he had poisoned poor Kitty, for she dropped dead out of nowhere, and Dr McTavish was a master of all sorts of potions. And that Dr McTavish was sorely fed up with his wife and would do anything to get her out of the way.

'A chaste marriage, that's what you had, and that's why you employed the services of Mrs Rose. Your wife would not give you your conjugals and was, by all accounts, a harridan to you, to boot.'

And although I could not see his face, for he was behind me, remember, I could tell by the rapid way he breathed that he was suddenly feeling very grave indeed.

What things we say, what promises we make, when we are pleading for our lives. But the way Dr McTavish stared at me, open-mouthed with horror, told me I was right. And that Mrs Rose had been right in her suspicions.

'Sir,' I said, 'here is the thing. I do very much fear that if you don't help me survive the gallows, then I might scream your secret to the world, and those would be my last words, for all of Edinburgh town to hear.'

'No one will pay any attention to the last pathetic words of a baby-killer,' Dr McTavish spat.

'You will loosen my hands,' I said, ignoring him, 'for they'll be bound at my chest, not behind my back – you will make sure of that. You will help me slip them up, under the noose. And you will make sure that the noose is not going to strangle me or break my neck. And if you do *not* do that, but put that noose tight and firm around my neck, I will scream on that gallows and tell everyone you are a poisoner and that if they dig up your wife's grave and examine her, the body will be full of laudanum.'

I knew about post-mortems by then, you see. I knew surgeons could make the dead talk, just as they had weighed my poor babe's lungs and seen that she had taken breaths.

'The folk of Edinburgh will listen with great intent to what I say on the gallows,' I went on. 'And the broadside-writers will be there, and everything will be scribed and put into news chronicles and books. If I tell them the hangman's wife lies in a Kelso kirkyard full of his poison, it will be an almighty scandal.'

A rodent scratched at the floor and we both glanced at it, but only for a moment, for me and Dr McTavish were coiled to each other now.

'Mistress Dickson,' he replied, 'I wonder if we might both do each other a favour. You remember Mrs Rose well. You know what she looks like, and you were clearly a confidante of hers.' I nodded. 'Well, as it happens, I have glimpsed her, here in this very town.'

'Have you indeed, sir?' I said, keeping calm and still. 'How very interesting for us both.' *Here? In Edinburgh? That wench has been here all along?*

'She is whoring again,' he whispered. 'Any gent will do, it seems, apart from me, who she refuses to see. I have tried, a number of times, but she will not conduct business with me. And I do have a particular hankering for her. A craving, if you understand me.'

We stood a moment – hangman and condemned – and considered the situation.

'Well, it looks like we are both in a bit of trouble and might be able to help one another out,' I said. 'Mibbie I might talk to your Mrs Rose and persuade her to see you.'

I feared then that he would laugh at my proposal, and even that he might put his hands to my throat and strangle me there and then. But there was a turnkey in the passageway and he would not have got away with it.

Instead he put his lips very close to my ears and said, 'I will hold you to that promise, Mistress Maggie Dickson.'

Later Ma, Da and Joan came, and we were put in a little visiting room where bluebottles rattled at the walls. They brought a creel with clothes and fresh bread and apples.

'We brought rum as well, but they confiscated it,' said Da. 'A rum would have helped you, too.'

'Do you want us there, when they do it?' asked Ma.

'We will have to be there,' said Da, 'or the anatomists will take her.'

Ma turns to me. 'And we've been promised the use of the parish coffin, so you'll have dignity on your final journey home.'

'I spoke to Kirk Session at St Michael's myself and it took some persuasion,' admits Da. 'Because of the circumstances. But coffins are expensive and we did not want to cart you all the way back home in a shroud.'

I shivered and they thought I was shivering for myself, and

the thought of being dead on a cart in a shroud or a coffin. But I was not. I was thinking that the anatomists still had my baby.

I wanted to tell my family, to give them a sign that I was going to try to survive the hang, because the sight of their faces was so horrific to watch. But the guards stalked the corridors, and the silence that fell over the Iron Room in the final hours leading up to Hanging Day was so still that overheard words could be plucked from the thick, sweltering air like fruit.

'I need you all to be there,' I replied. 'Get as close as you can to the gallows and then claim my body quick. Do not let the anatomists take me away for dissection. And then get us out of Edinburgh as fast as you can.'

They thought it was to get away from the body-snatchers. To get away from the shame and the boos, and the cruelty of being associated with me.

I could not tell them my plan.

I had seen the utter humiliation on their faces in that courtroom. Seen them look up at the jeering folk in the balcony and curl themselves as small as they could. Ma and Da were petty criminals, tea-hoarders. But they had always got away with it. Mibbie they thought my crime and punishment were a retribution of sorts for what they had always done.

Ma bent her face to me and whispered, 'The Lord will take you, and your poor babe will be waiting for you. Think of them as you go. Don't worry about us.'

Those were strong, kind words.

But also they probably thought it was best that I hang quietly, so they could try to put the scandal behind them. I let them hug me and cry and weep and I gave Joan the glass ring, and

I let their wails rise up above me, out of the Iron Room, up to the street above. I hoped everyone out there would hear them and know what this world and its laws had done to my family.

Joan clasped my hand. 'Sister,' she whispered.

I clasped her hand back. We held onto each other, a tightness in our grip, and eventually it was only when Da dragged Joan away that we let each other go.

On Hanging Day, like all the other condemned, I rose from my mat after a night of no sleep. I put on the gown Ma had brought – my navy wedding gown.

But unlike all the other men and women who were with me down in the Iron Room for those wretched days, I went to the gallows with hope.

PART THREE
AFTER THE HANG

Chapter Twenty-Three

Edinburgh
3 September 1724

O ur life events change us, of course they do. But there is
nothing that will change you like a brush with death.

It is the day after my Hanging Day.

Morning shatters on the Tolbooth Jail like dropped crockery
on tiles. The women around me wake furiously and swarm at
the gate, begging for clean linens and water and medicines
and visits; and then, when they are ignored and ignored, they
collapse back into the cell and fight over the pocket mirror. I
lie on my mat. I am so exhausted I can hardly move. If anything,
my limbs feel even sorer today than they did when I woke up
in the parish coffin. I touch my throbbing, agonizing rope-burn
and keep my fingers on it, feeling the pulse of me through it.

I am alive.

That promise I made to Dr McTavish seemed all very well
and good when I was pleading for my life. But now I owe him.
And he is not a man I should displease.

I am safe from him, here in the Tolbooth, but I must wait
whilst the sheriffs come back to me with their decision.

The breakfast gruel-pot clatters in and the women are
doled out their slops. The pickpocket takes Molly's gruel, for
Molly doesn't need it. She has ways of getting a bit of bacon

and a boiled egg. I have barely eaten in days and I am starving now, and I take mine and the watery mess does not even taste half bad, which goes to show how desperate I have become.

Molly watches me eat. When I catch her eye, she looks away, fiddling with her stockings. She is not a whore like Mrs Rose. She is not even a whore like the girls who loll around the Mussel Inn for sailors and fishermen. She is an Edinburgh whore. Her eyes swivel, surveying the room for dangers and opportunities. Before, I even heard her speak filthy words to the turnkey as she did her business with him – some words I recognized and some I did not, and others she put on in a foreign accent, and he seemed to like that.

Finally she approaches me.

'How did you do it?' she asks, her voice low, for of course the women are silent, listening intently.

'It was an Act of God,' I tell her, rasping, as my voice still croaks. She laughs at that, the rich laugh that turns into a hacking cough.

'I heard the other woman who hanged yesterday morning jerked like a marionette,' she says. 'And one of the men even fainted on the gallows and they had to revive him and manhandle him to the noose.'

'You know a lot, for someone who wasn't there,' I tell her.

'The turnkeys always talk of hangings,' she replies. 'You went calm and docile. At peace with your maker – that's what they said about you. Yet here you are. Was it a trick?'

'It was no trick. I am not the first and I will not be the last person to survive the gallows.' Dr McTavish had told me what to say to anyone who asked awkward questions. He saved his instructions for the last minute, as I'd stood on the gallows. Said this kind of event had happened before, from time to time, and even though a hanged convict might seem dead, they could revive some hours later.

Molly scrutinizes me, looking for untruths. I carry on, repeating his words. 'Hanging is a craft, but they can't always get it right with the measurements and weighings and the drop, and so on. My hangman was supposed to be one of the better ones, but here I am. Mibbie it's an Act of God, like I said. Or mibbie it was just that he got it wrong.'

I think that satisfies Molly, for now. She turns on her heel and goes back to her mat. The rest of the morning is long and is filled with bluebottles swarming around chamber pots. The rest of the women continue to avoid me, but I catch them all looking at my neck. It throbs, and I wait. But a long wait is a good thing, for the sheriffs are likely debating whether or not they can hang me again; and the longer it takes them, the more likely they will concede that I have served my sentence.

Dr McTavish had said as much. 'The sentence is hanging and that will have been served,' he'd murmured from behind his hood as his parting shot, before he'd loosened the rope around my hands and made sure I had wriggle room. 'The sheriffs have recently been debating whether to change the wording of the statutes to *hanged by the neck until dead*, but that has not been written in yet. So if they try to hang you again, you must argue that they cannot do it twice. Now, Mistress Dickson, act meek. The sheriffs will be watching you from their vantage point at the first-floor window of the White Hart Inn. By the time you regain your senses they will be drunk and easy to argue your case with. I will see you very soon, and you will help me reunite with Mrs Rose.'

And then he hanged me.

*

I can't remember everything about being dead, for there must have been a space in time, a gap of nothingness. But I can piece together bits, as if it were a dream. I remember Dr McTavish, and the rope, and the snake. Sometimes the snake and McTavish are one and the same. His hands coil around my neck and when I look at them, they are made not of skin, but of scales; and then when I look again, they are made of rope. Best hemp. And then I am back at the House of Correction again, beating the hemp for my own noose.

But that is a story about a dream. Usually I find stories about dreams boring. Joan used to tell me her dreams. 'Oh, last night, Maggie, I dreamed a funny one, and you and I were mermaids and then we turned into sea creatures and I was a dolphin, nimble as anything, but you were a big, ugly whale and you swallowed all of Fisherrow.'

But this was not one of those.

I do remember the moments before. Seeing Ma and Da and Joan near the foot of the scaffold, ready to rescue my corpse from the anatomists and take my good gown. Joan wearing the glass ring.

I remember looking up at the building tops, and down on the crowd, seeing the world as a bird might and praying to God, 'Don't take me yet.'

And although there were hundreds of men and women there, children too, with all manner of hats and flags and banners, my eye was drawn to a man standing at the edge of it all, under a tree, for he stared directly at me with a look of sorrow and regret, and I recognized him.

And he had no trace of a sea-beard or weather-tan about him at all, but the clean, pale look of a man who has been hiding away from the world for months.

My husband, Patrick Spencer.

And that was not a dream. It was real. Spencer had returned.

Chapter Twenty-Four

The heat of the September sun has warmed the women's cell to a humid broth, high up into the afternoon, when the turnkey eventually calls my name. The lust is still gone from his eyes.

'Mistress Dickson,' he says, unlocking the gate and avoiding looking at my throat, 'it's your lucky day. I've received instructions that you are free to go.'

I can hear the change in the air behind me as I leave the women's cell. The exhalations. The murmurs. I can feel them watching my skirts whisk beyond the gate. I do not ask questions of the turnkey. I can only assume the sheriffs have come to the conclusion my sentence is indeed served.

'You are blessed, Mistress.' It is the little pickpocket, who has done nothing but ignore me all morning as she ate her gruel and asked the other women to whip her back gently, to get her flesh used to it. But I cannot even reply, for the turnkey is bustling me back outside. *I am free to go!*

I did not expect a gathering at the Tolbooth door, but there is one. No sign of my family, but instead there are half a dozen men and women there, who fall silent when I am let out. It is bright and I am so elated I think I might faint and it takes moments for my eyes to adjust to the light, so I try to steady myself and not scream or cry or kiss the ground. This goes on for a few minutes and I notice that I am being watched. At first I assume these folk are waiting to visit their kin. But as

I pull my shawl over my rope-burn and think of a direction to
walk in, a girl approaches me. She holds her hand out.

'Are you the half-hanged one?' she asks, staring at my neck.
'You are, I recognize you from the gallows. Oh, Mistress
Dickson, can I see it? I'll give you a penny if you let me touch
your neck.'

The news has flown around Edinburgh. Passed from the
turnkeys to the water caddies, from the sheriffs to the landlady
of the White Hart Inn, to her other patrons and the ale
merchants. I back away from this girl. I have had too many
people – parish officers and matrons and hangmen – come at
me these past weeks and I have not been able to refuse any
of them. But my movement only triggers the rest of the group
to come forward, and I turn and hurry away, heading I do not
know where, down the High Street, trying to close my ears
against the cries.

'Half-Hanged Maggie, did you see the Lord?'

'Let me touch the wound for luck!'

'Was my husband at the Pearly Gates? Did you see a handsome man with a terrible pox, although the pox might have
cleared from him on the other side?'

'Mistress Dickson, how did you do it? Is there a method?'

'Are you a witch?'

'I saw her hands in the noose!'

'That hangman will never work again!'

I march as fast as I can, caring not about bumping into folk.
In my haste I send a caddie flying, his barrel of well-water
spilling over the street. I cry, 'Sorry' over my shoulder. I can't
keep up this chase for long.

I turn into a close and see the poky hole of a gin shop, its
open door revealing a peek of its depths, a flickering yellow
haze of old pipe smoke and bottle-gleam. I make straight for

it. I slam the door shut behind me and find the bolt and
pull it across, then put a chair in front of it for good measure.

There is only one person in there, it only just having opened
for its day of grim trade: an elderly woman with a wizened
face. She regards me in a considered way, as though wondering
whether to call a constable, but with no apparent fear of me,
then wipes her rheumy eyes.

I sit down at a spindly table, out of breath. Is this what is
to become of me? Hounded? Am I like a human curiosity in
a travelling fair of rarities? One came to Musselburgh once,
and folk queued with pennies to see two men: one the height
of a small child and one with no hands or feet. Joan was
desperate to see it, but Da forbade us from going.

There's a hammering at the door and I jump, and the woman
and I lock eyes. She makes her way to the door faster than I
would have thought, being of some considerable years, and
shouts through the timber planks, 'Away with all of you, we
are closed.'

I wonder if the crowd will simply batter down the door, but
things quieten and she nods, seeming satisfied, then turns to
me.

'You can have rest for a while in here, and let them get
bored waiting and get on their way, but I do not hoard thieves
or servants who are running from their masters. Are you either
of these?'

I shook my head.

'Well, what are you then?'

And that is a good question, to which I have no straight
answer, for I could tell her what I once was, and what I was
accused of.

But what I really am, I do not know.

I know what I wish to be, though, and that is free of this

grief and this mark on my neck and of the name 'Half-Hanged Maggie', which is abhorrent to me. But I don't say that.

Instead I say, 'I am in need of a drink', and the woman's eyes, faded though they are, light up, as I have given her all the excuse she needs to pour two drops of gin into two grubby glasses. 'I can't pay you today, but I will pay you back,' I go on, and she shrugs.

'That's what they all say, but you need a tot of medicine.'

Well, gin is not a medicine. Ma would not have gin in the house, and even Da avoided it. Whisky, yes. A glass of Spanish sherry after kirk on Sundays. Smuggled tea galore. Even rum. But gin is an unregulated liquor, not like whisky or rum, and anyone can set up their own shop and distil it; and it is cheap too, which means only the poorest of the poor drink it. Gin is nasty and potent and it will rot your guts. Gin is the road to hell.

Today, though, I am the poorest of the poor, and yesterday I avoided hell, and so I drink it.

We get through three glasses before Aunt Jenever – as that is what she says everyone calls her – pulls my story from me. It unravels, although somewhat back-to-front and with the looping repetition, in some parts, of a liquor-laced tongue. I tell her almost everything except the part about my pact with the hangman, for that is a dangerous secret I would not trust a stranger with.

'You are a sorry soul,' she says, over and over. 'And the poor babe.'

I weep then, heaving and ugly, and feel I will never stop. The emptiness of it, and the shame of my bleeding in the carriage ride from Kelso, and the way my milk bloomed at my breasts, and how the men talked of Jacobites to distract them-selves. And, finally, the guilt. Not the guilt that the law men put upon me, but my own guilt about failing to bear a healthy babe and failing to save her. And my own guilt is a monster that eats me.

'I should have done more to try to save the babe,' I tell her. 'To try and stop the labour happening, or to revive her. I should have told Mrs Baxter.'

'Babies succumb,' she replies tightly. 'We mothers know the grief. But she is in heaven now.'

'She is in a jar,' I say. 'At the surgeon's college. She does not even have a name. She was not even christened.'

'Well, name her,' Aunt Jenever says, 'the pour nameless soul. You are her mother.'

I blink at that, for I had been desperate to name her, but was embarrassed at the thought. The baby had become such a *thing*, so dehumanized by all who were caught up in my own scandal – myself included – that I had held off naming her.

'You will never mourn a babe properly if you don't name her,' Aunt Jenever says. 'Trust me, I have tried. It helps. Even the tiniest ones.'

'I will think of a name,' I agree, for I had not even settled on one, but the thought of it makes me feel a little brighter, which I had not thought possible. 'But I have other worries. I am a freak-show, and folk want to touch my rope-burn for pennies.'

'Well, let them,' she says. 'Let folk touch you for pennies and ask you if you saw God, and give them the answers they need, for you are a sorry soul and they are sorry souls, and the world is a cruel place and surely you can give some hope to one another. Besides, you can save the pennies for a proper grave for the babe.'

Oh, I had not thought of letting people touch the rope-burn.

Aunt Jenever blinks once, twice, and watches me consider it.

'I have a spare bed upstairs,' she tells me, 'and you can use it for a while if you like. I dare say you could pay the rent easy as anything if you charge folk to use you as a lucky charm. And I have a man that minds the door to make sure no one too rowdy gets in or things get out of hand. You will like him; he is decent, despite being rough around the edges. But what of your kin, the fisher people, will they not take you in?'

I do not wish to think of my kin at all. The few hours I spent with them, after my delivery from death, from the Sheep Heid Inn back to the High Court of Justiciary were plenty. They did not want me causing trouble by coming back to Fisherrow where, by now, I will be scandalous. Besides, I want to find Spencer – who had come to see me hang! – and the best chance I have is sticking around town to see if he reappears.

People with all manner of superstition and grief will soon start to come and find Half-Hanged Maggie when word goes out that I am living above Aunt Jenever's Gin Shop.

One of them will be Dr McTavish.

'There is a chance that certain gentlemen may come looking for me,' I tell Aunt Jenever, who rolls her eyes. 'It is nothing untoward,' I go on. 'One of them is my husband, Patrick Spencer, and I am most keen to speak to him, for there is a mystery about his disappearance that I would like him to answer for me. The second gentleman is a Dr McTavish, a physician and my hangman.'

At this she shudders and blesses herself.

'He is not dangerous to strangers,' I say, 'but he might be a danger to me. I survived his noose, you see. I might need protection from him.'

'My doorman will keep an eye out,' she tells me. 'He loathes the hangman, who has seen off more than one or two of his own pals. And my Cornelius is a burly sort and keeps trouble away, so folk can get on with the business of gin-drinking. I will warn him to look out for you. It will cost you, mind. He will want a tip. But you will have the means to pay.'

'Is it like whoring?' I ponder, thinking of the prospect of making myself into a half-hanged curiosity that folk can touch and ask questions about.

'Heavens, no, it will be much better paid and you can keep your drawers on,' Aunt Jenever replies. 'Come, untie your shawl and let's have a look at this bruise.'

She stands up unsteadily and leads me over to a large, grubby mirror. I am glad I've had three gins. I've not seen myself since the River Inn and I look how I feel. My face is dirty and my bonnet askew, my hair a grease-slick. My shawl is a grubby shade of grey. But worst of all is the bruise. The rope has made a clear, wide line all the way around my neck and the bruise spreads above and below, up to my chin and my ears.

I wail.

'Shush, shush, it will subside,' Aunt Jenever says. 'But you should gird your loins and make the most of it, before it does.'

So that is what I do.

Aunt Jenever sets me up in the other bed in her living quarters, which are one flight of steps above her shop and consist of two rooms, one where she sleeps off the gin, and the other where she takes a tenant when she sees fit. She is not a poor woman, nor particularly rich, nor particularly generous, for she wants a shilling a week for the rent, but I do not think her a schemer or a liar. And I have come to be an expert in those. She makes her living from selling Mother's Ruin and has no shame in it. She is industrious in her trips to the fruit market for juniper berries and blackberries, and labours in the tiny workshop at the back of the shop that she uses as her distillery. And I have come to a point in my life when I have seen a lot of what the world is about and have found out that there are some people who will pretend to be good, but really they are not. Aunt Jenever makes no pretence.

So now I have my own bed in my own room, but little time to lie in it and ruminate, for I need to make my rent.

Chapter Twenty-Five

The best way to attract attention is to go on a long walk through town, neck exposed. Aunt Jenever helps me dress, my old shawl soaking in a barrel of soap and water, for I am not to wear that now. Instead I wear one of the eye-catching gowns she used to wear when she was younger. It is her brightest one, in a murky shade of yellow, and she cuts a new neckline into it, so there will be no mistaking the bruise, which clashes horrifically with the dress. She gives me a small, fine shawl in a similar yellow hue and says I am to wear it as loose as I can.

'I look a sight,' I cry, when she shows me my reflection.

'The crowds will certainly part for you,' she agrees. 'Someone must tail you, for we do not want you coming to harm. Cornelius will be a few steps behind.'

I agree, relieved to have a chaperone as hefty as Cornelius, who is as bulky as I had hoped, but bows when he meets me, most respectfully. I step out of the shop into the shock of the High Street and make my way up towards Edinburgh Castle.

'My God, what happened to her?' a passing caddie cries to the pal he is walking with. 'Have you been beaten?'

I shake my head, though that smarts when my neck moves, and walk on. But the other caddie knows.

'It's the fishwife,' he says, 'the woman they couldn't hang. We saw her likeness in the *Courant*.'

The pair stop and tip their caps and give low whistles. I

stand for a minute or so and let them do this, holding my shawl loose so they can take a good look at me, then continue walking. More men stare. Women stare. Pedlars and children, and mothers with babes-in-arms. At the bottom of Castlehill someone makes their first attempt to touch me. It is a pretty girl in a loose dress, who has the rouge of a whore about her high cheekbones. I step back and grip my shawl close.

'Let me have a look at it, hen,' she pleads. 'There's chaps who've tried to do that to me. How sore is it?'

'It aches like nothing else,' I reply.

She bites her lip and stares. She is fragile about the face and neck. I imagine her being strangled by a nasty sort and wonder at the horror of the world.

'What waits for us, on the other side?' she asks. 'You must have seen a glimpse of it?'

'I saw something of it,' I tell her. 'But I do not talk of it in the street, for free.'

And this is how a line is formed, of stragglers and misfits and folk who are grieving a loved one, and folk with a spare penny in their pocket and not much else to do. They follow me, a dozen or more by the end of my saunter, back down to Aunt Jenever's Gin Shop, and I am glad to take a seat in a corner and see folk one by one. They queue mildly, without pushing and shoving, and await the answers to the questions of life and death.

There was a mystic that used to knock at the doors in Fisherrow, and some would take her in. Others, like us, would not. For my ma is Presbyterian, all the way from her striped apron to her Sunday sherry. Ma said the mystic was a confidence trickster, and Da said she danced with the Devil. The fishwives who saw her muttered of her claims in hushed, awed tones: 'She said my old ma was looking down on me', 'She said

I will find a husband if I go to the Mussel Inn next Tuesday and wear green.'

I find I am somewhere in between. Somewhere in between the Presbyterian and the confidence trickster, which, given my roots, makes sense.

I say that the world next to death, next to God, is a dark void and there is neither fear nor anger there, nor regret of things said or unsaid. It is a great peace. Folk like to hear that. It lights up their faces. I admit that I have not seen their dead kin, but I say that I feel, *with all my heart*, they are with the Lord now. I suppose that is the trickster in me, for they look at me with a bit of awe and consider me delivered from death, which gives great importance to my words.

I do not talk of the snake, for he is my particular nightmare, and mine alone.

I do not tell them of my deal with Dr McTavish, or that I pissed myself on the gallows in fear under my best dress. Or that the hangman loosened my bindings and I gripped onto the noose, clinging on for dear life, until everything went black.

I do not tell them that I think I searched for my own babe and did not find her there, in the beyond, and that terrifies me.

I don't need to go out wandering again.

Over the next week or so it even gets into the *Courant* that Half-Hanged Maggie takes an audience at Aunt Jenever's Gin Shop on weekday mornings: a penny for a five-minute private sitting. '"But do not be tempted to stay and drink the gin, for this craze of taking these cheap medicinal waters is leading to a generation of drunkards",' cries Aunt Jenever, reading out the article, before slapping the news-sheet down on the table.

But she is pleased, I can tell, for the woman I first encountered with a greyish visage and sombre eyes now has a lightness about her, now that she has a new project to run. And run me she does. The pennies pour in, and she takes her rent and sends me to a dressmaker in the Luckenbooths for nice gowns – 'Nothing gaudy, you are not a trollop' – then to the milliner for a decent bonnet, and so on.

'You look quite respectable,' Aunt Jenever tells me, as I come downstairs one morning, ready for my customers. 'You must feel back to your old self again?'

'I will never be back to my old self again,' I say. The ropeburn has left a weal, calmer now and more like the lash of a whip. Cornelius picks up the *Courant*. I do not think he can read, but he muses over it for a while, looking at the sketches, before putting it down.

'I suppose you are branded, of sorts, aren't you, Mistress Dickson?' he says. 'Like what they do to some of the criminals – vagrants and the like – who don't have the funds to pay fines. They brand them with irons on the cheek and banish them out of town, so they can't get back in at the turnpikes. Happened to a pal of mine, not seen him since.'

I put my hand to my cheek in horror.

'Now, now, Cornelius,' murmurs Aunt Jenever. 'Maggie's situation is nothing like that.'

But Cornelius is right. My situation is exactly like that. Only worse, for I am forced by circumstance to live a life that Ma and Da – petty criminals though they are – would look down on. Letting strangers touch my neck. Telling them half-stories to please them.

I think of my pile of coins that grows slowly. My piles of coins always seem to grow slowly and shrink again, and never quite come to anything much.

I think of London. The city paved with gold and bodice-makers' apprentices and cheap theatre seats.

Mibbie I should try to get there again. I could be anonymous there.

After my morning's customers have been served with tales of the afterlife and peeks at my neck, I slip up the close, hiding under a large shawl, for I want a bit of solitude and a walk. The stalls and shops of Edinburgh never cease to be a wonder to me, but I am not tempted to splash my pennies, despite the wares. They have lost their gloss. Painted pots and fur shawls and silk gloves sit side by side with stands selling pies and live chickens and blood sausage. The air is eye-watering from chimney-smoke and old piss, and worse things, and everyone all in a rush to be somewhere. I pull my shawl further up my face, covering my mouth and nose, and breathe the scent of soap-soaked wool instead of the reek from the street. Perhaps some rosewater might help. I look for a shop that might sell it. I finally chance upon one, seeing bottles stacked in a window. But just as I am about to go in the door, the lettering above it catches me.

I am not a learned woman. I had to get a scribe to write a message to my own family. But I have grasped the meanings of some letters over the years, as we all must do, to get by. And there are four words etched above the shop door, four words I recognize, for I have seen all of them written down in one form or another, in what seems another world entirely.

Patrick Spencer's Perfume Emporium.

I am dithering about whether to go in or whether to flee back to Aunt Jenever when someone grabs my arm and pulls me towards the wall. I have no good vision to the side of me, for my shawl is up about my head, and I have to fight to see who has grabbed me. I think it will be Spencer of course, as I am right outside what seems to be his new shop.

But it is not my husband.

It is Dr McTavish.

Chapter Twenty-Six

D r McTavish's arm coils around mine and he drags me through wynds and stairways until we reach a building at the top of the hill. He does not let go of my arm, even as he opens the front door and drives me up two flights of spiral steps. All the while he is muttering, 'I will not harm you, if you come quietly' and although we must look a suspect pair and we attract many looks, no one intervenes, which says it all about this town.

Finally he shoves me into his rooms and stands wiping the sweat from his hands and brow, with his backside firmly against the door.

'If I come to any harm, there are folk who will come looking for me,' I tell him. My voice is shaking.

'I own you, Mistress Dickson,' he warns. 'And I am better connected in this town than you are. I could have anyone jailed or hanged, if I wish it.'

We regard each other for a moment or so. A longcase clock ticks lightly in the corner. We are too high up to hear any street-babble. Dr McTavish wears a brown wool coat with a matching waistcoat and luminous pearl buttons. There must be good money in hanging. He puts his hand out and touches my rope-mark. I am so used to people touching it that I do not even flinch or try to stop him. I even lift up my chin, the way I have become accustomed to doing, so that he might see it all the better. He has a gentle touch. Some do not.

'It is a fine-looking mark,' he says, pleased.

He has such a distaste for human life, this man, that he ought not to call himself a doctor.

'I am indebted to you for sparing me,' I tell him. It's better to play to his pride than to challenge it. 'I do plan to spend the rest of my days repenting and doing good deeds, sir.'

He nods. 'Come,' he replies, 'sit down and have a drink with me. I only have Madeira, although I hear you've taken to gin these days.'

He busies himself pouring us drinks in crystal goblets. I have never drunk from a crystal goblet before, although I have seen them for sale in wine-merchants' windows. He sits on a low couch and beckons me to come and sit next to him. I do so, taking care that our legs do not touch.

'It is gin, isn't it?' he goes on. 'You've taken refuge at a gin palace. Ho!' He shakes his head and sips. The ruby liquid leaves a little stain about his silvery moustache. 'I could not count the number of gin-soaks I've hanged. It drives them to crime. Poisons the mind. And you are selling yourself, I hear? Letting the waifs and strays touch you, and talk to you about the afterlife? What a great enterprise, what a great caper, Mistress Dickson. I am in admiration.'

He makes me furious, but I have to keep it to myself. Not just his arrogance, but the fact that I know he is right. I do not like what I am becoming.

'It's difficult to make a living otherwise, when you're scarred like this,' I tell him.

'I dare say,' he agrees, with no emotion. 'But you were spared, and you argued your legal case with the sheriffs successfully, just as I suspected you would be able to do. Now, I have news for you. My Mrs Rose is doing well for herself. So well, in fact, that she has taken rooms a ten-minute walk south-west of here, near Greyfriars. I have the address, for I have followed her, but she doesn't know this, and I think she needs a delicate touch. I can't simply turn up unannounced or approach her in the street.'

'And that is where I come in,' I said warily.

'You most beautifully do.' He coughed and wiped his mouth with a pristine kerchief. 'I desire her, Mistress Dickson, like I have wanted nothing else in my life. I crave her artful ways of the bed.' He leaps to his feet. 'Come, he insists, 'I have even prepared her a chamber.'

I follow him towards a small room off the parlour, my fear making me feel quite sick. The Turkish carpet beneath my feet is thick and soft. Enough to muffle a girl's cries. The door swings open. The room beyond is appointed as one might decorate a room for a princess. The four-poster bed is of walnut, with carvings. A heavy-looking bedspread is folded across it, tightly and expertly. There are gold tassels everywhere too: dangling from the curtains and the bed canopy. A dressing gown hangs from a coat-stand, decorated with snarling brown snakes with red tongues, and I nearly jump out of my skin when I see that.

'That, I bought from a trader who'd had it shipped from the Orient,' Dr McTavish states, with pride. 'Do you like it?'

'I do not,' I say. I cannot take my eyes off the snake-gown, for it is exactly as I see the snake in my dreams, swirling and coiling. I put my hand on the door to steady myself.

'Well, it is not for you anyway,' he replies. 'It's for Mrs Rose. She will be my special guest. She will soon realize that she will want for nothing.'

I drag my eyes from the snake-gown and look around me again. This room would be a chamber of delights, were it not for two things. First, he has had the window secured, which means there is no natural light at all, only the light from the lamps. By 'secured', I mean boarded, and the boards look to be nailed into the wall. And over them are iron bars that remind me so much of the Tolbooth Jail that I can't look at them for too long. Second, he has fastened to the wall, by the bed, a pair of iron chains.

'Do you mean to keep Mrs Rose your prisoner?' I gasp.

'Only if I have to,' he says. 'I hope she will stay willingly, but she might not. I hope she will be enticed and will find the idea of being my plaything quite entertaining. But if she does not, that is our problem, not yours. So don't worry about that side of things. Instead tell me: is this not the most luxurious room in the whole of Edinburgh town? There is a drawer for her rouges and another for sweetmeats – she has a tooth for candied fruits – and somewhere she can keep her laudanum to hand. She can have all the laudanum she needs here – tell her that. And I have purchased a set of dominoes too, best bone and ivory.'

I have been more terrified in my life, but not often.

'You do not mean to let her escape, do you?' I say. 'You will keep her here until you tire of her and then she will likely end up overdosed on laudanum.'

He pretends not to hear me, and leaps from the room back into the parlour and paces the Turkish carpet. I follow him, desperate to be out of that chamber.

'Now I shall give you Mrs Rose's address, and clear directions, so there's no danger of you getting lost. But do not go to her lodgings. There is a coffee house she frequents after dark. It is where she plies her trade. Go there and simply bump into her. And this is what you are to tell her.'

He pauses here, his eyes roaming the ceiling, the window, the floor.

'Tell her you forgive her the theft. Tell her that you are delivered. From death. And that in the afterlife you had a vision, and that you are to forgive all those who have sinned against you, like in the Lord's Prayer. Tell her that you have a fine place where you are living now – from your earnings – and invite her to take tea with you. Two old pals from Kelso, finding their way in the big town. Then you are to bring her to this apartment. Not the gin shop. Tell her that is where you work, if she asks, for she might have heard tales of you and we do not want to scare her off. But do not take her to the gin shop. Instead, bring her here. And when she is safely in this parlour, taking her tea, you will excuse yourself and leave.'

'And you will be here, I suppose?'

'I will await you leaving. Then I will announce myself to her. When you leave, make sure the door is closed and lock it behind you. I will give you a key so that you can get in, so use that. I will put some powders by the tea leaves and you can put some in her cup. It will make her sleepy.'

There is no question of, *If I don't?* Or, *What happens if Mrs Rose doesn't come?* Dr McTavish had decided it all.

'And after this,' I venture, 'are we settled, you and I?'

He looks me straight in the eye. 'After this, we are settled. My reputation as a hangman is caught up with the sensational story of your revival but I expect that to ease in time. There are plenty more condemned criminals for me to hang good and proper. And it will all be worth it for my Mrs Rose. So once you have helped me capture her, put the front-door key under the mat and walk away, and think no more of me or her.'

Chapter Twenty-Seven

Dr McTavish says I am to do the deed tomorrow evening, and he will be waiting. He lets me out of his apartment and I run down the stairs.

When I get out onto the street again, I could kiss the foul ground with relief, for I thought he might tie me to that bed and do all manner of horrors. Then I remember my dreadful task – the task that will free me from him, but will put Mrs Rose in her own hell.

I wander like this for an hour or more, my thoughts spinning too wildly to go back to Aunt Jenever's. There are dark things that a person can be driven to. You never know, until you are faced with such choices. What price, my own survival? I suppose some folks who came to see me hang would not be surprised if a woman like me goes off down to Greyfriars the next day hiding a secret plot, as one might cover a baby in a creel.

I thought Dr McTavish might keep me in that chamber of delights. Fasten me by the wrists and have his wicked way. Probably strangle me afterwards too and enjoy it, in private this time. Human life is cheap. They die on street corners, in rags, an empty bottle rolling around beside them. They die of poxes and plagues and starvation and hangings. They die in childbirth. Or shortly thereafter. Whispers of the afterlife are sometimes the only hope we have.

Mrs Rose will be caught in a trap of her own making. Were

it not for her selfish, self-serving act of theft, of taking everything I had, I would have been off to London, and I am quite certain that I would not have been left dangling on a rope.

But I do not want plots and wickedness. I don't want to go back to the gin shop and face the queues of soul-searchers. I don't even want London or riches, or any of that. I want home comforts and a roaring fire, and good stories and the feel of a warm blanket over me as I get into bed of a night. My feet ache and my neck still troubles me from time to time.

And I don't know if this is a coincidence or if something is pulling me along the streets like a baited line, but as I am nudging my way through a crowded wynd, pinching my nose against the high stink, I hear a cry that rises like a gull above a tide.

'Fresh fish!'

I follow the cry, for I am just by Fishmarket Close, and when I turn into the close there is a sight so familiar – of striped aprons and white caps and silvery fish – that I start to weep. Tears prickle at my eyes and flood down my cheeks, tears for lost families and lost fishermen and lost babies, and I stand – *what a sight I must look!* – and breathe in the tang of it and it feels like home.

By and by, the fishwives notice me standing there, for I am a sorry sight by now, and one shouts out, 'It's Maggie', and they rush to me and I am embraced and held, and fussed over and murmured over.

And all the things I feared – like being shunned and called a baby-murderer, or worse, by my neighbours – well, they simply do not happen.

'When are you coming back?' asks one of the women by the name of Betty. 'You always had fast hands and a good singing voice when we used to all sing together while we were collecting cockles.'

I have not sung for months. Joan was the singer really, in the choir, and I always thought myself a drone, for that was what she said I was. But I liked a sing-song; I don't even know that I could sing again, for my voice is even huskier now. Mibbie Dr McTavish broke my singing voice.

'I don't think you will have me back in Fisherrow,' I say.

There is a flurry of protest at that, and more stroking of my head and petting of my shoulders, and I feel entirely gathered into a press of striped bosoms.

'You have had a terrible ordeal,' says Betty, 'and your ma misses you something shocking. Your sister too. She is quite at a loss without you.'

'I am making something of myself here in Edinburgh,' I reply. 'I have a room above a shop.' I do not say 'gin shop'. I do not say there is a madman waiting for me to bring me his Mrs Rose, to play with until he bores of her.

'But is Edinburgh home?' asks Betty. 'Does it feel like a place where you could live out the rest of your days?'

Well, of course it does not, for I know that if I stay in Edinburgh I will put Mrs Rose in a lair, and I will drink more and more gin and live out my days as Half-Hanged Maggie: half-woman, half-myth. And the thing with Dr McTavish, well, it will always be staring me in the face every time I walk past his well-appointed rooms. I will always look up and think I catch a glimpse in the boarded-up window of something awful.

I turn to Betty.

'Let me come back with you today,' I say suddenly. 'If there's room on the cart. I'll squeeze in and come home and see everyone.'

There are shrieks of excitement at that, but I urge the

fishwives not to make more of a fuss, for I do not want word leaking out and somehow getting back to Dr McTavish that I am running away.

The Fisherrow carts leave town at three of the clock. At five to three I go back. I have my belongings from Aunt Jenever's, and she was unsurprised to see me flee. I told her I was going home, but if anyone should ask, then the story is that I have finally gone to London, to make my fortune there.

Dr McTavish will come looking for me, see, and I want to muddy the trail. I did not tell Aunt Jenever about him. I do not want her to try to talk me out of it, or get her into any of my own trouble.

By five past three I am back with the fishwives, tucked amongst them and hidden under my scarf. The cart rolls out of Fishmarket Close and off down the High Street. The women rub their feet and roll their shoulders and pat my arms, and tell me what a good choice I have made, coming home.

I think of Mrs Rose going about her business in Greyfriars, none the wiser to any of this. I think of Dr McTavish waiting for me to arrive tomorrow with her, waiting and waiting and growing more restless and urgent and furious, and finally realizing in the small hours that I am not going to come.

He will look for me. I know it. He will search the streets and quiz Aunt Jenever and eventually he will hear word that I fled with the fishwives.

I think of Patrick Spencer.

But for now, home is the safest place I can be.

It is the only place I want to be.

Chapter Twenty-Eight

Fisherrow
October 1724

It is not quite supper time when I arrive home, and the cottage looks smaller than I remember, with no sign of life and no smoke billowing from the chimney. I don't know what greeting I will be met with.

I am suddenly aware that my hair is escaping from my bonnet in wind-pulled knots, and my dress is a merry shade of pink that has never been seen in Fisherrow. I don't know whether to walk straight in or announce my arrival. In the end I tap on the door with a gentle knock, bracing myself.

It is Joan who answers and, when she sees me, it takes her a moment or two, but instead of all the things she could do – like shriek or frown or shout for Ma, or say my dress looks trollopy – she puts her hand to her throat and shakes her head.

'I did not think you would ever come back,' she says.

'I did not want to, for a while,' I tell her.

We stand and look at each other for a bit. Then she puts her hand to her throat again. 'The mark looks better,' she tells me.

It is her way of trying to be nice.

She walks inside and I follow her in. The cottage smells the same, but mustier than I remember. But the familiarity of it:

the scrap of Turkish carpet. Little Paws waking and stretching and stalking over to me, her tail in the air.

'Da is at the Mussel Inn, and Ma is having a nap,' Joan whispers, nodding at the bed-curtain. 'She has not been well these past weeks.'

I stroke Little Paws and let her rub against my legs. I know that if Ma is unwell, it's my fault. But I say nothing as Joan pours me a mug of lukewarm tea.

'We heard stories you were selling yourself. Letting folk touch you. Ma thinks you might be whoring,' she goes on. She looks me up and down, taking in the dress, but seems to swallow back any comment about it.

'Not whoring,' I tell her. 'But something like it, I suppose.'

'Your coming back here will be a scandal,' she begins. 'Da has only just got back in favour with his gang at the Mussel Inn, and this will upset everyone again.'

'It has not been a scandal so far. I have been welcomed by the Fishmarket Close sellers and I will be accepted back by everyone else, I believe. This is my home after all, and I have the right to live peacefully here. They might have called me all manner of things in Edinburgh, but I did nothing wicked. I lost my baby, Joan – you were there.'

At this, her eyes fill with tears. Mine too.

'I am sorry that I was not stronger in the courtroom,' she says.

'Joan, I am furious that you did not try harder to defend me in that courtroom,' I reply, my voice rising.

'I know it. But that Lord Leith was a bully,' she says. 'I have nightmares about him.'

'You've been a terrible sister,' I go on. 'More an enemy than a friend. And some of the things you've done have devastated me.'

'I am weak,' she admits. 'You were always the strong one.'

'That nonsense has to stop now,' I tell her. 'You are a grown woman and need to take responsibility for yourself.'

'Oh, Maggie,' she weeps, 'I think of the babe all the time. She was a perfect babe and I should have done more to help, but I was so shocked I didn't know what to do. I should have fetched the Baxters. I should have watched over you both.'

'Yes, you should,' I answer. 'You are reckless, Joan. One day you will come to some harm yourself, if you don't stop.'

She nods and looks awful, and I suppose she has suffered too. But we are both here now, and we are sisters, and I have troubles enough without falling out with her again.

'The babe was perfect,' I say. 'The most beautiful babe I have ever seen in my life.'

'What did you call her?' asks Joan.

'She did not have a name. I couldn't think of one, for all the terrible things that happened next.'

'But you must have thought of one by now?'

I have. It has taken a while, but now I am more certain of myself I feel I can name my own daughter. 'Her name is Susanna.'

'Oh, baby Susanna – our babe,' says Joan. It is bitter and sweet to hear the name spoken. 'And where is she buried, so we might visit?'

'She has no grave that I know of. The anatomists have her.'

'Our Susanna cannot rest like that,' cries Joan.

The commotion wakes Ma, who rises from the bed and opens the curtain, rubbing her eyes and reaching for her kerchief. When she sees me, she has to put her hand on the wall to steady herself. Her kerchief drops to the floor. Ma's hair is greyer and wirier, and her face is thinner and her body saggier, as though it has had some of its life drained out of it. Even the knuckles of her hands have aged and knobbled.

I did this to her. I could cry out for the shame of it, for as I sat and sipped gin and promised strangers that they would reunite with loved ones, and all things were forgiven beyond the grave, I knew nothing of the sort. I was not delivered. I am not God. My own mother withered as I sold stories and, if I had not come home now, forced to flee, I might have stayed in Edinburgh for years and she might have withered away to nothing.

'Ma,' I say, almost choking on her name.

'What a relief to see you,' she replies. 'We didn't know what to do, and when we heard you'd been released from jail, we knew you needed to be left to make up your own mind about whether to come home.'

'I needed time to think,' I tell her.

'Mibbie Joan can put a fresh pot of tea on,' says Ma and she sits down at the table.

Joan busies herself – Joan *busies* herself! – and Ma regards me with a pucker to her lip.

'Are you back to stay?'

'I am back for the time being,' I answer, for truthfully I am here to hide from Dr McTavish, all the while knowing that a half-hanged woman cannot hide for long.

Ma sits, chin in one hand and the other hand running idly up and down the wood grain of the table. Her hands look bonier and more scarred than ever. I take a deep breath.

'I have let you down badly. I have shamed you,' I tell her.

Ma's gaze doesn't lift from the table, but there's a flicker in her jaw. 'I have not been a good enough mother to you, Maggie Dickson,' she says. 'You ran and ran, didn't you? Ran until you were dragged back.'

'No one dragged me back today,' I reply. 'Motherhood is hard, Ma. All the world looking upon us, waiting for us to put a foot wrong. I did not want it – the babe was an accident. I was feared of childbirth, and of the hard work of being a mother. But it seems there is another side to it altogether, and that is the way we are judged.'

'You can judge me all you like,' she tells me. 'You are my daughter, after all.'

'I do not judge you,' I answer.

Ma makes to say something, but her voice sticks in her throat and what comes out is something else entirely. A sob, a heave and she puts her face in her hands. My heart rises in my chest and I don't know what to say, so I say nothing. Eventually she wipes her face and clears her throat.

'I have mourned you so many times, I am frightened to take you back into my heart again,' she whispers.

Oh, Ma!

'When you ran away, I didn't know if you were alive or dead. And when the letter came – the letter you had written to us from Kelso – I ran down to the Mussel Inn myself to have someone read it out to me, for I thought it would say you had died. But you were still alive, and then the only thing I could think to do was ask Joan to fetch you. It should have been your father, but he is in no fit state to do anything responsible, for he drinks and loses his temper. So there was a time when both my girls were miles away from me, and all I could do was hope and pray.'

I open my mouth to say something, but Ma has an urgency to her, a compulsion, and I think that I must let it take its course. Even though I hate what I am hearing, for it fills me with shame.

'And when those constables came' – here even more shame erupts, in a rush – 'all I could think was that if you had been here, and if I had been looking after you, none of it would have happened. For we would all have taken care of the babe, regardless of whatever had become of Patrick Spencer. And the fact that you felt you could not come home, well, that was the worst thing about it.'

'It was not for hatred of you that I didn't want to come home,' I reply. 'It was because I had my own wishes for how I wanted to live my life.' I do not say anything about what happened between Joan and Spencer. I think that is better left unsaid.

'But we have failed you,' she goes on. 'For this has not been much of a home to you, has it?'

'Mibbie not,' I admit.

'And when they said you were to *hang*, Maggie, that was my biggest failure of all.'

'I thought you were relieved to see me hanged,' I say. 'When I watched you all, for a minute or two after the hanging, and when I came alive again at the Sheep Heid Inn.'

'I was relieved your suffering was at an end,' confesses Ma. 'I was relieved to be bringing you home to rest. But I knew that the end of your life would bring the end of my life. And I was relieved at that too. For I did not want to live much, after that. And everyone was decent enough – we were not shunned or told to leave Fisherrow, or anything like that – so I knew your sister and your da would be fine. But if they could have hanged me on the gallows beside you, I would gladly have let them.'

My poor broken ma. She sinks back into her chair – her rickety chair in her smoky parlour – her only home comforts stolen crockery and meat bought with the profits of smuggled tea. She wipes her face with her hands again, her red-knuckled hands scarred with cuts from fish hooks and gutting knives.

'I came home to make things right again,' I tell her. It's not quite the truth, but I do earnestly mean it now.

'How did you survive that hanging, Maggie?' she asks. 'All of the others that were hanged that day died. Only you survived. Do you think we were given a second chance – our family?'

'I cannot tell you how I survived,' I say to Ma, for that is the truth. I cannot tell her I bribed a hangman, for I do not want to burden her with that knowledge. 'All I can say is that I sit here today with you, and we are a family once again.'

Joan comes back with the tea, and with something else.

'Look, Maggie, some sage from the garden – we can make a poultice for your neck.'

It is likely a bit late for poultices now, but I let her do it: chop the leaves and mix them with hot water, and put it all in a muslin cloth. I tell them I've put no poultice on my neck, nor did anyone in Edinburgh offer, and Ma tuts and asks does no one in Edinburgh know how to do anything right, but drink gin and haggle over the price of fish?

And then we three talk. Ma tells me that Joan has her eye on a mill man, and Joan blushes and says let's change the subject. Then we talk about our lost Susanna, like I had never imagined we would. Joan tells Ma about Susanna's delicate skin and little face, and Ma talks about her own lost babes, and for the first time I feel I can talk openly about my babe. And even though the poor soul still floats somewhere in Edinburgh, in a physician's jar, I feel as though she is part of my family.

All this lasts until Da comes home.

I first know he is here by the way Ma's face falls at his footsteps outside the door, which are so faint I cannot hear them myself, but her ears are trained to listen out for them. Joan stiffens.

Da walks into the parlour and drops his bag. It thuds onto the mat. He is smaller than I remember, and rougher-looking too. He needs a haircut and his smock is filthy.

'I thought you were living in Edinburgh now,' he says.

'I have come home for a while,' I tell him.

'Well, there is no room for you,' he replies. 'We cannot have us all sharing a bed, now you are married.'

'Indeed we cannot,' I say, standing up and walking towards my father. I take my purse with me and open it in front of him. I pull out a handful of coins and hand them to him. 'Take these and get yourself back to the Mussel Inn,' I tell him. 'You can stay there for a few days whilst we women sort things out here. We have much to catch up on, and you won't want to hear our silly gossip, I am sure.'

Da lets me press the coins into his hand. He looks at the three of us – three women who are not necessarily the three finest women in the world, nor the strongest, and certainly not the fanciest. But we are in unison, and we do not want him spoiling our evening.

'I shall on my way then,' he replies and picks up his bag. 'But you cannot wear that pink gown about the place. It is too bright for around here.'

'I shall wear what I like,' I say. 'It is my gown, bought with my money that I earned from my own hard work.'

Da does not like that at all. He blinks and swallows and looks at Ma, but she just folds her arms. When he retreats, he doesn't look like a terror or even much of a bully, for I have seen worse. He looks like an angry man with nowhere to put his frustration and sorrow, except on those around him. Well, we are having no more of that. If our neighbours on Fisherrow have not shunned the Dicksons after a hanging, they will not shun us for barring our da from the door.

Afterwards, when Da's footsteps have long disappeared, Ma closes her eyes and smiles, and her face looks a little lighter. Joan does the rushes and says how about a tipple of rum? And we all nod, and Ma hums as Joan fetches the bottle.

We are not desperately bonny, we Dicksons, not really. In a good light Joan is pretty, and a sight prettier than me. Pretty enough to lure the son of one of the mill owners at Eskmills. But we do not light up a room. Even in pink dresses, we do not gleam like the Mrs Roses of this world, nor pose like the ladies of Edinburgh in their carriages. We wear no jewels, aside from my glass ring and the odd paste brooch, and we are comfortable elbow-deep in fish guts.

But there is a stoicism in fishwifery.

We are bold and brave and built for battle.

We do not stay up late really, the three of us. We have tea and there is a bit of ham in the pantry, and we slice that up and talk more of all that has happened. Joan and I do not look at each other when Ma mentions Spencer's name.

I do not tell either of them that he is living in Edinburgh and that I saw him on Hanging Day, and that he runs a perfume shop now.

I do not tell either of them that I was planning to walk into that perfume shop, for I do not want to hear their questions about it. I don't know myself what I would say to Spencer, or how that conversation might go.

We go to bed around ten of the clock, as tomorrow we must gather bait.

Ma snores almost as soon as her head hits the pillow and, by the rattling depth of her snores, she is in a deep and well-deserved sleep.

Joan folds into herself and I know that she lies awake a long while, as I do too.

Finally, I sleep.

I dream of snakes, and Mrs Rose and Dr McTavish. Today has been a good day, in the end.

But as my dream-snake uncoils itself in the grass and stretches its scales and flicks its tongue and feels a hunger, an insatiable hunger, that can only be satisfied with a kill, I feel Dr McTavish sit in his plush apartment, aching for his beloved Mrs Rose and growing angrier and angrier that I have not brought her to him.

Dr McTavish will come for me.

Chapter Twenty-Nine

They say Da is having a fine time down at the Mussel Inn. He keeps himself to himself and drinks in the lushery, and goes out in his boat as usual, and we do the bait and the lines, for nothing has changed in that regard.

'We have only just got the trust of the tea men back. If your da stays out at the inn long enough, folk might stop coming here and giving us things to look after,' worries Ma. 'They might not think their tea is safe, being looked after by women, with no man about the place.'

'Well, mibbie it's time to put an end to all that,' I say. 'Take it from me, you don't want to keep hoarding illicit things. You don't want to get caught and have to spend time in jail.'

'What if your da runs up a big bill at the inn?' Ma looks better now that he has gone, but she has a habit of disappearing into herself, rubbing at her chin or her bonnet or the table top and gazing into the mid-distance.

'I will settle his bills,' I tell her. 'I have enough saved.'

I have not gone hawking my half-death here in Fisherrow or Musselburgh yet, but I will if I must. Instead I would rather get a proper trade, so I dress well for the next Friday fish-market, which is always the biggest of the week.

They come for miles for their Friday fish, and that brings out all the other traders too. Fisherrow harbour is lined with stalls and barrels and crates, filled with loaves and autumn harvests of apples and pears and carrots and parsnips, along with the lobsters and salmon.

After a busy hour of selling our fish, I leave Ma and Joan and take a walk up the harbour, which sings with the cries of gulls and traders. A wind comes off from the Forth, a fresh wind, and I sit on the wall and feel it. I would take off my bonnet and sense it whip my hair, were it not for the fact that I am far too grown-up for such frolics. This is what it is to be alive. To feel the weather and to blink at the sun's harsh glint off the waves. To look at the sea, full of Navy ships and pirates, and wonder where the world ends. To feel as small as anything.

Before the hanging, I barely noticed any of it. I was too busy studying maps and daydreaming.

I get up and walk over to the harbourmaster's office. I do not like smartly dressed men, but I have come to learn how to talk to them and make a case for myself. I knock sharply on the door, and a deep voice calls at me to come in.

The harbourmaster sits at a large desk, smothered with papers and cups and quills, and he is plainly puzzled to see a woman walk into his office. He is not a Fisherrow man – I can tell by his rakish frame and his well-cut vowels.

'Can I assist you?' He frowns, as though he fears I am here to report a theft or drunkenness, or the usual trouble the Friday market brings.

'I am Mistress Maggie Dickson,' I tell him. 'Of Fisherrow.'

The penny drops, but he is too much of a gentleman to gawp.

'Are you the – ahem – the *hanged* woman? Ah yes, I see you are; there was a likeness of you in the *Courant*.' He looks me up and down, then blushes as if I were naked.

'They call me Half-Hanged Maggie,' I say. 'But I'm not fond of that name.'

We wait for his blushes to cool a little.

'I would not be fond of a name like that, either. They call me Harbourman Jim, which is not quite as bad, but I don't like it. My name is James Munroe,' he tells me.

He is trying to be decent, so I take the plunge. 'I should like to ply a trade at the market,' I say. 'My own folks have a fish stall, but they don't need the extra pair of hands, as my sister works with them now.'

'Yes, the Dicksons' fish stall, which is one of our most reliable. I understand the Dickson fisher folk go back generations. Do you want your own fish stall?'

I shake my head. 'I want to try something different,' I reply.

He frowns. 'But what other knowledge do you have?'

'I lived in Edinburgh awhile,' I tell him. 'I learned the gin trade, but I would not wish to bring that to Fisherrow.'

He shakes his head vigorously. A good Presbyterian man.

'I told stories about my hanging for pennies, but I do not wish to sell myself like that, either,' I admit.

He considers me.

'You have been through an ordeal,' he admits. 'Many ordeals, if what I read in the *Courant* is true.'

'But I am still here,' I tell him. 'And I have learned a lot. Folk in Edinburgh would touch my neck for luck. They would think it would save them from their own hardships and perils.'

'It is easy to be superstitious,' Mr Munroe says. I can tell that he would not be as willing as other folks have been to believe my stories. His stare is frank. I dare say I could not tell this man any untruths, for he would see right through them.

'But sometimes superstition is all we have,' I go on. I sit down now on the spare chair, even though he has not invited me to do so, but he does not object or tell me to get up. 'I have seen men stand at this very harbour and kiss cauls before they get onto their boats. I have seen their wives pray on their knees as the storms come, watching and waiting for the boats to return. I have seen storms come out of nowhere. I have seen folk ply their own secret trade in trinkets and tea and perfumes, and all sorts of smuggled goods, just to get by, for there is not much of a living to be made selling fish, once they have paid their rent for their stalls and a place to keep their boats overnight.'

He does not nod or shake his head, but looks serious.

'All I should like to do,' I go on, 'is have my own little corner of the market where I can sell bits and bobs – enough to get by and make some sort of a living out of and not disturb anyone, nor be disturbed.'

He sits back in his chair and scratches his chin. 'Have you brought any trouble with you from Edinburgh? Any constables looking for you?'

I shake my head. I do not tell him about Dr McTavish, or the fact that my own husband is alive and well there.

'And do you have a trade, other than fish?'

'Not yet,' I say. 'I have worked in an inn, but I don't fancy that again – all that cooking and cleaning. I was thinking of selling salt or spices, something like that. Mibbie making some connections in that regard and taking it from there.'

'That might take a while,' he muses. 'The setting-up of connections in trade is not an easy one. Not in honest trade anyway.'

'I want an honest trade, more than anything,' I tell him.

The fire burns in the grate and the gulls cry distantly. I cast my eye around the room and think it a cosy one, despite the pamphlets and the chaos of papers. On the desk is a paper bag and the remnants of a pie crust, and I wonder if Mr Munroe has a wife at home or takes his meals alone at his desk all the time.

Finally he seems decided.

'I could use an assistant here in my office,' he says. 'Someone to keep the place neat and tidy and take messages and make tea for visitors.'

'Oh,' I reply, taken aback. 'I had not thought of an office job. I have not worked in any kind of clerking job before. I don't read well, sir.'

He smiles. 'But, as you say, you want an honest job. Well, this is honest work. Keeping things ticking over here. Now, will you take it?'

I say I will take it.

When I close Mr Munroe's door behind me, leaving him to scribble and scrape the details of his new appointment into his books, I must confess I feel proud of myself. The old Maggie Dickson would have been horrified of course. She would never have worked in the office at Fisherrow harbour. But she never reached the London of her dreams, which likely does not exist anyway and is not as decent a place as Fisherrow.

An office assistant! I cannot wait to tell Ma and Joan. I could skip for joy. But then I remember Dr McTavish and my heart sinks.

That night the fishwives come to our cottage to hear their fortunes and to touch my neck.

I had known it was bound to happen sooner or later. They weren't invited, for Ma would not have welcomed the attention, nor Joan. But rather word got out and I was seen that day at the Friday market and, it being a Friday night, the men were down at the inn and the women were at a loose end, so they came wandering up to ours.

Ma lets them come in, dribs and drabs of them, until the

parlour is full and hot and close. They've brought sherry and fruit baskets and slabs of cheese, so we can't really turn them away. They take off their boots at the door, and by and by the doorway is so piled with boots that I don't know how each will manage to find her own pair at the end of the night.

At first their questions are easy to answer.

'Are you glad to be home?' they ask. 'Did you miss your ma's cooking?'

Then, as they tip back their drinks and their eyes begin to glaze, the questions turn into an interrogation.

'We only want to *know*, we are only *asking* – she doesn't have to answer if she doesn't *want* to.' But their questions are no different from anyone else's. How did the babe die? Do I miss the babe? What was the jail like? What was the Iron Room like? Is it true you get a good last meal?

What happens next, after we die? Have I been delivered, have I been spared, have I been resurrected?

Can we see the rope-bruise? Oh, it is not as bad as we feared. Oh, you can hardly see it, not really – not in this light.

Can we touch it?

I do not want to embarrass Ma. I do not *want* to embarrass Ma, but their words and faces and fingers probe at me until the only thing I can do is close my eyes; and when that doesn't work and doesn't drown them out, I put my fingers in my ears; and when that doesn't work, I stand up. Plates clatter to the floor and a hush falls over the room.

'She has had a terrible time,' says Joan. 'And you are all making it worse.' I have never heard her so stern.

'Then we shall change the subject,' they cry, and the subject is changed. And I sit back down and they all go back to talking about the weather and the price of wool, and the best time to slaughter their household pigs.

Under the table, Joan reaches for my hand and squeezes it.
I squeeze it back, grateful to her.

Afterwards, when I get embarrassed thinking about my
outburst and wonder why it happened, I realize that it is
because I do not want to tell tall tales any more and, truthfully,
I was never dead, was I?

I was out for the count. Unconscious. Similar to a fainting
fit, I suppose. The noose constricted my breathing for a while,
and Dr McTavish pronounced me dead, though he knew full
well I wasn't.

There is nothing special about me at all.

But everyone else wants me special, for it gives them some
sort of hope. Hope of reunion with lost loves, and hope of
salvation. They want it by touching my neck, and Dr McTavish
wants it by me bringing him Mrs Rose.

Chapter Thirty

For my first day I am at Mr Munroe's office a quarter of an hour early, which means I must wait for him in a downpour of rain, and it soaks through my bonnet and lashes onto my skirts.

'Oh, my dear Lord, I should give you a key,' he mutters when he comes down from his apartment above the office to open the door. 'Come inside and dry yourself by the fire.'

In this way, my first day as his assistant gets off to a slow start, as he spends more time assisting me than I do him. He helps me to dry off and fetches me tea, and sits me in a chair and asks, 'How are you doing?' and 'Are you all right?' and 'Are you quite comfortable?' over and over again, as though I am a visiting lady. When we have firmly established that I am very happy indeed and really most comfortable and pleasantly warm, he suggests that I might start by tidying the bookshelves, which are in quite a mess, with books strewn all over the room, so I do that and take my time over it.

Mr Munroe is a busy bee of a man, humming over his papers and occasionally shaking his head and saying in his deep gravelly voice, 'That will never do', but I quite enjoy the company of him, for he never goes into a mood or talks braggingly of what he is doing, even though he is in charge of all sorts of things, from the markets to the moorings.

As I tidy, I decide to take a duster and sweep the shelves as I go, and although I do not understand most of what is written on the covers of the books or maps, I have a few words, and it is not a bad task. And I think of Ma and Da and how they get by, dabbling in the smuggling trade, and whatever Spencer was up to with his perfumes. And all of these crimes are probably problems that occasionally land on Mr Munroe's desk, causing him to puzzle at his cleanly shorn chin and say, 'That will never do'; and I think that it is a life better lived if we do not have to turn our hand to crime.

'Mistress Dickson, you are a blessing,' he tells me as he watches me tidy the shelves. 'You see, I can walk past those books time and time again and think, *I must put them back,* but I never seem to find the time to do it.'

'Well, it's a good job that you have me in your employ,' I say.

He nods and busies himself again and gives a small sigh, and I wonder if he has a wife, but I have not seen one, and I would never ask. Mr Munroe is an interesting fellow, but I think the thing I like most about him is that he has never asked to look at my rope-bruise, or asked me questions about the afterlife, and I do believe there is something straightforward about him that means he never will.

At one of the clock he tells me he will be out at the Mussel Inn for his lunch. He pauses, walking cane in hand.

'Should you like to join me?' he asks. 'I usually dine upstairs, with a fine view of the harbour.' It comes out in a blurt, and despite the fact that his voice is usually deep and serious, it cracks a little and he blushes.

'Oh,' I reply, as a fear washes over me. A fear of that very upstairs room he is talking about. A fear of sitting in that room in the Mussel Inn with a handsome man, and how that might lead a girl into a nightmare. 'Perhaps I might do that another time,' I say. 'For my ma has given me a slice of ham-and-egg pie today.'

'Of course,' he replies and bolts for the door.

Oh Lord, that was embarrassing. What was I thinking? *Ham-and-egg pie! Urgh, of all the things I could have said.*

- But I believe I could have sat and talked to Mr Munroe about things and he would have listened, and I would have been interested to hear what he might say.

And that frightens me. It frightens me to let go of myself and allow a man to be nice to me. I might get very hurt again. Besides, am I not still married to Patrick Spencer?

The office is not quite spick and span yet, but it will get there, I am sure of it. There's a big looking glass over the fireplace and I stand on my tiptoes and look into it. I think it is the biggest and brightest looking glass I have ever seen in my life, for it reflects the light from the window. I am a dark figure in the middle of it at first, until my eyes adjust.

I once had a fear of my own reflection, but I don't feel fear now. I cannot help who I am. My hair falls in two neat plaits down to my breastbone. Mibbie I should curl it in papers. I used to brush it and put powder on it, but I seem to have forgotten to do that. Mibbie I'll buy some powder at the market, although I will have to hide it from Joan.

My face is pale, but it looks better for a bit of Ma's cooking and less of the gin. I wonder what happened to Mrs Rose's rouge, for it got lost in the way of things. The rope-bruise has changed. In fact it is the most changed thing about me. It has faded, as a fire does at the end of an evening, so that it still glows, but with less heat. I touch it gently and feel no pain or tenderness at all.

I wonder what Mr Munroe thinks when he looks at me.

I am quite lost in contemplation of myself when there is a commotion and two men burst in, making the door slam open with a bang.

I spin on my heels, but before I do that, in order to face them, there is a moment – a split-second of time – when I know they have come for me. Neither of them is Dr McTavish, but I know he has sent them. One stands with a rope in his hand.

'Mistress Dickson,' he says, 'now you shall come quietly with us in our carriage, or we shall hang you from the rafters of this very room. Those are our instructions from the doctor.'

I edge away from the men as much as I can. They do not move, but remain blocking my only way of escape.

'There's no point trying to run,' the other observes. 'We are paid for a job and we are doing the job.'

And that is when they grab me.

They make me sit on the floor of their carriage, with the rope around my arms and waist, trussed up like poultry. They put metal cuffs on my wrists.

I sit there, watching the world flash by at the carriage window for the whole hour into Edinburgh. The men say nothing. No small-talk or even anything to scare me. I wonder how long it will take before someone misses me. Tears prick at my eyes. When Mr Munroe comes back, when I am not home for supper, they will think I have run off once more.

Ma will think I could not face the fishwives' questions again, and Mr Munroe will think I ran away at his invitation to lunch. They will think I preferred the anonymity of Edinburgh.

Then I think, *This will be my last journey*.

Dr McTavish will punish me and will enjoy it too.

Chapter Thirty-One

Edinburgh
October 1724

The men hand me over at the door and, after taking a payment from Dr McTavish, they disappear.

I am still trussed. Dr McTavish pushes me into the bedchamber and throws me onto the bed. I bite my mouth to try not to weep.

'You should never attempt to run away from me,' he says. I can hear the boards creak as he stalks around the room. He lights candles and paces, and lights more candles. There is a difference in his voice; it is hoarser. He sounds as if he has not slept. 'It has cost me a small fortune to have you brought back here. And that was money I could have spent on something nice for Mrs Rose.'

He is a madman.

I open my eyes and watch him. He paces and his eyes dart everywhere. His mouth moves from snarl to grimace.

'I only want one thing of you. I have tried to approach Mrs Rose myself, and she simply will not accept my offers. And now you have made everything worse by showing me you are not to be trusted. What am I to do with you?'

He sits on the bed now, resting his weight on the thick bedspread, leaning over me. He puts his hand to my throat.

'A thick neck,' he murmurs, 'so unattractive on a woman. And you smell of fish bait too. What man would ever want you, Mistress Dickson. You are disgusting.'

I weep, for fear and for the fact that I think he speaks the truth.

'I would not even enjoy fucking you,' he says, 'but perhaps I will do it anyway.' He pulls the chains down from the wall and secures them to the cuffs on my wrists. 'You are tied now,' he keeps saying. 'I bet no man has done this to you before. Some women enjoy it. Mrs Rose will enjoy it, I am sure of it.'

'Do not touch me, please,' I beg him. 'I will do as you ask. I will do whatever you need.'

But Dr McTavish ignores all of that and runs his hands from my throat to my breasts, and then down further. I cannot say what he does next, for I close my eyes, but I know that he satisfies himself looking at me like this.

He does not fuck me. Instead he pleasures himself whilst watching me whimper.

'I would not fuck you. I would dirty myself,' he whispers.

He leaves me for a while afterwards. It must be all the afternoon, for I grow hungrier and more distraught, and my wrists ache from the cuffs. I have no sense of time, for the windows are boarded. I hear him creak the floorboards in the next room and I smell a fire start in a grate, and I wonder if he will just leave me here to rot.

Eventually he opens the door again. He comes in with a silver tray piled with food. Bread and eggs and cheese and fruit, and a crystal glass of wine.

He takes off the cuffs and watches as I rub my wrists.

'You will be free to go, once you have had some supper,' he

tells me. 'Free to go anywhere. But you know what you must do before that, don't you? And if you don't do it, then I will track you down again. Now there is a good gown in the wardrobe, and your pick of bonnets and boots and all sorts of girlish things. Get dressed and go and fetch me my Mrs Rose.'

'And what if she won't come with me?'

'She will come,' he soothes. 'She is weak-minded and opportunistic, and she will be desperate to see what she can get from you this time.'

'And what if I can't? I have friends. Family. They will come to my rescue if I need them.'

He laughs, tilting his head to the ceiling. His Adam's apple bobs in his throat, and I think I would like to hang him myself.

'You will do me the one single favour I ask, or you won't see your friends or your family again,' he replies.

The coffee house where Mrs Rose plies her trade is full of men who look like university scholars and physicians, all talking politics. They gather on long benches, but the proprietor nods me towards a stool at the side and sits me down, then sets a cup of cocoa and a dish of walnuts on the shelf beside me. I am not the only woman here. There are one or two others, rouged and cross-legged, dangling from their stools and looking unimpressed by me.

I have a kerchief about my neck, a white lace one, to cover my rope-mark and I am wearing what the whores do: gaudy skirts with a flash of petticoat underneath. But as I sit on the stool, I come to understand that I really am no great beauty, for the debating intellectuals remain more interested in their conversation than in the new arrival.

I never thought I was beautiful, but it smarts to see them

ignore me. I finish my cocoa and my mouth waters for a gin, but there is no liquor in the place. None of the other women drink their cocoa, their little cups and saucers growing stone-cold on the bench. I pat my mouth with my fingers and feel quite awkward.

But all of this is swiftly overtaken when, in a sweep of skirts, Mrs Rose arrives and I remember the enormity of the awful task ahead.

She is much changed. Her face is drawn and painted in brighter hues to compensate. She looks as though she has had molars pulled – that is how sucked-in her cheeks have become. She wears strings of cheap glass beads across a white bosom. Her hair is piled too high and is set with too many red ribbons. Joan would say *she has gone to rot*.

Mrs Rose sits down, right next to me, not recognizing me at first, and is served not cocoa, but a tincture of reddish-brown liquid that I assume to be laudanum, and a small cup of coffee.

It takes her a few heartbeats to realize it is me, but when she does, I think she might fall off her stool.

'Mistress Dickson, from the River Inn at Kelso,' she breathes.

'Do not try to leave,' I warn her, 'or I will follow you and make a fuss.'

She grips onto the shelf. Her blue eyes dance. 'I had no choice but to run away that night,' she says. 'I knew you would come looking for me. *Oh! I am such a fool. A silly goose. A selfish, silly mess of a girl*. Here,' she starts to fumble in her skirts and pulls out a drawstring purse, 'I can pay all the money back. Some now – look, here is half a crown, and some English coins too. Are you set for London still? I can recommend lodgings near Covent Garden.'

She carries on in this fashion for minutes, tipping coins out of the purse and sniffing, as though she might burst into tears.

'People are watching us,' I warn her. 'Stop making such a scene. Put the purse away. They will think me your procuress or somesuch.'

'You're right, of course,' she replies, scrabbling the coins back into the purse. She places it on the shelf. 'It is yours, though – all yours.'

There are many things I wish to say to her about the peril she left me in with her thieving, but now I find that I can't. I suppose I built Mrs Rose up in my head to a bigger thing than she really is. But isn't that often the way, with those people who cause us ill?

Instead of telling her these countless things, I take a deep breath. 'I have had a most terrible ordeal,' I tell her. 'I don't know if you've heard, but I was nearly hanged at the Grassmarket Gallows.'

She had heard clearly, for she nods enthusiastically. 'The story of your half-hanging is still the freshest news in town,' she gossips. 'I put two and two together that it was you – the Maggie Dickson I met at Kelso – when the gents in here were discussing the botch job the next day. They said a hanging must be done in a certain way, and you either bribed the hangman or he was drunk. So tell me what happened, for I am agog.'

She stares and awaits the tale. She says nothing of Dr McTavish. Her eyes are wide and her face blank. She has no idea that he's a hangman. He has kept his secret well.

My God, the poor fool.

'I did bribe the hangman,' I say.

She edges closer. 'And with what?'

'I bribed him with sex,' I lie.

She sits back, satisfied. 'I am in admiration,' she answers. 'You must turn a marvellous trick, for you are quite plain to look at, but they say it takes all sorts and the quiet ones are the naughtiest.'

'I am a magician in the sheets. But tell no one of my rope-trick,' I whisper.

She is earnest now, leaning in again, looking at my belly. 'So you were with child then, back in Kelso? Well, you said nothing to me.'

'I did not know it then,' I reply.

She pauses to take some laudanum, her eyes watering at the bitterness of it.

'I have had two pregnancies,' she says eventually. 'Many years ago. I take a tonic now – a draught from the apothecary – but I had to have two aborted. I was so young, you see: fourteen the first time, and then the second one only a year later. I was frightened the childbirth might kill me. I went to a midwife. She had me wear a tight girdle and, when that did not work, she gave me a purgative.'

She slides her eyes at me. They are beginning to glitter, now that the laudanum is taking effect. The lanterns glow and the pipe smoke billows and the scene becomes her. Her skirts rustle and the strings of glass beads about her throat twinkle. She is far from gaudy and gaunt now. Mrs Rose is the sort of lady who lights up at night. Luminous, with her sad tales and her sorrows.

'I am not a good woman, as you know, Mistress Dickson, but I was not dealt a good hand in life,' she goes on. 'I try to make the most of what I've got. I am pretty to look at, but spiky underneath. It's survival. It's why I call myself "Mrs Rose". It's not even my real name! My real name is Dorothy Donaldson – how dreary is that. Now I know a secret of yours, and you know a secret of mine.'

Oh, she is marvellous. I think, if I were a man or a sapphist,

I would fall in love with Dorothy Donaldson, or Dorothy Rose, or whoever she is. But I am neither of these. So I admire her honesty and pity her melancholies, but I do not want to have her or possess her. She cannot be possessed.

When Dr McTavish realizes this woman is her own woman and cannot be possessed, he will snuff her out like a candle-stub.

'What was the hanging like?' she asks. 'I was not there on Hanging Day, for I stay away from that side of town. If I was caught working up there, I'd be put in the tolbooth for *whoring*.' She mouths the word 'whoring' as though it were a secret between the two of us, when in fact we are in the midst of the Greyfriars whores right now. 'We night-blooms are safer down here. But what was it like? What did you think, when you were standing there on the gallows, my dear?'

I have answered this question day after day after day for pennies, and I lost my temper and my sensibilities when the fishwives started. But for Dorothy I give the real answer. She is a woman who will not see old bones, after all.

'I thought I would shit my drawers in front of all Edinburgh town,' I tell her.

She roars with laughter. I knew she would.

'Show me your rope-mark,' she says. 'They say it is a belter.'

I loosen my kerchief and she puts her fingers to it. They are warm and gentle. I do not mind it at all.

'Oh,' she responds, 'it is red like garnet. It will slim down soon to a silvery mark, I think. It will not look like a rope-burn for ever. One day it will look like a simple line. A jewel, my dear – a mourning necklace. For your dear departed babe. We all have them, you know, we women who have carried a babe in our womb that has not had the chance to live, or that we could not give the chance of life to. We all wear our own mourning necklaces. Some more apparent than others.'

I bite my lip. I had not thought of it like that. I had not thought my rope-burn was ever about anything but me. But it is not just about me. It is about the baby, and the loss of her. For the flutters and the kicks she gave me, all still now. She is long gone. But we are linked through my rope-mark. It is the only thing of hers I have left. They said I would swing for the crime, and I did. Now I wear the rope-mark like a mourning necklace.

Time passes well enough in an Edinburgh coffee house, but Dorothy is so lustrous, so vivid, and her counsel so wise that she deserves a starrier night than this – we both do – so I take her to a wine shop next door, where candles twinkle on shelves and the glasses are crystal, which I have come to prefer.

'Let's share a bottle of French wine,' I say. 'Like we did in the River Inn.'

We perch, looking like two silly whores, on two rickety chairs in the window, the wine bottle resting on an upturned barrel. If tuts and shakes-of-the-head were pennies, we would have become rich women that night. We talk of lost babies and lost lovers, and I get weepy about Spencer, and Dorothy gets weepy about so many of her old lovers that I could not count them on both of my hands.

'My husband's here, in this very town,' I confess. 'Patrick Spencer runs a perfume shop now. And I don't know whether to go and see him or not.'

By this stage in the evening Dorothy has begged a pipe from someone and a pinch of tobacco from someone else, so she puffs and thinks. Then she puts the pipe down and puts her hand on my arm.

'There is a restlessness about you, my dear,' she tells me.

'Rushing to marry Mr Spencer, then trying to run to London, then running from motherhood and now look at you, wandering the streets, not knowing what to be at. You are like a knotless thread. You can go and find your Spencer or you can leave him well alone, but he will likely not give you the answers you need. If he had wanted to find you, he would have found you by now.'

'And where will I find my answers?' I ask mournfully. My neck starts to ache again, and the words 'knotless thread' made me think of ropes and snakes. I am not good on wine.

'Well, my dear, if I had the answers to all of life's questions, I would be a wise woman indeed,' she cries.

I hope I will find my answers, but I cannot think of any of them now, for we are still spending our evening together. In other circumstances I do believe Dorothy could be a friend to me, and we could have endless nights putting the world to rights, where I am as far away from snake-dreams as I have ever been.

But, alas, tick-tock. The time comes for me to lead her to Dr McTavish's snake-nest.

Chapter Thirty-Two

The next day is a bright one, with rain scattered about the closes. A warm wind brings the drop of leaves and the rise of the last of the wasps. It is a day for making fruit pies and chutneys. In Fisherrow, as they string fresh bait on lines, my second disappearance will be the talk of the harbour.

I walk to Fishmarket Close and when the fishwives see me there are questions and some relief, and I explain that I had to make an unexpected return to Edinburgh, but they should reassure Ma and Joan and Mr Munroe that I will be back soon, once all my business is complete. They give me a pair of haddock to take away with me and I take them to Aunt Jenever's. 'Fresh fish calls for a fry-up,' the fishwives call.

Aunt Jenever's shop is dark and quiet when I get there, but last night it shone like gold. I put the fish in the pantry and take a seat by the window. By and by, Cornelius drops in. Good Cornelius – Aunt Jenever's boy who will do anything to keep the peace around here. Anything that needs doing.

'There's a nice bit of fish out the back for supper,' I tell him. 'I hope you're sticking around that long.'

'Not got much else to do,' he says. 'It's been very quiet around here of late.'

Then there's a bit of a swish and swirl of skirts, and a tippy-tap of pointy boots on the stairs, and we both fall silent, for down comes Mrs Rose, my pal Dorothy, looking radiant despite our late night out. She yawns and asks if there is any coffee.

'It is a habit I have got into,' she says, continuing to yawn. 'A nice little cup of coffee when I wake up, although I usually wake much later than this. It is noisy in the mornings at this end of town. Greyfriars is more genteel, I dare say. And might there be somewhere I can get a tot of laudanum?'

I raise my eyebrows and Cornelius and I exchange glances. Cornelius has the shadow of a late night about his eyes.

'Shall you be heading back to Greyfriars after your cup of coffee then?' I ask Dorothy.

'Perhaps, or I might stay here a while,' she answers. 'I feel quite safe here, you see.'

Cornelius stands up and goes to the kitchen to brew some coffee. Dorothy plays with the rings on her fingers and at last has the decency to look embarrassed at herself.

'You did me a great favour last night,' she says. 'Dr McTavish had been a pest to me, begging me to do business with him again, but there was no way I'd consider it. I knew in my bones what he'd done to his wife. I would have left Edinburgh altogether, but the trade is so good here and the laudanum easy to get. I was worried he would do me a mischief one of these days, but I had no idea about the depths of his plot. Planning to keep me a prisoner – chained up.' Her face is pinched.

'He is no longer a threat to anyone,' I tell her.

Cornelius comes back with three china cups filled with steaming coffee.

'I feel a proper gent drinking this,' he says. He hands a cup to Dorothy. He can hardly keep his eyes off her. 'We will talk of what happened last night once more – and once more only,' he goes on, 'to get our stories straight, as it were. After that we shall talk of that scoundrel Dr McTavish no more. Some things are best buried.'

*

We talked then and got our stories straight, but here is mine: the real one.

I am not a woman of parchments or books or written words, but as I come to look back on these events – on this time of my life – I wish I was, for I do think the story of Half-Hanged Maggie, the woman who survived her own execution, is only half my story. I admit I feel quite melancholy that my other memories will die with me, on the day of my natural death. For though not quite as macabre or dramatic as the story of my hanging, these events are quite a tale too.

It begins with Dorothy that night, on the walk from Greyfriars, a ten-minute walk at most downhill to the Grassmarket, then uphill to the High Street. Late at night, it is a walk past inns and taverns and shuttered apothecaries, and beggars and vagrants under blankets who might be asleep or dead – you don't care to check. As we passed the Grassmarket, the gallows spot, I knew without question that I was not going to lead Dorothy to her doom. For had I not been led to my own doom at this very place?

On Hanging Day they had carted us from the Tolbooth Jail down to the Grassmarket Gallows, which is only a short ride, but felt like eternity and a blink of an eye, all in one.

The streets were lined many-deep, for our hanging had been advertised, you see, all over town, as is the custom. The crowd went with us, as we ricocheted over the potholes, our hands bound so that we could not use them to steady ourselves and we had to plant our feet anywhere they could rest.

I even laughed quite hysterically, once or twice, at the nonsense of it all, trying to avoid being battered by stones and vegetables and potholes as I was about to meet a hangman. The others wept and prayed and closed their eyes. The chaos made the carthorses nervous and they lifted their tails and shat, all the way down the street, and I thought of how the dung would lie there and be trodden in, long after I was coffined.

I didn't know whether I would live or die. Dr McTavish might do anything on those gallows. What if I survived the hanging, only to wake up to find the anatomists cutting into me?

But I had been spared. And I do not believe in a life for a life, or anything like that. I just know that Dr McTavish is a man who thinks he is God. I have not met God. But I know he is not in Dr McTavish. There is more of God in me than there is in Dr McTavish.

As we passed the gallows last night I turned to Dorothy. We stopped then and there, under the trees, under the stars.

'This is where they hanged me,' I told her.

'I should like to see a day when no one is hanged for concealing a pregnancy,' she replied. 'For it doesn't seem right to me to put a mother to death when she is grieving for her lost child. It does not seem right to me that women are blamed for things they cannot help, and are told what to do with their own bodies.'

She began to weep. She had had a bellyful of wine.

'Men use my body, then shun me,' she said. 'I can have a man naked in my chamber all night, but should he see me around Greyfriars the next morning, he will not meet my eye. Imagine if we ruled the world, you and I. There would be no need for women to sell their bodies, for folk could be given an allowance, say, if they fell on hard times. And men like Dr McTavish would not be allowed to get away with wickedness like poisoning their wives.'

I knew then that Dorothy had so much wisdom and worldly experience that she must not be snuffed out. That would be a terrible sin. More so than anything else I had ever done.

Then I told her. I told her who my hangman was, and her eyes widened and I thought she would gasp herself into a fit.

'That awful, awful man,' she said. 'That *murderer*. All those times I went to his cottage in Kelso. He sat and played dominoes without a care in the world. And oh, I shared a bed with him. I have been intimate with a hangman, Maggie.'

'You were not to know,' I soothed.

'I am utterly relieved I ran away from him. For he is revolting and one day he would murder me too,' she added.

Then she looked at me and realized.

'You bribed Dr McTavish. But not with sex. You bribed him with *me*.'

'I had no choice,' I told her. 'I was gambling on my life. I threatened to tell everyone that he killed his wife, and he said that if he spared mine, I was to help him get you back. But I didn't realize quite what a monster he is. He means to take you and keep you prisoner.' I couldn't stop myself now. 'He sent me up to Greyfriars to find you. He wants me to deliver you to him. If we don't go to his apartment, he will find us both. We are in danger, Dorothy.'

'We must run away this instant,' she hissed, gripping my arm. 'Both of us now – what do you say? We can get a night-coach to London. I know where they depart from. It's not even far from here. We have good clothes on and we have the money in my purse, and we can take lodgings near Covent Garden. What say you?'

'I am not running away from anyone, ever again,' I insisted. I grasped her arm back. 'And neither are you. Come, we will go to Aunt Jenever's Gin Shop for a nightcap and we will talk this over. Dr McTavish is not expecting us 'til after midnight anyway.'

I knew Aunt Jenever would help. Even more so, I believed Cornelius or some of the lads he knew would help. For if there is one thing men like Cornelius loathe, it is a hangman.

Cornelius made us stay at Aunt Jenever's, so the truth is that I do not know what happened up at Dr McTavish's apartment last night, only that a couple of lads got together – one of their own dear pals had been hanged a year or so past, just a small-time thief – and they felt that whatever might happen to Dr McTavish would be well deserved.

'I don't think I am a lover of coffee,' Cornelius declares now.

Dorothy takes delicate sips of hers, but I have no thirst for mine.

'If we are ever asked – if the constables should come knocking and asking questions about whether we saw anything unusual last night – the answer is that we all had a nightcap of gin in this very room and then went to sleep,' says Cornelius. 'Are we clear on that?'

We nod solemnly.

'Is he quite dead?' whispers Dorothy. There is a tremble on her lip.

Cornelius places his hand on hers and she looks up at him. I think she is startled by his gentleness.

'Hanged from his own rafters, by a length of good hemp rope,' mutters Cornelius.

I blink away the image. I do not want to think of it. I decide to leave them to their coffee and go upstairs. Aunt Jenever is getting herself ready to face the world. Her room is a chaos of robes and bloomers.

'I shall open a window,' I declare, picking over the detritus on the floor and pulling wide the shutters.

'I think I am getting too old for all the dramatics of this town,' says Aunt Jenever. She wears nothing but her nightgown and is putting fresh plaits in her silvery hair.

'Here, let me,' I tell her and lead her to the chair, where she sits quite meekly as I pick up the brush. I need to do something simple and human, like fix hair.

'Is Cornelius all right?' she asks. 'For whatever passed last night, he is my best doorman and I do not want him out of the game.'

'No one was harmed, except for the man who was causing trouble,' I tell her. 'And he will cause no further trouble.'

'This is a harsh town,' Aunt Jenever muses as I pin her two plaits over her head. 'I dare say you are not staying here long.'

She is right. I need the Forth and calm, and my family.

'I have one or two more things I must do, then I will be back home,' I tell her. 'But I have been touched by your generosity. You have saved me somehow, when I had nothing. Less than nothing. You picked me up and gave me somewhere to live and a chance.'

Aunt Jenever shrugs, for she is not a woman who likes too many compliments. Her plaits are tight now and pinned to her head. But her hair is so thin I can see her pink scalp through it, and I wonder at her fragility, despite her coarse voice and ways; and at the fragility of us all.

Then I powder my teeth and wash my face and hands with a bit of lavender soap and head out. If I catch him, Patrick Spencer will be opening up his perfume shop about now, and I want to have a nice scent about me.

Chapter Thirty-Three

It is eleven of the morning, and the wiggers and shoemakers are already doing a roaring trade. I stand in the street and let the crowds wash around me as I look through the emporium window.

The last time I saw Spencer was at the gallows when he was standing under a tree, the type of which I cannot recall, as I was too occupied with my own peril. Why would he come, when he could have spent that morning doing anything else? He risked being seen by Ma, Da and Joan.

I still wear his ring, silly fool that I am. It reminds me of glowing rush-light and whispered words, and discovering that my own body could experience blissful things. It reminds me of the intimacy of nakedness. It's only glass, but it does twinkle in a world that has often been dark.

The perfume shop is as I once imagined ours might be in London. Glassy and musky. It is furnished with cabinets of a dark, expensive-looking polished wood, almost the colour of cherries, the like of which I saw in Dr McTavish's apartment. On the shelves are all sorts of stoppered bottles. Spencer is doing well for himself.

He is alone. I take a deep breath and walk inside. I shut the door behind me and wait for him to notice me. The scent is intoxicating and brings me straight back to our cottage, his smuggled packages, our first kiss. I almost walk straight back out again, but I mustn't. He is intent on arranging things on the counter and he looks just as he always did, except that now he wears a velvet waistcoat in a deep burgundy to match the wood of his shop. I am much changed, and he is not. I wonder, uneasily, if he has a woman upstairs, lying abed, taking her *Women's Tonic*. If he does, I imagine her to be viciously pretty with an accent like cut-glass. A soft delicate throat, unscarred, with a hint of expensive musk about it.

Finally he looks up and clears his throat, expecting a well-heeled gent or the neatly turned-out maid of someone from a top-storey apartment. When he sees me, he gulps and then quickly recovers himself.

'I wondered how long it would take you to find me,' he comments.

I say nothing for now, just slide open a cabinet door, pick up a bottle of something and take off the stopper, then put it to my nose. I hope he does not notice that my hands shake.

'I can only apologize for disappearing the way I did,' he adds.

Well, that makes me cross.

'Apparently that was not your fault,' I tell him, my blood rising. 'They said you were dragged off by a press gang.'

'That was part of what happened,' he replied. 'I was taken onto a boat, but I was able to bribe one of the Navy men. Another boat came into the port, from Gothenburg, and I was expecting a consignment on it, so the Navy man took that in lieu of me. I would never have made a decent Navy officer anyway.'

Oh, he never even made it out to sea! And I had spent all those days and nights pining and aching, and wondering if he might be whipped or drowned. But I don't pine and ache now, I just twirl the glass ring on my finger. It is light and cheap and thin.

'So why did you not come home?' I can hear the fury in my raised voice rattling off the cabinet-glass.

He shifts from one foot to the other and fiddles with his waistcoat pocket.

'I think I had got myself in a bit deep,' he replies. 'What with one thing and another. Marrying you so soon.'

'You certainly had got yourself in a bit deep. You were fugging my sister,' I retort.

Spencer sits on his stool and rubs his face. He looks embarrassed.

'Joan was a bit of a seductress,' he tells me.

'Joan is an idiot, who knew nothing of the world,' I say. 'She was as green as I was. You were older and wiser than both of us.'

'You thought I'd help you escape your fishing life for a life in London,' he replies. 'That was your real ambition. But you didn't need me to help you, in the end. You managed that all on your own. In fact you are a great escape artiste – you've escaped the noose! And doing all right now, are you not? I've seen you talking to folks and being passed coins. I've read stories about you in the *Courant* and heard gossip in the taverns. They say you saw God. They say you have the power to give folks a second chance.'

I could almost laugh at his nonsense. He has said nothing of our lost child. No *how have you survived?* Or *how is your ma?* Or *how have you all coped?*

'I suppose our marriage contract has come to an end,' he adds. 'What with you having legally been dead and all?'

I ignore that. 'Your *Women's Tonic* certainly does not work,' I tell him. 'So mibbie, if I were you, I would not give that to your conquests so confidently.'

'I am sorry about the babe,' he says. 'I know you did not want one, so perhaps its passing was for the best.'

I pick up a bottle of scent and consider smashing it on the floor.

'Nothing that has happened these past weeks have been for the best,' I reply. 'The babe was held and adored during her short little life, and she knew nothing but love.' I do not tell him her name. I do not give him Susanna. She is mine.

Now he sees how upset I am. 'What can I do, Maggie – what can I do to make things up to you a bit?' he says. 'What do you want?'

'I have no idea about our marriage contract,' I tell him. 'But mibbie I should go to the sheriffs and ask their opinion. We might be still wed, in God's eyes. Or you might be a widower. But they would enjoy nothing more than to ponder over that question as they make their way through a bottle of wine at the White Hart Inn. It would give them something to do. And perhaps that would make its way into the *Courant* as well. The illustrator does a good likeness of folks, and I could get him to do a nice sketch of this perfume shop too.'

Spencer's mouth falls open.

'You would be famous all about town,' I add slyly.

'There is no need for that,' he says. 'We shall proceed as you wish. We can settle our marriage in a way that is satisfactory to us both.'

'This is how we shall proceed,' I tell him. 'We will consider our marriage ended with my hanging. For there is a death-certificate after all. And you are a widower, and I – well, I am not sure exactly what I am, but as far as I am aware, my dear husband is lost at sea, presumed dead. But I should like a settlement from you. Enough so that I might go back to Musselburgh and live again in that cottage we had, or one like it, and so that Ma and Joan might join me if they wish, for it is no life for them living with my da and keeping smuggled tea beneath the bed, and waiting for a knock on the door from the Excise men.'

'That sounds like an awful lot of money, Maggie,' he begins. 'And there was a decent stash in the safe, wasn't there? I presume you found that and put it to good use? Surely you don't need anything more from me?'

'That stash is long gone. Stolen from me. And anyway you can manage to spare more,' I assure him. 'You are a man of means, as I can see from this shop; and you are a man of cunning ways, as I have learned from knowing you a bit. Second, I should like an extra sum of money from you in order that I can bury our poor babe in a kirkyard, so that she may finally rest in peace.'

'The babe is not buried?' At this he looks horrified.

'I believe her to be kept by the anatomists,' I say. 'And that is no way to spend eternity. We must both do better by her.'

Patrick Spencer is not a good man. I know nothing of where he came from in life, for I made the mistake of marrying a man I barely knew. I can only guess at his fate, which will be well heeled and lonely, I believe. But in the moment of our final conversation he does his best by me, which is to give me the settlement I ask him for.

He disappears upstairs for a while, and I hear the creaking of floorboards overhead and the murmuring of two voices.

Oh, I do feel the pierce of cut-glass in one of them.

But it is only a momentary twinge of pain at knowing that Spencer trots from woman to woman as easily as a ship calling at ports. I brush the dust off my skirts with my hands and think ahead, to seeing Ma and Joan again and mibbie, hopefully, Mr Munroe the harbourmaster, if I might still have my job.

And Mr Munroe might take me out for that lunch.

Spencer thuds downstairs and puts a purse on the countertop. 'This is enough for the burial and six months' rent,' he tells me. 'It's all I have, and after that you would need to come back.'

'But you might not be here,' I say. 'So I shall take some bottles of your perfume, and that will see me for the year.'

'But my perfume is worth a lot of money,' he replies.

'And so is my silence,' I warn.

He sighs. 'You are a witch. A wench. You are not the mild fishergirl I married.' Then he nods at my glass ring. 'That's not worth much money.' He grins. 'In fact you'll not believe how I got it. It belonged to a girl in Gothenburg. Lovely girl, she was. Eighteen or so. She was dying of the pox. It gave a mottle to her skin and a hacking cough. Two or three summers ago now. A pox went around the whole port. All the physicians could do was sell bottles of medicine to take the pain away. There were no cures.'

I look down at my hand, seeing the ring differently now. *Lovely girl.*

'I paid her enough for the ring to get her a decent bottle of medicine, but I think that ring could have got her two bottles. Maybe three, if she'd had a mind to barter for them. But, Maggie, she was in no state to barter. She was likely a gonner. You could tell by how fast she deteriorated. She wanted hardly anything for the ring. There was no point giving her more than she asked for, was there?'

I wonder whether she died or mibbie even survived, and whether she looks at her hand from time to time and misses the glass ring. I wonder whether a sweetheart gave it to her too, and what became of him.

I should never have taken Patrick Spencer into my heart.

I am quiet as he takes a dozen bottles of perfume from the shelves. 'I hope this is the end of it,' he grumbles, 'and you are not planning to come back to blackmail me for more.'

'None of this is blackmail,' I say. 'The devastation you caused can never be compensated for. But I shall go and fetch our babe now and leave you alone.'

'Should I come with you,' he offers, 'down to the anatomists? Might you need a man to speak on your behalf, to the learned gents?'

I laugh then; it bursts out of me, half-mirth and half of it a release of tension. Spencer's face is pale, with a sheen of sweat at his upper lip, and I know he is craving a rum already, to take the edge off his terrible morning, even though it's not yet noon.

'I am more than capable,' I respond. 'In fact I think I would do a better job of it than you would. A better job than you, or my da, or any of the men who are supposed to have looked after me. And instead of looking after me, you have behaved dreadfully. Now, Spencer, might you parcel this lot up for me, and the purse too, so that I can carry it with me when I go down to the anatomists' hall?'

He does as he is told and ties a looping bow at the top of the parcel. It is a heavy load, truth be told, but I am of broad-shouldered fishwife stock, so I lift it with confidence.

'That'll be that then,' he says. He is furious under his noncha-lance, though. I can tell by the way his upper lip sweats.

'That will be that,' I reply firmly and I take the parcel out of the door, into the clamour of the High Street, and head to the south side of the city.

Chapter Thirty-Four

I might have shown a bit of bravado with Spencer, but when I stand before the imposing doors of the Incorporation of Barbers and Surgeons on the southern edge of Edinburgh, that bravery slides away.

There is no bell or door-knocker of any sort, so I push the door open and walk into a high-ceilinged hall that smells of pungent medicines and ointments. A man in a bottle-green coat is standing by a bookshelf, inspecting its contents, but comes to a standstill when he sees me.

'Do you have an appointment?' He looks me up and down, then up and down again, as if not quite believing what he sees. I don't know what he disbelieves – the fact that I am shabbily dressed, or evidently poor, or a woman, or carrying a huge parcel – but, in any case, I put the box on the floor.

'I have no need for an appointment, for I shall not be taking up much of anyone's precious time,' I say. 'I have come for something of mine, sir, that I believe has been kept here for a while.'

He frowns so deeply that I fear his face might stay like that, if the wind were to change.

'Something of *yours*? This is a library and museum, and a medical place. Perchance have you got it confused with another building? Might you have thought us a shop, or a workhouse?'

I shake my head. 'This is the place where the surgeons do their dissections, is it not, sir? Well, a few weeks back the surgeons took something of mine: my babe, sir, after it had died. They performed a post-mortem on it and now I should like to have my poor babe back.'

'An infant post-mortem,' he says, still frowning and with no hint of sympathy. 'And what was wrong with the infant? Was it defective or conjoined, or somesuch?'

'She was born too early and passed not long after her birth,' I reply. 'And I was accused of concealment and hanged, but survived the hanging, and I am here to claim my child. In fact I have heard that after my hanging, great efforts had to be made to stop your lot from bringing my own corpse here, into this very building, to endure God knows what indignities.'

'You are the half-dead woman!' he cries, his eyebrows shooting up, and opening his mouth to display a row of good white teeth, so perfect that I wonder for a moment if they are his own or if they have been pulled from one of his cadavers and glued onto his gums.

'I am not half-dead, sir, I am very much alive,' I assure the horrible man.

'My colleagues should like to talk to you,' he says. 'Very much indeed, for there was much excitement at the fact you survived.'

'I am not having any of them touch my neck or ask me of God,' I answer.

He shakes his head, most vigorously. 'None of that, but more so the technique by which you escaped strangulation. We pondered over that and concluded that perhaps you had a breathing technique, or a way of easing your fingers beneath the noose? You quite confounded the sheriffs. I hear they are changing the wording of the death-sentence altogether, so that now it reads, *You will be hanged by the neck until dead!*'

'I have no recollection of my hanging,' I lie, 'so I am afeared I would be of no interest to your colleagues.'

He looks crestfallen at that. 'Perhaps an error by the hangman,' he comments.

'That is your guess, not mine,' I reply. 'I am only here to collect my own flesh and blood, which I fear is on one of your shelves.'

He considers the request for a moment or two.

'You see, Mistress – Dickson, isn't it? – everything in the collection is recorded, and so I would have to officially release it and might need permissions from my supervisors too. The infant cadaver is our property now. We use specimens like that for teaching purposes.'

The man is awful. The ointment-stink and the waft of warm air that seeps through the building make me feel I might vomit, and I put my face in my hands. It has all been too much. Really it has. To have come this far and not get my Susanna. Mibbie I should have brought Spencer with me. My neck starts to ache again.

'Oh, well,' I say, more to myself than to this man, 'at least I tried my very best.' There is a chair by the bookshelf and I sit down on it, for if I don't, I am sure I might collapse.

He watches me all through this, folding his arms across his waistcoat. I look up at him.

'I shall tell you something, sir,' I say. 'I did not spend long in the world beyond ours. I can't tell you what heaven looks like, for I do not think I truly got there, but I knew, when I was preparing to meet God on that gallows, that I did not have any fears that I had sinned against anyone. They said concealing a pregnancy is a sin, but I held that babe in my arms and loved her. In fact the *infant cadaver* you speak of is called Susanna.'

He swallows.

'Mibbie my Susanna will give you and your scholars lots of teaching. But it is truly something to go to the Lord with a

clear conscience, and if you do not give me back my Susanna –
if you do not let a mother and her daughter be together – let
us both be on your conscience until the day of your death, sir.
And that is the price you will pay for such teaching.'

He opens his mouth and shuts it again. He hovers and his
fingers flit about the bookcase for a moment or two longer,
then he nods his head, tells me to wait, turns on his heel and
makes his way through another set of doors.

It is a long trudge from the south side of the city back up to
the High Street, especially carrying half a dozen bottles of
perfume, a heavy bag of coin and Susanna.

The anatomist gent took a while over the task, mibbie even
an hour, but eventually came back through the doors with a
wooden box.

'Is she still in a jar?' I asked, feeling all of a sudden squeamish
and horrified.

'Your Susanna is in a shroud and a small sealed casket now,'
he said. 'I have placed her there myself. And she looks perfect.
Perfectly at peace. Have no troubling thoughts about her
at all.'

I liked the man after that. Mibbie he had a babe of his
own. He handed her over to me with such gentle respect, I
think that he might. It is astonishing what a bit of persuasion
can do.

It is a strange feeling to have Susanna back. Like a weight
has been lifted, even though the load of carrying her is heavy.
Like I have saved her, yet failed her. I talk to her all the way
up the road of course, the tears streaming down my face, and
folk staring at me as I pass.

I thank her for waiting so patiently for her mama, but say

that I had matters to attend to. I tell her what a good babe she has been, and what sights she must have seen in that anatomy museum; and all about what I have seen, and that the first thing I did – in that half-world between life and death – was to search for her. *I tried to find you, Susanna, I knew you were there somewhere.*

And other things, like how sorry I was. Sorry she had been born too soon and had slipped from me, and sorry she could not get to know Joan and Ma. Sorry we did not fetch the Baxters to help us. Sorry I had been so stupid as to try to keep her a secret. At some point the kerchief comes loose from my neck and folk stare at my rope-bruise, which is not much of a bruise any more, but more of a mark; but they do not cry 'Half-Hanged Maggie' at me, so mibbie it is not so apparent now, how I came to be marked as such.

It is a long trudge from the anatomists' place to Aunt Jenever's, heavy with tears and sorrow and relief, and I feel a passing of sorts as I do it, from Half-Hanged Maggie – the person I was for a while – to just plain Maggie; but no longer the girl I once was. Now I am a bereaved mother, finally allowed to grieve.

Can you believe this? When I get back to Aunt Jenever's Gin Shop, which must be a full three hours after I left this morning, Dorothy and Cornelius are still sitting together at the same table, in rapt conversation. Cornelius is looking at Dorothy as though she is the only woman in the world, and she is flirting like mad with him. But it is not the silly-goose flirting I have come to expect from her, all fluttering eyelashes and tossing of curls, but more of an open sort of a way with him. She wears no rouge, and the morning sunlight streams though the

window and makes a play on her skin, showing up her shadows
and her flaws, but she looks like she could not care less, a
smile on her lips and her eyes flashing with life.

My goodness, I think, *they are falling in love.*

'She is back!' cries Dorothy, putting her hands out to me,
and I sit down beside them like a little gooseberry, taking care
to put my precious parcels on the next table, where I can have
them in plain sight. She puts her arm around me. 'Where on
earth have you got to all morning? We were just saying we are
peckish for a spot of late lunch, and Cornelius here knows a
place that does all different sorts of game pies.'

'Pigeon, rabbit, hare – you name it, Mistress Dickson,' he
says. 'Down by the White Hart Inn. And all the condiments
you could imagine too.'

Dorothy looks brightly at me. 'Fancy it, my dear? We could
share a pigeon pie.'

'You two go, but not me,' I reply. I have no wish to go to
the White Hart Inn, for that is the place near the gallows. 'I
must get back home to Fisherrow, for they'll have no idea what
has happened to me.'

Dorothy looks solemn now. 'My dear Maggie, is this to be
goodbye?'

'I think so,' I tell her. 'I cannot see myself returning here,
for all my family are by the Forth and that is where I belong.'
I suddenly want to talk to her about Mr Munroe, the harbourmaster, and that I felt something for him, an affection towards
him that I haven't felt towards a man for a while. Dorothy
would understand and would tell me what to do, how to behave
with him. But I can't say anything like that in front of Cornelius,
and anyway Mr Munroe might not even wish to see me again.
Not after I left him in the lurch like that – upped and off on
my first day working for him.

'But you must return for visits, and we can take a night out together and drink a bottle of wine, can't we?' she pleads.

'Indeed we shall,' I say. But I know, in my heart, I will not return. And that is nothing to do with Dorothy, for she is a most amusing and entertaining woman really. But I am not at home in Edinburgh, the town that tried to hang me.

'I shall find a boy with a cart,' says Cornelius, 'whilst you say goodbye to Aunt Jenever.'

The woman herself is just emerging. Ready to fill her customers with gin and make their troubles disappear for a few hours. She comes creaking down the stairs, her skirts sighing with age.

'The very woman, for I have something you might want to buy from me, at a very good price,' I say, reaching for the perfume box. 'Patrick Spencer sells these bottles in his perfume emporium up the street, and terribly expensive they are too. But I have obtained a few and I am sure you can do something with them.'

Aunt Jenever picks up a bottle of the perfume and unstoppers it and dabs some on. The scent of musk and spice rises from her wrist.

'Oh,' breathes Dorothy, 'that is magnificent.'

'Can you take them?' I ask Aunt Jenever.

She sniffs her wrist and nods her head.

'It is mighty strong, though. I might need to water it down – what say you, Cornelius? I'm sure I have something in my gin shop we could dilute it with. We'd have twice the bottles then, would we not? And make much more coin!'

We agree a nice price, and it is not long before my cart is waiting, with an impatient boy and an impatient horse, and I am saying my goodbyes to Aunt Jenever.

She comes outside with me and fastens a threadbare shawl round me.

'You want to look poor,' she says. 'So that no one guesses at the fortune you carry. You have quite cleaned me out, my dear, but I dare say it was a good investment. I will make a tidy bit from that perfume, and I could do with it too, for what is to come.' She grows solemn. 'Now I am nobody's fool, but I don't think I will see you again. I'm not in my first flush of youth and winter is coming, and the Edinburgh winters are wicked. I might need a nurse, and medicines. I nearly succumbed to the past winter, and I do not fancy my chances with this one.'

'Oh, don't talk of such things,' I plead.

'Age makes us face up to such matters,' she replies. 'One day it will make you face up to them too, but that day will be a long time coming. You are not just a survivor, Maggie Dickson – you are reinventing yourself. I see it in the way you carry yourself with confidence. So when you go back to Fisherrow, do not let them dwell on your past. Make them see that you have a bright and shining future.'

She watches as I clamber onto the cart, and the wisps of her hair float in a breeze that sweeps up the street, bringing a few golden leaves with it, and her hair dances around her face.

That is the way I will look back and remember Aunt Jenever, when the snow falls in a few months' time, and the windows ice up and the winter coughs start.

But for now, forward! The cart leaps into life.

My money is fastened tight under my skirts where no one can reach it.

I have travelled too far in this world, and met too many of its inhabitants, to risk letting it out of my sight.

Chapter Thirty-Five

Fisherrow
October 1724

They say many things of fishwives. That we are gossips, and that we are rough and coarse and loud. That we are greedy, and that we berate and browbeat our poor husbands. That we pile our coins high, and that we strive to break out of our place in the world, although we really know nothing but fish. And that we stink.

Many of these things may be true of us, from time to time. But we know of far more than just fish.

We know of freezing mornings, monstrously dark, standing on the beach as the sun rises and the boats go out, picking up shellfish with our bare hands. We know of grit under our fingernails that never scrubs quite clean, and we know of waiting for boats to return as the storms rise. We know of back-breaking work.

Proud as I am of that life, and though it has taught me much about being resilient, I want more now, for me and Ma and Joan.

When the cart drops me back home, early evening, the pair of them spill out of the front door to meet me.

'Oh, dear lass,' murmurs Ma, clutching me. 'We thought you'd had enough of us and done another flit.'

I lose myself for a moment or two on her shoulder and let myself be enveloped. I feel Joan's hand pat my head, and I stand back and say we ought to go inside, for it's dark and cold out here.

I can't tell them what really happened.

I feel far enough removed from the events of last night that I do not fear a constable will come. It is not likely. How many enemies must a hangman have? And certainly I was not one of them, for Dr McTavish quite failed to hang me altogether.

'I had some unfinished business,' I tell them. 'And it is finished now.'

'I feel like I don't really know you, Daughter, disappearing off like that and coming back as if all of it was perfectly normal,' Ma says, sitting down at the table. The remnants of a half-eaten meal of bread and cheese lie on it, and it looks as though it has not been tidied and wiped since the meal before that.

'I shall try not to do it again,' I promise, 'but I have friends in Edinburgh now and sometimes they might call on me, for I do not fancy going back there again. You must trust me to live my own life, Ma.'

'That chap came looking for you – the harbourmaster,' Joan says, watching me unwaveringly. 'He was terribly upset and was off to call the constables. One minute you were in his office and the next minute gone, and no one had even seen you leave. I said to give it a while and that you had not simply vanished into thin air. I had a feeling you had something to do in Edinburgh and that we would see you before too long.'

My sister knows me better than anyone, it would seem. But oh Lord, constables are the last thing I need.

'I shall go and let the harbourmaster know I am safe,' I reply. I hand Ma my parcels. 'You are to guard these with your life.

Do not open them; we will discuss what is in them when I return. We have plans to make.'

'You cannot go and see the harbourmaster dressed in that shabby shawl,' says Joan. 'You look a real fishwife in that. Worse than a fishwife, Maggie; you look like an Edinburgh beggar.'

So I am given a clean shawl and Ma wipes my boots, and I grab a lantern and off I trot down to the harbour. I have missed the fresh tang of it. It is not the kind of scent everyone likes, of salt and fish and horses and carts and the cold north wind. But it is mine.

Mr Munroe is standing on the doorstep of his office, looking out across the darkness of the Forth as if it holds some answers or some secrets he is trying to work out. As I approach, I can just about make out the details of his face from the light of the harbour lanterns. He looks as though he has not had a lot of sleep. He is a smart-looking man, handsome enough, but not showy with it. Decent, I'd say. I call out to him and, when he sees it's me, he stares, as though he can't believe I'm here.

'I am sorry,' I begin. 'Terribly sorry, but something happened to me when you went out yesterday and I had to go and deal with it urgently.'

I think Mr Munroe will say something – scold me or tell me I am not welcome back in his harbour or in his office again – but he nods at me to go inside and sits me down by the fire.

'I was about to call the constables,' he says. 'Your sister said to trust you a little and that, with everything that has happened to you these past few weeks, you have become flighty. But even so, I was very worried about you.'

'I had no choice but to leave for a while on urgent business,'

I reply. 'But I can promise you I've no more plans to go away again. And if I do, I will give everyone proper notice.'

He takes his pocket watch from his waistcoat and fiddles with it, then wipes his lips and paces up and down for a few minutes, as men do when they are pondering what to say next.

'I did enjoy my morning's work with you here,' I tell him, 'even though it was cut short. I should like to keep working here, with you.'

He stops and glances at me.

'I did enjoy your company,' I add shyly.

'I dare say my company is not as exciting as some of the company you have kept,' he says.

'Mibbie that's what I like about it,' I answer.

The cottage in Musselburgh has been vacant since Spencer's lease expired. The landlord, who turns out to be a friend of Mr Munroe's, gives me the key so that I can go back and take another look at it.

It's always the smell of a place that brings back the memories, is it not? The Musselburgh cottage smells of the ghost of Spencer's perfumes, as though they have seeped into its very bricks and boards. It also still smells of freshly laundered linens and rush-light smoke and rum; but oh, it is still. It is empty of people and laughter and stories.

It needs to be filled with these things again.

I go back to the landlord and tell him I shall lease it for the next quarter – see how I like it. Then I tell Ma and Joan that we have a new place to live.

And that is how, by and by, Da returns to Fisherrow, for I was not happy to pay for him to live in an inn for the rest of his days. And Joan and Ma come to live with me in Musselburgh.

And we do cause a scandal, I can't deny that. All over Fisherrow, and Musselburgh town too, they talk of how we upped and left, and how my half-hanging and my high ways had made me into a different Maggie than the meek one they had long known. But we do not care, for me and Ma and Joan fill the place with chatter and laughter and stories. Happy stories and sad stories, and here is a sad little one.

It is a cold October day when I finally lay my poor Susanna to rest.

The gravediggers at St Michael's do not have much of a job of it, for the coffin is tiny. But one day I will rest with her. I made sure to buy us space.

It has rained and the east-coast wind has made quick work of the kirkyard trees, stripping them down to their bare branches and making my heart feel stripped bare too. It is the yellow part of autumn, when there is so little of the season left, and such bitterness in the air that we might as well call it the start of winter. But now Susanna is finally in the ground, at home, near to me, where she can close her eyes and take her blissful slumber.

Chapter Thirty-Six

Fisherrow
November 1724

I t's late on Friday afternoon and the market is starting to die down. I am waiting on the harbour-front for Mr Munroe, who has asked me to join him on a walk around Musselburgh golf links. The golf links are not a part of town that I'm familiar with. Fishing folk have little time for pastimes or pursuits and, if we do, we prefer the indoors to the outdoors. 'The golf links!' Joan had said, when I had told her I'd be late home. 'That's where the ladies and gents go for romantic walks.' Joan knows all about the golf links too, as she's been busy with her own affairs of the heart. Her lad's not a mill owner's son as such, but has a highly regarded clerking role and hopes of being a manager.

I can think of no reason other than a romantic one for a gent like Mr Munroe to want to walk out with a lass on a Friday afternoon, and my heart dances a bit at that, for we have got closer, day by day, in his office; and rather than talk of books, we have talked of our lives. His has not been as wild as mine, but he has a decent profession and sees it as his calling to watch over our little harbour and make sure it runs as well as it can.

Yesterday we had a glass of port after work, sitting by the

fire, and he said he hoped I did not mind, but he had something of his late mother's and could he give it to me?

'Would you be offended?' he asked. 'My mother liked this, and I have kept most of her bits and pieces, but frankly it is just lying in a purse now and I think it would look most beautiful on you.

I sat and waited for him to fetch it, wondering nervously what on earth he might think to give me of his late mother's. I sipped my port and then watched it swirl in the crystal glass, and then I relaxed a bit and enjoyed the feeling of being with a man who wants nothing more than my company and to make me feel happy.

Mr Munroe came back downstairs carrying a small velvet purse, and opened it and showed me what was inside. It was a necklace, a gold necklace with red gems strung on it that gleamed like little berries.

'I think it suits your colouring,' he said, blushing almost the same colour as the gems, poor man. 'But do not feel you must take it, or that you must wear it.'

I let him put the necklace on me. It was cold and his hands were warm and deft, and I could smell the port on his breath and had a sudden thought of him touching me most intimately, and I blushed too.

'A good friend of mine, a lady called Dorothy, once told me she thought my rope-bruise would fade to look like a necklace – a mourning necklace,' I told him. 'She's a lovely lady, Dorothy; gents adore her.'

My eyes prickled at that: at what Dorothy had said, and that I miss her a bit and think I would like to send her a message to come and visit me one day and see if she and Cornelius are married yet, which I am sure they will be before the year is out.

Mr Munroe hesitated before he brushed my rope-mark with his finger. The patch of skin, which still aches from time to time and no doubt always will, tingled at his touch. I had not been touched there for a long time and I did not mind Mr Munroe doing it at all.

'This is not a traditional mourning necklace,' he said, 'for they are usually made of dark jewels. But I suppose I thought of you when I saw it. Well, you could wear this for any reason. As a mourning necklace or as a trinket, or just to have something of mine, if you like.'

And then there was a moment when I thought he might kiss me, but he did not. Instead he asked me if I might walk out with him tomorrow after work, to the golf links.

When I got home with that necklace on, Joan gawped and gawped.

'Look at this, Ma,' she cried. 'Maggie's got some fine jewels about her neck.'

'Oh, Maggie,' breathed Ma, 'those look like real gems.'

'Not paste, like Spencer's ring,' agreed Joan. 'Those are the real deal. Was that Mr Munroe? Are you to marry him? Can you marry, Maggie – what with you being married before and now legally dead? Do you still need your glass ring? I could have it now. Mr Munroe will buy you a gold one.'

She has never let up about that bloody glass ring.

'You can have the glass ring when I am dead, Joan, but not before. I have no idea of Mr Munroe's intentions, for all he said was that he should like me to wear his poor deceased ma's necklace, and I think it covers my rope-mark quite well and I might wear it as a mourning necklace for Susanna.'

'And why should you cover your mark?' asked Ma in a low voice. 'It is part of you, and speaks of your past and all that you have survived.'

'I feel I am branded,' I said. 'And my mark is my punishment for the mistakes I have made. It makes me feel ashamed, Ma.'

'Do not wear the necklace to hide your shame. Of all the reasons to wear it, do not let that be the one. Wear it to honour Mr Munroe's request, and to let him remember his ma, and to let you remember Susanna, and to give this piece of jewellery a new lease of life. But mostly wear it because it suits you, my girl, because it makes you sparkle.'

I said I would.

'It does make you sparkle, Maggie,' said Joan. 'She looks bonnie, doesn't she, Ma?' My sister had never said that before.

'She looks bonnie, but best of all, she looks content,' agreed Ma.

So now as I wait for Mr Munroe, as he ties up his loose odds and ends in the office for the weekend, I touch my mourning necklace and consider that if he should ask me to marry him, my answer would be yes; and as I am legally dead, I need not worry about whoever I was married to before.

By and by, a young lad aged about twelve or so, with seemingly nothing much better to do on a Friday afternoon, bobs along and regards me with curiosity as he picks up pebbles and throws them at the harbour wall.

The pebbles bounce and land here and there. There is no point to his game, only to keep himself entertained for a few minutes while his ma and da finish up their business at the market, or empty their drinks at the Mussel Inn, or whatever they might be doing.

I try to ignore him and continue to look at the harbour. But he edges closer and closer until he is finally a few feet away from me, staring firmly at my throat.

'That's a sparkly necklace,' he says. 'But what's that mark on your neck?' He comes even closer now, the pebbles abandoned. 'Oi, Missus, are you Half-Hanged Maggie?' he asks. 'Only that mark, Missus, it looks like a rope-burn. What happened then, on the gallows? Is it like they say and you woke up in your own coffin at the Sheep Heid Inn, and walked into your own funeral wake and your own family nearly died of fright?'

I turn to him, sighing. 'I am she,' I reply. 'And my story is not for the likes of little lads like you.'

'A little lad!' He scoffs at that and pulls himself up to his full height, which is not much. 'Tell me,' he begs, and I roll my eyes, for I have heard this question a hundred times or more. 'Tell me what happens to you, in the afterlife.'

I sigh and shake my head. 'You will not like the answer,' I say.

His eyes widen at that.

'But you must tell me anyway – here, have a shiny pebble.' He rummages in his pocket and brings out a fine-looking little stone. 'I don't have pennies, Missus, but this here shiny stone would look grand in a collection, if you collect such things.'

'I do not collect stones, for I am not a child,' I reply gravely, but I am developing a soft spot for the fellow and I suddenly have a terrible hankering for Susanna.

'Oh, you should,' he says, sounding dejected. 'They are free on the beach and look good, all lined up in rows. I have rows of whites, greys, reds and blacks.'

'Well, carry on making your colourful collection, and I will not take your nice pebble from you.'

'But you will tell me, won't you?' he pleads.

I will.

'The answer is that all the things that you do in your life

come back to you, when you reach your final moments. And you think of all sorts of strange things – of the conversations you never had time to have and of the mistakes you made, but mostly of the people you love. Above all things is love.'

'Oh,' he says, sounding disappointed. 'I had thought there might be Pearly Gates or somesuch, or even the Devil come to see if he can drag you down to hell, with the serpents and the fire and all that.'

'Well, mibbie that happens too,' I suggest. 'But I was only half-hanged, so I never got there.'

We are interrupted then by Mr Munroe, whose appearance makes the boy scarper away with his pebbles.

'Mistress Dickson,' he says, 'you look pretty as a picture in that necklace.' He offers me his arm and I take it, and off we walk, just two ordinary folks taking a stroll.

With my other hand, I touch the gems about my neck, and the rope-mark too. For the first time in a long time, my skin feels dazzling and luminous and glorious.

And for the first time in a long time, I know exactly who I am, and I am at peace with it.

I am Maggie Dickson. I am walking up to Musselburgh golf links before it gets dark. I am two-and-twenty years of age and I am the first Dickson girl in many generations to leave the fishing trade. I didn't want that harsh sort of life. One day I will be Mistress Munroe, the harbourmaster's wife. One day I will be a mother again. One day my raw grief for Susanna will fade a little, like my neck bruise. But that is all to come.

EPILOGUE

Musselburgh
Forty years later: May 1764

It is a spring day when it finally happens. A wet and windy day in early May, which starts with the first drop of all the pink blossoms that have bloomed around town. A drop that makes everyone sigh and say, 'Blossoms are bonnie, but they never last very long.' I don't see the blossoms fall, for I have not been able to leave my bed for a while, but Joan tells me about it and I don't wish to see it.

I do not feel the wind or the rain, either, for I am under blankets and kept warm by fires and the holding of hands. Joan's hand is so old now that to see it startles me sometimes. My husband, the finest harbourmaster that Fisherrow has ever known, is here and his gentle voice hums like a bee. Our children are here, all four of them.

But you are not to feel sorry at this scene, for I would not have wished for a better, kinder passing.

It has been a winter death-rattle, similar to the ones that took Aunt Jenever, then Da, then Ma, then Dorothy. We do not make old bones in Edinburgh, nor in Fisherrow. Mibbie one day there will be an easier way to earn a living. One that does not break our skin and our backs, or cause us to battle the weather. So I am not ancient, but I am not too young for death. Death has walked with me for many years, but I am suddenly afeared of it, afeared of pain and what lies ahead, and of Judgement.

But that fear passes, right at the moment that I become aware that I no longer feel the weight of the blanket, or my husband's hands.

Oh, it is different this time. Different from the day they hanged me and different from how I'd imagined it too. And if you want to hear this part of my story, you do not have to touch my neck for luck, or pass me a coin to find out what happens in the hereafter, for it is a short but simple tale and is the very truth.

I'd thought there might be Pearly Gates, as I'd talked of them and been asked of them often enough, but I do not see any. Not yet.

Nor snakes. And that is a relief.

Instead a small basket lies just ahead. It looks like a fishing creel, my old one, the one that saw me through my hardest travels. As I approach, I see there is something inside it, moving. *Oh!* It cries and raises its fists to its mouth and suckles, as though desperate for its mother.

I bend down to look at her. Susanna. My neck moves freely for the first time in years, for my neck-mark is gone now. And the red-gem necklace too. I must have lost it on the journey.

I am not sad about that. Although that necklace had become part of me, its time is over now. Joan will mibbie wear it for a while, along with that glass ring she always admired.

Oh, goodness, Susanna is as beautiful as I remembered.

I pick her up and bring her to my breast.

Our embrace, when it finally happens, has been half a lifetime coming.

HISTORICAL NOTE

Sometimes truth is stranger than fiction. From 1690 to 1809 the Scottish 'Act Anent Murthering of Children' meant that mothers who kept their pregnancy secret could be tried for murder if the baby died. A similar law existed in England. The laws were written onto the statute books amidst concerns about undeclared births, abandoned children and illegitimacy. The women who were tried were often those who had given birth to illegitimate babies.

Maggie Dickson was a Fisherrow fishwife who fell foul of this law. After her husband was press-ganged, she left her home and travelled to Kelso. There, she gave birth to a child, telling no one that she had been expecting, and abandoned it on the banks of the River Tweed. It is unclear whether her baby was stillborn or died after birth, but Maggie always maintained her innocence and said it had been born prematurely and that she didn't know what had caused its death.

Although she was hanged aged twenty-two, by some trick of fate she survived her execution and was allowed to go free. She went on to live a long life and died of natural causes, some forty years later. Various versions of her life story have become folklore and she became known as 'Half-Hangit Maggie' or 'Half-Hanged Maggie'.

Whilst I have taken liberties with some of the elements and have added family members and smugglers and new characters to the story, *The Mourning Necklace* is my reimagining of Maggie Dickson's life – before, during and after her hanging.

The smuggling of the increasingly popular drink tea to avoid paying expensive import duties was prevalent up and down the East Coast of Scotland and England during the eighteenth century, although there is no suggestion the real-life Maggie Dickson or her family were involved and this is my own invention.

Although Maggie is renowned for escaping death, as I wrote her story I was more moved by the other themes it brought up, such as women's reproductive rights, working conditions, poverty, heartache and grief, which – despite the passing of hundreds of years – are still so very prevalent today.

Maggie's story is well known in Edinburgh and there is a pub in the Grassmarket named after her, near the spot of the old Grassmarket Gallows.

ACKNOWLEDGEMENTS

This book would not exist without my literary agent, Viola Hayden, who heard me talking about 'Half-Hanged Maggie', one of Edinburgh's notorious historical characters, and said I must write her story. Thank you, Viola, for helping me bring Maggie to life. The more I got to know Maggie, the more I felt compelled to bring her extraordinary story into the world.

I am also greatly indebted to my team at Curtis Brown Books, Ciara Finan, Atlanta Hatch and Nadia Farah Mokdad, for your tireless work and support.

Thank you, Mantle Books and Pan Macmillan, for continuing to publish my stories and helping me to shine a new light on the overlooked or infamous women of the past. To Maria Rejt and Madeleine O'Shea, for being the most incredible editors I could hope for; and to Chloe Davies: you are a brilliant publicist and make everything so much easier! Thank you too, Natasha Tulett, Rebecca Needes and Mandy Greenfield for your amazing work.

The Fisherrow fishwives were a magnificent breed: stoic, hard-working, bold, brave women. Their lives are celebrated at the John Gray Centre, Haddington, and I am grateful to their archivists.

Massive thanks to the booksellers and bloggers and writers and reviewers who have helped make a vibrant and supportive community around what can often be a solitary craft. And to the Women's Prize Trust, for all the work it does to promote women's writing.

Thank you to my family: Dad, Frances, Harry, Simon, Jane, Sophie, Jasmine, and to Tom and Ruby who make me proud every day. And to Mum, who is in everything I do.

To Paul, who always knows what to do for the best, and to my friends, who are more like family and inspire me with their love and warmth and joy: Sarah, Lesley, Cara, Fiona, Alison, Linda.

To Nikki, with whom I have been friends friends for longer than anyone and with whom I share the most treasured memories.

And to Denise Verth, a bold, brave woman who was fascinated by Scotland and its history and its bold, brave women.